Saving Grace

Also by Janie Bolitho

Kindness Can Kill (1993)
Ripe for Revenge (1994)
Motive for Murder (1994)
Dangerous Deceit (1995)
Finger of Fate (1996)
Sequence of Shame (1996)
Snapped in Cornwall (1997)
An Absence of Angels (1997)
Framed in Cornwall (1998)
Exposure of Evil (1998)
Buried in Cornwall (1999)
Victims of Violence (1999)
Betrayed in Cornwall (2000)
Baptised in Blood (2000)
Plotted in Cornwall (2001)

SAVING GRACE

Janie Bolitho

Constable · London

First published in Great Britain 2001
by Constable, an imprint of Constable & Robinson Ltd
3 The Lanchesters, 162 Fulham Palace Road
London, W6 9ER
www.constablerobinson.com

ISBN 1-84119-317-8

Printed and bound in Great Britain

A CIP catalogue record for this book is available from the
British Library

For Jo Anderson who makes
life easier

GRACE

Time, which had once seemed elastic, now rushed forward at an alarming speed. On Monday Grace's future would be decided by twelve total strangers. She was drained, a cipher, no longer human, her body an automaton obeying the subconscious instructions of her brain. She ate and slept and worked and even socialised so that no one would guess at the terror within her. Over the years she had become adept at hiding her emotions. When the dark rooms of her mind threatened to open their doors she slammed them shut relentlessly and went out to dinner or played squash with Ruth.

It was Friday. With a sigh of relief that she wasn't on call, Grace Cornell left the surgery at seven thirty and headed out of Exeter on the B road which would take her across Dartmoor. Freezing fog enveloped the car as soon as she was clear of the city's lights and it was cold, even with the car heater full on. All around was a blanket of grey moisture which the headlights barely penetrated. She drove carefully but she was not afraid. The moors were a part of her and she craved their solid permanence. Although they were invisible now, Grace could still sense their brooding presence. The fog pressed in around her and tried to invade the womb-like cocoon of the car. Needing this weekend of solitude she was still aware that the next two days provided only a reprieve.

The turning was invisible. Grace would have missed it but for the white finger of the signpost which loomed suddenly out of the fog. She braked very slowly, pumping the pedal several times to prevent the car from fish-tailing as she turned into the narrow road. It had not been gritted. In second gear she rounded the next sharp bend and felt the wheels slide. There were no longer any road markings. Grace steered with the nearside wheels brushing the verge. She could have walked faster than the speed at which she was travelling.

Matt had rung before she left work. His call had upset her. Today, of all days, he had chosen to rake up the past. She was exhausted, it was the last thing she had needed. Matt, to whom she had been engaged when an almost normal life had seemed possible, used to claim that he preferred intelligent, independent women. It was a myth. In theory he did, when it was anyone other than Grace, but he had expected her to drop everything on his behalf if he felt the occasion warranted it. He had accused her of neglecting him which, she accepted, was not without some truth. Well, she thought, there's no going back, he has, as they say, had his cake and eaten it.

The practice partners, along with Ruth, had wanted to book a table for dinner with Grace as their guest but she had dissuaded them. This show of support having failed they tried to insist that she stay in Exeter over the weekend where they would be on hand if she needed them. 'I just want to be on my own,' she had told them. 'Honestly, a couple of days at the farmhouse is all I need.'

Weeks of snow and sub-zero temperatures had created a surreal stillness even in Exeter itself. Memories Grace usually managed to suppress flooded her mind painfully. There was no escape from them and she knew that, over the next two days, they would fill her waking hours as well as her dreams. But it was time they were faced.

It was never clear to her how the gloomy periods she suffered dispelled themselves but they went suddenly and without warning. It happened then, symbolically, just as the fog rolled away like tumbleweed and exposed a black sky with every star a pinprick of ice. Around her, like a moonscape, stretched the crystallised countryside. The irradiated white light of snow went on for ever. Without the muffling quality of the fog the plaintive bleating of sheep carried clearly through the sharp air. Ahead, but in the distance, was the farmhouse. With only a mile to go she thought of the decent wine and the well-stocked larder which awaited her, thanks to Judith whom she had rung in advance to warn of her arrival. Judith is my saviour, Grace thought as she negotiated the sharp bend into the lane.

Without her inheritance Grace would not have been able to afford the flat in Exeter and the farmhouse which had become a sanctuary. The two properties had only in common a set of her favourite toiletries and some of her clothes. She loved them both equally.

The flat was modern, luxurious and secure; the farmhouse had stood with its back to the hill for over two hundred years, withstanding whatever the elements had chosen to throw at it.

As the chimney stack drew nearer, silhouetted against the night sky, the tension in her neck and jaw began to slacken.

There was no drive and no garden. The moors swept down and surrounded the house and would have swallowed it up were it not for the dry-stone walling on three sides. The area was too exposed for anything much to grow. The snow crunched beneath the tyres as she pulled in and parked on the open verge.

'Oh, Judith, dear Judith,' she muttered as she unlocked the front door and stepped into the warmth. The oil-fired central heating was left on low all winter because of the risk of frozen pipes but, anticipating Grace's arrival, Judith had turned the thermostat up to its highest setting.

There was fresh milk and food in the fridge and a table lamp left burning in the sitting-room. Judith had come in response to an advert for a cleaner, but she had turned out to be far more than that. Friendship had developed and, despite being three years younger than Grace, Judith had a tendency to mother her. Her thoughtfulness was touching. In the summer there were flowers and vegetables from her sheltered garden, or a salad, ready made, in the fridge. When the weather changed there were doughy buns and saffron cake which, much to Judith's amusement, Grace sliced and toasted before buttering it. Once, after several gales, a badly stitched draught-excluder in the shape of an overlong dachshund had appeared. Judith had promised to stay on until after the trial then she would be joining her husband. Until recently he had been a prison warder at Dartmoor but he had had enough and had bought a market garden in the Tamar Valley. No longer able to remain in their living quarters, Judith and her daughter, Zoe, were staying with Judith's mother. Another fortnight and they would be gone.

I shall miss her, Grace thought, and Zoe. I'd like a daughter like that one day. Zoe was five and amused Grace with her serious, adult observations and her knowledge of fashion and music.

In the kitchen Grace threw her handbag on to the worktop and opened a bottle of claret. Then she lit one of the menthol cigarettes she had taken to smoking lately, cursing herself for her hypocrisy because she gave frequent warnings of their danger to her patients.

The casual clothes she wore at the farmhouse were kept

upstairs on a permanent basis so there was nothing to unpack. She carried the drink through to the sitting-room, the wine bottle in her other hand, and sat down, still wearing her thick woollen coat. With her head resting against the back of the squashy settee she went back over the events which had led her to that point.

There had been the letters, of course, three of them, sent to the flat. The police had them now. They had told Grace that they would be used as part of the evidence but she could have them back afterwards if she so chose. She never wanted to see them again.

'It's you and me, Gracie. For ever. The past is over and done with,' the first one had said. But it wasn't, far from it. The letters, naturally, had been unsigned. Grace had known who had sent them and why they had been sent.

She smiled, relaxed by the wine. No one but her father had ever called her Gracie and he was dead. Lately she thought of him often and how their lives had been when she was young; unchallenged, peaceful and happy, notwithstanding Olivia's growing dissatisfaction and her eventual departure.

Grace had been a summer baby, born on a sweltering day in June. Her mother, Olivia, whom Grace always thought of by her given name, had stayed in hospital only one night before insisting she returned to Gorstone Manor where the food was superior and she could be looked after equally well by her own staff. Gerald Cornell had been prepared to pay for his wife's private care indefinitely but she could not bear to be away from Gorstone or from Gerald for long. The house and most of the furniture had been in the Cornell family's possession for four generations although it was not entailed. It had been a happy place which each following generation had been only too pleased to take over without making changes. Grace and Luke had once felt that way too. Her biggest regret was selling it after her father's death but it had been unavoidable, neither she nor Luke could envisage going back there again. The only keepsake she had chosen was the large, ornate mirror which hung in the hallway of her flat without managing to appear incongruous. That, alone, held more memories than she could often bear.

When she and Luke were children a constant stream of people had flowed through the house, individual or joint friends of their parents or Gerald's business associates. Once, when Grace was eleven, she had travelled up to Paddington by herself. While she was waiting for her friend's mother to come and collect her she had studied the crowds milling around the concourse. The scene had seemed vaguely familiar until she realised that so much activity reminded her of Gorstone. It had made her a little homesick.

Grace recalled the long summer holidays when female voices would drift from the upstairs drawing-room or the garden where Olivia would take her guests if the weather permitted. Gerald tended to show his colleagues into the library, a room always filled with cigar smoke and deep, male laughter. By some unspoken agreement the family and guests would contrive to gather for drinks about fifteen minutes before dinner was served. It was rare to sit down at the table as just the family. Grace realised it was not an orthodox upbringing but it had taught her how to mix. She was not a precocious child, Olivia would not have allowed her to be, but she had gained the strength and confidence she had required for the time when Luke depended upon her and she was left to deal with the estate.

Grace's hand shook as she leant forward to refill her glass. Claret spilled on to the polished surface of the small table beside her. She watched the ruby droplets settle and hold their convex shape, then closed her eyes tightly. But the scene was inside her head, she could not shut it out. Warm blood seeping into snow, melting it, becoming pink as it was diluted. But was this a memory or imagination? Eight years was a long time. The picture was ingrained, as when someone tells a lie so often it becomes the truth for them. 'I have to face it,' she whispered. 'I have to remember the details. It's my only chance. I have to try to remember my father as he really was.'

Gerald Cornell had married Olivia when she was very young and very beautiful. When she left she was still young, only thirty-four, and even more beautiful. Her olive skin complemented her black hair and her almond eyes were almost as dark so it was ironical that when she ran off with an Italian associate of Gerald's and went to live in his country she was mistaken for a native. One of the few things for which Grace was grateful to her mother was the bequest of her looks.

At the time no one had fully understood why she had left, except possibly Gerald who refused to discuss it. They were a striking couple and wealthy, and they had laughed a lot together until the last couple of years when Olivia's laughter had become brittle. It had taken Grace a long time to work out what had been wrong and the reason why her mother had been unable to stay. But by then it was too late, all contact had long since been severed by Olivia.

And then, last September, had come a letter from Italy. How Grace had trembled when she saw the thin blue envelope with its foreign postmark. It was the first time she had heard from her mother since the day she had left. The letter had been sent to the surgery and said little other than that Olivia had heard what had happened and hoped that Grace was all right. She had given her address and telephone number and added that, although Grace might not believe it, she had thought of her every single day. Grace had not believed it. As much as she wanted a reconciliation, her reply had been terse; Olivia had not written again.

Olivia's leaving had traumatised Luke. He was seven at the time and adored his mother and, so everyone thought, she him. It was this, the leaving of her children, which no one could believe or understand. Luke's girlfriends, who did not last long, all resembled Olivia in some way. Ruth Ferrers, a clinical psychologist, Grace's best friend, once suggested that he was searching for his mother's lost love. She's probably right, Grace realised, she very often is. But as close as she was to Ruth, her friend had no idea what it had also done to Grace.

Luke had been their mother's boy, a little shy of his father, but she had idolised both her parents. Gerald had possessed an unequalled zest for life and such a total disregard for the conventions that he was fun to be with and drew people to him automatically. To her school friends her parents had seemed like film stars. The girls were made welcome and Gerald treated them as equals by discussing their ambitions and talking of his own and, to their delight, pouring them wine with dinner as if it was the most natural thing in the world. He was one of the few men who could entertain teenagers without appearing patronising.

After Olivia's departure fewer people came to Gorstone and for a while there had been some embarrassment amongst her former female friends because of what she had done. They feared Gerald might no longer welcome them because they were reminders. However, it was never quiet and many foreigners came and went because Gerald's wealth, apart from the money his father had left him, came from building luxury hotels all over the world. Grace used to sit and listen as he spoke on the telephone, fascinated as he switched from English to French or Spanish and back again. His linguistic skills had not been handed down to his children although Grace had made a point of keeping up with Latin because she had always intended to become a doctor.

At fourteen, not long before Olivia's departure, Grace had believed her mother to be affected and stupid but that she managed to conceal the latter. Begrudgingly she admired the way in which she thought it was done. If her father and his colleagues were discussing abstract theories or politics or something Grace imagined to be beyond her mother's comprehension, Olivia would light a cigarette, raise her eyebrows and blow a cloud of smoke out of the side of her mouth in a manner which suggested that what she was hearing was ludicrous. These actions were often accompanied by the crossing of her long, shapely legs which had a disconcerting effect upon the company and occasionally made the speaker stumble or lose his thread altogether. Grace recalled the strange expression which would pass over her father's face but she had never been able to read it with any accuracy.

My opinion of her was incorrect, Grace told herself as she refilled her wineglass. It was mostly due to the stirrings of adolescent rebellion which I never had the chance to go through with because by then she had gone. It was I who was stupid in my teenage arrogance. Olivia was both beautiful and intelligent but she played the latter down because she was aware that, in one so decorative, it undermined the masculinity of her father's acquaintances in some peculiar way, although why this should be she did not know.

Grace knew that this nostalgic catharsis was necessary even if the pain finally drove her crazy. For that's what they think, she told herself, my partners and my friends, they think I'm crazy already. My sanity is at stake here. She had begged not to be disturbed over the weekend, claiming that she would refuse to answer the telephone if it rang, yet she had a sudden desire to speak to Luke. Breathing deeply she knew that she must remain calm, that this had to be endured alone. What was Luke doing right now? She glanced at her watch. It seemed impossible but

11

it was already after eleven and she had not yet eaten. It did not matter, she could sleep late, if sleep came.

Luke had been sent away to school, as planned, which, at the time, although at boarding school herself, Grace had thought to be a heartless decision. Yet, astutely, Gerald had known it was the right move, that the change of environment and meeting new friends would help to distract him. In its way it had worked but she knew how much Luke still hurt, how much harder he found it to forgive their mother than she did.

Gerald Cornell died when Grace was in her second year at Southampton, reading medicine. Some time later she saw that it was almost fitting for a man who had lived so enthusiastically to have died so dramatically. Even if his whole life had been a lie.

The wine bottle beside her was almost empty yet she did not feel the effects of its contents. Her head ached only because of a hard week and the effort of facing the past. She wondered why she was so hot until she realised she was still in her coat. She stood and took it off and laid it over the back of a chair.

In the kitchen she opened the freezer then closed it again. So often the thought of food made her nauseous. She managed one slice of bread and butter spread with pâté. Upstairs she ran a bath and sank into the hot, scented water which Judith had remembered to switch on. Her limbs became weightless and she almost fell asleep. Stepping over the high side of the bath Grace was shocked to notice her ribs poking through her skin. She shivered although she wasn't cold. Above the tank, on the slatted shelves of the airing-cupboard, lay piles of clean, white linen, the towels carefully folded, possibly even ironed. Grace reached for a bath sheet and wrapped it around her. She felt faint from a combination of a lack of food and lying too long in the hot water.

She slipped a cream satin nightdress over her shoulders and felt it glide softly down her warm body to her ankles. She got into bed between crisp cotton sheets, the top one folded neatly back over the bedspread, and longed for Judith's company. Her cheerful freckled face was always a welcome sight and she had a knack of knowing exactly what to say to put problems into perspective. It was the last thing she remembered thinking before falling asleep.

When Grace opened her eyes she found it hard to believe that the night had been dreamless. It had to be after seven because a rectangle of greyish dawn light was running along the floor beneath the lined curtains which stopped short four inches below the narrow sill. The novel she had brought with her lay unopened on the bedside table. She sat up and stretched. The room was warm and familiar, the dark wood of the furniture perfectly suited to the low-ceilinged, whitewashed walls of the bedroom. All I want is for the trial to be over, she thought as she got out of bed and reached for the dressing-gown which matched her nightdress. The deep pile of the pale blue carpet was soft beneath her feet. Under the bed were her slippers, peep-toed velvet with a swansdown trim. She stepped into them and went downstairs to make a jug of coffee, unable to understand how rested she felt.

There was crusty bread in the earthenware crock, Devonshire butter in the dish and a pot of the marmalade Judith's mother made every winter. Grace's weight had dropped by over a stone and she knew she had to rectify the matter if she wasn't to become ill. And as she intended taking a long walk fuel was essential. What irony, she thought, if, having survived all those years ago, I was to be found on the moors a second time, but this time dead. Anyone who had been brought up in the Dartmoor area knew all the dangers and did not leave home unprepared, even in a car. Mists could descend unexpectedly, shrouding the wild expanses until there were no landmarks from which to take your bearings. The only thing to do was to stay put and wrap up warmly and pray that the mist lifted quickly or that someone found you before you died of exposure. Snow still lay on the ground, feet deep in places and piled against the walls where Judith had cleared it away from the back door. The sky arced over the moors, as high and as blue as in summer, but the temperature was well below freezing and Grace was aware how foolish it would be to stray more than a yard or so from the roadside. Drifts and hidden boulders could cause a broken leg, the sky could darken in seconds and surround you in a dis-orientating blizzard until you were completely lost. Grace felt lost enough already.

The fragrance of coffee and toasting bread filled the kitchen and made Grace's stomach growl in anticipation of food. But when she bit into the buttered toast with its chunks of Seville orange marmalade it was tasteless. Waves of nausea washed over her but she swallowed hard to stop herself retching. The coffee was strong. She drank three cups then forced herself to eat the cold toast.

When she had washed she dressed in needlecord jeans, a thick shirt and a heavy sweater. On her feet she wore fur-lined boots which could never have been described as a fashion accessory. For work her hair was tied back or pinned on top of her head. She left it loose, enjoying the feel of it around her face.

In the scullery off the kitchen hung a body warmer and a padded waxed jacket. She put them on. With so many layers she felt like a bundle of washing. Grace had never felt comfortable in a hat but in concession to the wind which was rattling the window panes, she tied a scarf around her long hair. She would be unrecognisable to anyone who knew her in Exeter because there she was always chic and elegant. Picking up her mobile phone she stuffed it into her pocket. It was not switched on, it was for emergency use only. In the other pocket was a Mars bar.

Snow had fallen again during the night. With a heavy shovel Grace scraped it from the front path knowing it was a pointless exercise because more had been forecast. Surrounding the cottage the dry-stone walling had a topping of four or five inches of pristine snow. Sunlight caught the frozen particles, which glittered brilliantly. From the side the walls had the appearance of chunks of wedding cake. Icy air took her breath away and carried it forward like a thinner version of the previous night's fog as she made her way down to the main road. She wished that she had some sunglasses to combat the glare of the sun. Dirty slush lay at the sides of the road, which was now passable again. There was very little traffic and only sheep for company. From a distance they looked white and fluffy, like the clouds which were building up on the horizon. The reality was a lot different. A ewe, half in the road, saw Grace approaching and eyed her nervously. Its coat was long and thick and matted with clumps of mud and worse. Against the snow its fleece was yellow, like the teeth of a hardened smoker. It bleated half-heartedly.

She had been walking on the verge rather than the road and, unused to the uneven terrain, her legs began to ache. Spread above and below her was the beauty of the moor, as breathtaking now in its blanket of white as when the heather bloomed and the streams trickled over water-smoothed stones and the hills cast their dark shadows. Only when she saw the high walls looming ahead of her ominously did she realise just how far she had come. Dartmoor prison, or the Moor as it was known with an odd sort of pride to those who had been incarcerated there, was a bleak and eerie place even in the height of summer. Wherever it was viewed from it had a chilling aura and even the stonework emanated foreboding. It was a constant reminder of another side of life, and a reminder of death.

'How stupid of me to have come this way,' Grace said aloud. Prison. Trial. A child could have worked out the word association.

That close to the village of Princetown there were cars and people around. Grace had no wish to be amongst them. She turned back. Ponies had gathered at the side of the road hoping to be fed but, cute as they looked, she steered clear of them. They could kick out viciously.

Even walking fast and with a downhill journey it took her well over an hour to reach the farmhouse. Once there, she removed her outer layers and put on the kettle. Now that she was out of the biting wind her face began to burn with the sudden change in temperature. It had been a long time since she had felt the blood pumping through her veins so efficiently.

With a mug of coffee in front of her Grace sat at the kitchen table and lit her second cigarette of the day. She toyed with the ashtray, recalling how much she had smoked at university, unsure whether it was because everyone else had done so or because she had needed it to get through the days after the funeral.

She had always been what was now termed an achiever and had passed every exam with good grades. And, Grace thought, to give Olivia her due, whilst she was there she always turned up for speech days and sports days and parents' evenings and praised me when I did well. But her father had been puzzled when she clamoured for his approbation because he had never doubted that she would do well in whatever she set out to achieve. Grace was, after all, his daughter. Her chosen career had come as no surprise to anyone who had known her as a child. She had conducted major surgery upon her first teddy bear at the age of six and later on dolls, one of which, unbeknown to Grace, had been a Victorian heirloom. On each occasion she had been disappointed to find nothing but sawdust or stuffing inside them. If Luke fell and grazed a knee or an elbow, it was his sister rather than his mother to whom he went to have it bathed with antiseptic. Grace had loved the smell of it, and still did. Having already decided upon her career she had applied to several universities and was accepted by Southampton, her first choice.

It was there she met both Ruth and Fay. And Lance Harrington. Ruth had decided she would prefer to treat people's minds rather than their bodies and had switched to psychology but Fay had always been a natural doctor and was now completely at home at one of the teaching hospitals in London. Grace knew from the start that she wanted to become a GP and as soon as she had finished her hospital training she had applied for the vacant post with a small practice in Exeter. It had seemed so perfect, the job of her dreams, her flat and, soon afterwards, the house on the moors. Then, just as she was settling in and beginning to put the past behind her, it had all started to go wrong.

With surprise she realised that she was hungry. What she was experiencing was a normal, healthy desire for food. Sitting on a shelf in the fridge in a film-covered dish was a steak, its fat thick and creamy, just as it should be. The sight of it no longer revolted her. She would eat it later. For now a sandwich would do. The butter was hard; she dabbed it on the bread in slivers. The thickly cut ham with its golden rind had come from the butcher in Tavistock where Judith bought her own and Grace's meat. She picked up a broken corner and put it in her mouth. The tender strands fell apart. It tasted of her childhood, of the joints Mrs Collins used to carve after baking them herself studded with cloves or glazed with mustard and honey. It was a long time since anything had whetted her appetite. There was salad in the container. Grace added tomatoes and lettuce then sat down at the kitchen table. In front of her was another mug of coffee, its rising steam broken by a slight draught from beneath the back door. She got up again and fetched the dachshund from the larder, vowing to cut down her caffeine intake once the trial was over. A carpenter had told her not to bother replacing the door. The weather would soon warp the wood and the age of the building meant a new one would have to be custom made and fitted. Grace had decided to retain the original, the top half of which she left open in the summer.

She picked up the sandwich and bit into it. Her stomach accepted the food without complaint although her mind was still on the past.

The smooth progress of her childhood ambition was interrupted when she was twenty. During the Christmas vacation of her second year at Southampton, Gerald Cornell had, as always, organised many entertainments for his children and their friends. By then Luke was nearly fourteen and claimed he was too old for the annual pantomime. He was at the awkward age when childish things were behind him but he was not quite ready to join the adult world. Some of his friends came to stay and Gerald took them shooting or they made their own amusements, but mostly Luke took himself upstairs to the self-contained flat occupied by Mr and Mrs Collins who ran Gorstone Manor in their own way now that Olivia was no longer there to give them instructions. There were dinners for Grace's contemporaries and trips into Exeter. It was then that I knew, Grace thought. It was that Christmas when Aunt Monica came to deliver our presents and stayed only long enough to drink a glass of sherry. It had taken only the smallest gesture for her to see what should have been obvious to her for years.

It was two days after New Year's Eve when the telephone call came, the one that took both Gerald Cornell and his daughter out into the frosty night. But only Grace came home.

Numerous times the police had made her repeat her story but they had never been totally satisfied. Lately she had repeated it all to Inspector Jordan, or Harry as she had come to call him since, out of necessity, they had spent a great deal of time together. It had, she admitted, been foolish not to have done something about the letters as soon as she had received the first one but Harry soon understood her reluctance in showing them to anyone.

Grace frowned at her plate in surprise. It was empty. The moors were already weaving their spell. Her appetite was returning and she felt marginally stronger. Mentally stronger, too, she realised because thinking about her father and the night he had died had not made her panic.

This lovely old place has never failed me, she thought. She loved her work but an endless stream of patients took their toll.

Coming to the farmhouse refreshed and relaxed her and acted as a buffer against reality. Grace had never been sensitive to atmospheres in the way in which Ruth was. Ruth could walk into any house and shiver, saying she couldn't possibly live there, or yes, this is a happy place. But on the day the estate agent had unlocked the door and Grace had stepped into the flagstoned hallway she had known immediately that she would be safe and contented within these four walls and as happy as she was ever likely to be. It had been easy to picture how she would furnish the place because it had been empty, apart from the double bed which had been built in the bedroom because the doors and windows were too small to admit such a large item. The previous occupant, a Mrs Hooper, had died so there was no chain. Grace was a cash purchaser so the transaction had taken place very quickly. Mrs Hooper had died in the bed in which Grace slept but there were no ghosts. Living there alone, her life had been hard but she had survived until her ninetieth year and had died in her sleep. If she had left anything of herself it was only a sense of peace.

Grace had walked through the empty rooms with the estate agent on her heels, their footsteps echoing hollowly on the uncarpeted boards. Upstairs, the view from the main bedroom had made her gasp. There was no other dwelling in sight and the autumnal shades of heather and moss were all that could be seen as they spread for mile upon mile over the hills and down into the dips littered with lichened boulders. The sense of space had made her dizzy. And everywhere the sheep, their splotches of red or blue denoting their ownership.

Grace had taken three weeks off work in order to decorate and furnish the place but, despite her sense of achievement and the calmness she experienced when she was there, she did not invite guests or allow others to stay in the farmhouse. It was not some sort of holiday home, it meant far more to her than that. One of her partners, Anton Roach, and his wife, Carol, had a secluded place on the coast somewhere near Exmouth. Grace was more than fond of them both but she found their attitude to their weekend home amusing. They always went with an entourage of friends. Each trip involved countless journeys back and forth between their large house in Exeter and the car as they loaded the boot with food and wine and charcoal for the barbecue. Carol took the garlic press, a filleting knife and other such tools of the adventurous cook, one who, in Grace's eyes, returned to Exeter on Sunday evenings more exhausted than if she had stayed at home.

Matt had come to the farmhouse once, just after they had become engaged. Grace had tried hard to share her life with him but even then the warning signs were there. She had felt a small resentment at his presence which did not bode well for married life, but later she had seen that what she had really resented was his lack of interest and apparent boredom at being stuck in the middle of nowhere. They had not stayed the night as planned. It was around that time that she began to doubt that they were truly compatible. But it was Matt who was responsible for the final break-up of their relationship. Now she could think of him without hurting, but she wondered whether she had simply buried the pain, as she had done with so many other things. Matt was a doer, always on the go and unable to relax. But this was merely part of his make-up, an abundance of nervous energy. Grace's inabilty to relax came from an inner fear she had learned to live with and the dark places in her mind.

In front of her sat the empty plate, one of a set she had bought second-hand from a stall in the market in Tavistock. They were farmhouse blue and white and had cost Grace more than an equivalent new set of crockery would have done. Only once had anyone else eaten from them. It had been summer time, one of those days when the air was still and heavy and filled with the scent of dry vegetation. She had been sitting outside the front of the cottage with all the doors and windows open behind her. In the distance, where the main road rose out of a valley, sunlight had glinted off a stream of cars as each one crested the brow of the hill. The sight had mesmerised her. It had been like watching somebody signalling with a mirror at regular intervals. Way over there had been all that activity – tourists and picnickers, families with quarrelling children who were tired of being cooped up in a hot stuffy car, packed pubs and overcrowded tearooms and queues at the windows of the ice-cream vans in the lay-bys – whereas Grace was alone with the sweeping moor, the lazy sound of bees in the heather and the chomping of sheep at they tore at the grass. Then she had heard a car, its engine whining as the driver dropped down through the gears to negotiate the steep hills and the hairpin bends. It was heading in her direction. A two-door Metro rounded the corner and stopped opposite the farmhouse. The man behind the wheel had been red in the face and too large for the vehicle. Through his open window she had heard the American twang as he bemoaned the lack of air-conditioning to the woman sitting beside him.

'Hi,' he had called by way of greeting, as if he had doubted that Grace had noticed their arrival.

She had walked across to the couple, her arms stiffly at her sides, resentful of the intrusion. Because of their loud, golf-course type clothes she had wrongly mistaken them for stereotypes. However, they were hot and tired and, despite their map, lost.

'Do you do cream teas, honey?' the woman had said, leaning across her husband to address Grace from beneath a frizz of thin hair. Grace had smiled then because she had realised that she, in turn, had also been stereotyped.

'No,' she had replied and even now had no idea why she had invited them in. Perhaps it had had something to do with the look in the woman's eyes.

They had expressed their delight with the farmhouse and the coolness of the kitchen although they seemed to have the impression that every West Country home owner lived only to serve scones to visitors. Grace had apologised for not being the sort of woman who made her own bread and strawberry jam and hoped she had not disillusioned them by producing nothing more complicated than a pot of Earl Grey and a packet of digestive biscuits.

Once they were cooler and less parched they had talked about themselves and Grace had found them to be entertaining company. She would never forget them because, for an hour or so on a summer's afternoon, they had helped her to forget the things which haunted her. For Martha it had been her first trip to Europe and she and her husband had been doing a sort of whistle-stop tour of their own devising. They had flown to each destination then hired a car. 'We didn't want it to be this way,' Harvey had explained sadly, laying one of his suntanned hands upon the back of his wife's thin, veined one. 'We'd always planned to take at least a year after I retired and spend several weeks in all the major cities. You know, really get to know them? And we'd sure love to have spent some time in a place like this.'

'You might be lucky and find somewhere still vacant,' Grace had suggested. 'Why don't you ask in Princetown?'

The couple had exchanged a look and sad smiles. It was Martha who had spoken. 'I don't have the time, honey.'

Grace saw then, in her face, what she had failed to recognise earlier. As a doctor it was not something which was new to her and, had they been anywhere other than the farmhouse where she abandoned her professional role, she would have noticed immediately that Martha was dying, her life draining from her daily.

That was two summers ago. Six months later Harvey had written to say that Martha had died but that the kindness extended by Grace had made their day on Dartmoor one of the happiest of the trip. The letter had found her despite the inadequate address and the lack of her surname.

Grace got up and stretched. She had sat in one position for too long and her joints were stiffening after the walk. Putting the plate in the sink she felt wetness on her face but she did not know if she was crying for Martha, who was no longer alive, for Harvey, who had lost the wife he so obviously loved, or for herself.

From the window she noticed that a bird had left a track of clawprints on top of the snow on the dry-stone wall. It must be hungry to come so close, she thought. It was rare to see small birds near the farmhouse because there were only a few wind-stunted trees and bushes. Overhead the sky was darkening. It would not be safe to go out again that day even if she had had the energy to do so. The rest of the afternoon and Sunday stretched ahead of her. Now she wanted the time to pass slowly. How she dreaded Monday.

She took more coffee into the lounge and lit the fire in the grate. It had not been worth doing so last night. Judith had left it laid and although the central heating was more than adequate a real fire was a comfort and gave a focal point to the room. There was no initial warmth from the flames as they licked around the dry kindling but Grace sat back on her heels and watched the miniature display of fireworks as sparks crackled up the chimney. There was no television at the farmhouse but she could spend hours watching the changing patterns of the firelight and listening to the sap spitting and hissing. Her every-day world became an alien place whilst she was there. Nor did she bother to drive to the village for a newspaper. That she chose to isolate herself so completely only added to her friends' conviction that she was unstable and on the verge of a breakdown. Grace accepted that it was unusual but hardly a sign of insanity if a person could survive a weekend without being aware of the news. She argued that it was more insane to be in need of the continual fix of a television screen or half-hourly news bulletins on the radio and the manipulative editorials of the press. And Grace knew the power of the media, her family had suffered at its hands on more than one occasion. And is about to do so again, she realised, feeling her mind closing in upon itself. Her mental defence mechanisms, so often called for, blocked out all thoughts of Monday. We all cope in our different ways, she thought. That does not render us mad.

The sky had now acquired the peculiar pearliness which heralded more snow. If she was cut off she would not be able to attend court. No, she was tired of running, tired of looking over her shoulder all the time. She had to go through with it.

Wandering around the room she touched familiar things then picked up the telephone receiver to make sure it was working. If there was heavy snow on some other part of Dartmoor the lines might be down, but the dialling tone purred reassuringly from the earpiece.

On a shelf between well-thumbed books stood a picture of a smiling and handsome Matthew, squinting into the sun. It remained there because Grace had consciously decided not to change anything until after the trial. It was a silly superstition but it was as if the voice of Mrs Collins was directing her. She could almost hear her broad Devon vowels as she said, 'Leave things be lest you tempt the devil.' She had had a huge store of such sayings, many of which made no sense to Grace.

Like most people, Matthew and Grace had met by chance. They had been staying at the same hotel but for different reasons. He was a research chemist for a company which produced drugs but he also had an additional talent for being able to drum up sponsorship. He had been in London to speak to some influential people whereas Grace had had more hedonistic reasons. She and Fay, who had kept up their university friendship, had contrived to get the same weekend off. They went shopping, saw a matinée at the theatre and then had dinner together during which they arranged to spend Sunday sightseeing. Later, when Fay had gone home to her boyfriend, Grace had bought herself a brandy in the hotel bar. She and Matt were conspicuous by being the only solitary figures amongst couples and groups. There was nothing prurient in the striking up of a conversation and, afterwards, neither of them could recall who had spoken first. Their feelings for each other had grown slowly rather than burgeoning out of instant attraction. Grace had been amazed when Matt told her that his parents lived in a village near Exeter and that he now worked in the city.

'Two coincidences,' Grace had commented lightly when she learned how he earned his living. 'You produce drugs, I dish them out.' It was then that he had asked her for her telephone number. She gave him the one at the surgery. It was over a week before he telephoned by which time Grace had almost forgotten about him.

They began to meet regularly. Grace admired his dedication to his work and respected his intelligence, but more importantly, she enjoyed his company, he was able to make her laugh and the past seem less significant. And he was handsome. Loving him had been a gradual process and more satisfying than the headiness of mere sexual attraction. The Christmas before last Matt had given her an engagement ring and they had decided upon a date for their wedding. That date had since passed.

Grace had believed that Matt represented exactly what she needed and that together they would make one whole. But she had misjudged her needs or maybe Matt had been unable to fulfil them. They had enough similarities and differences to make the relationship interesting but it was not until it was over that she saw how Matt had steadily but subtly undermined her. 'You give them too much of yourself,' he would tell her, referring to her patients, when what he meant was that he begrudged them her time. But it was more complicated than that, she realised. He liked to think of me as a professional person but it was almost as if he wanted me to be a doctor without my having to attend the surgery. Once, at a dinner, Matt had given a speech and fluffed his lines. 'It wouldn't have happened if you'd been there, Grace,' he told her afterwards. 'You know how much I depend on your support.'

They had seemed like flattering words until she saw they were meant to induce guilt. She had been on call that evening. But he had failed to take into account Grace's own frailties. For this she

23

partly blamed herself. She wanted to prove that she could hold down a demanding job and run two homes and still have a full and active social life. Her vulnerability was kept hidden because she had been terrified of admitting to it in case she might admit too much.

'Did you sit at home and weep for me?' Matt had asked laughingly when he returned home from a week's trip abroad.

'Naturally,' Grace had replied with a grin, but deep down she wondered if he wished that she had. It was then that she saw more pitfalls and invited Matt to the flat for dinner. She wanted to clear the air, to explain that there were times when she felt helpless and useless such as when she could not provide a cure or find a specialist able to prevent the death of a very sick child.

'You're not God, Grace. You can only do your best,' he had told her, dismissing the subject almost at once.

But there had been some wonderful times and occasions when they had exchanged a look and laughed because they had both been thinking the same thing. However, she soon realised that once she had failed in the role of Matt's prop he had turned the situation around and made her the weak one. Now I know what real strength is, she thought. I have seen it in the shape of Harry Jordan. Grace bit her lip. She did not want to think about Harry.

Outside large snowflakes floated silently to the ground. It was not a flurry, there was no wind, and it was soothing to watch. They blanketed the landscape in the way Grace's denial of the past cloaked her consciousness.

The snow came to nothing. Within fifteen minutes it had stopped falling and darkness edged up over the distant hills to merge with their now shadowy shapes. The moor shimmered under a three-quarter moon and the frost hardened. It was a beautiful sight. Way in the darkness a car ascended the hill, its headlights beamed upwards like searchlights, then disappeared. Grace turned away from the window, unable to see snow without thinking of her father.

She took a deep breath and and walked briskly to the kitchen. It is definitely time for a glass of Bordeau, she thought, and then I shall grill that steak.

MONICA

Beyond the bay window with its cretonne curtains and padded window-seat, snow lay thickly on the lawn. Crisp and white, it showed no signs of melting although it glinted in the morning sunlight. Across it ran the tracks of birds, criss-crossing lines of tiny fleurs-de-lis, the single indentations of the back claw like a stem. They belonged to the blackbird whose territory it was and the robin which came to feed timorously from Monica's outstretched hand. Apart from half a dozen friends and acquaintances they were her main companions these days. She had come to know their habits well. Every morning she put out scraps and seeds and broke the ice in the old dog bowl from which they drank. When Poppy, the last in a line of red-setters, had had to be put down Monica had decided not to replace her. It had been another ending, another way in which she had altered because no one could remember a time when she didn't have a dog.

She now lived in Exeter in a sound and solid house, although it was not in the class of Gorstone Manor, her family home and where she had been born. As a daughter and the younger child she had always been aware that it would be Gerald who would inherit it. There was no animosity, she and her brother had loved each other deeply. He had told her she must still consider it to be her home. By that time she had just married Freddie and as he was about to do a tour in the Far East it had seemed perfectly natural for Monica to live in the lodge whilst looking for a suitable place for their marital home. It had not happened. Monica found fault with every property she viewed but deep down she knew this was because she could not bear to be away from Gorstone. Freddie, who adored her, finally agreed to live at the lodge. 'It doesn't matter greatly,' he had told her. 'We'll be out of the country a lot of the time. As long as we've got a base in England, that's all that counts.' This had shaken Monica, who had imagined she would carry on as before but with a sometimes absentee husband. They had compromised. Monica agreed to accompany him as long as she could come back whenever she found she was homesick.

Their father, Charles Cornell, had outlived his wife Elizabeth, by only two years. Before he died he had assured Monica that his children had been provided for equally. Her inheritance was in the form of the property in Scotland where he used to go to shoot, and the farmhouse in France which had been purchased long before such things had become fashionable amongst the British. There were also some stocks and bonds which had served her well. Monica hated Scotland and had put what she thought of as the bleak mausoleum on the market immediately, allowing the agent to arrange matters without travelling up there herself. The French place had been dealt with in a similar manner, although for different reasons. There were too many happy childhood memories for her to be able to bear to visit it again. After Gerald's death foreign travel had lost its appeal. So had many other things, Monica reflected with regret.

It had come as a surprise that Gerald had left Gorstone Manor to Grace, although she was his elder child. Tradtionally it was passed down to the males. But Gerald had known his son and had feared what might happen to the place in Luke's hands. Monica had cried when she heard that it had been sold but any resentment faded quickly. She would have done the same thing in Grace's position. The new occupants had extended one or two dinner invitations to Monica because they were aware of the history of Gorstone and imagined they were being kind in asking her back to her home. Monica had declined without excuses. It was impossible to return now that it belonged to someone other than Gerald. Yet here she was, staring out of the window of the house she had shared with Freddie as if the suburbs of Exeter did not exist and she could see over the moors to where they had all once been so happy.

'Is it really eight years since you died, Gerald? Yes, I suppose it must be.' Monica spoke aloud. One-sided conversations were not unusual. It was not a sign of senility, it was a way of filling the silence. Gorstone had been full of people and laughter; self-enforced solitude was Monica's penance.

Freddie's death, coming so soon after Gerald's, had not affected her nearly as much. Several people had commented upon this but Monica explained that as she was still grieving for her brother she was unable to take in the enormity of what had happened. 'It'll hit her one day,' her friends had said. But it didn't because her love for Freddie had always been incomplete.

It did not matter that she was seeing no one that day. Before she came downstairs Monica had bathed and dressed and applied make-up just as she did every day of her life. Her mother had instilled in her a rigid set of standards which she rarely allowed to drop although lately, instead of skirts, she had taken to wearing well-cut trousers with a blouse and one of her collection of elaborately embroidered sweaters. There were few left to admire her enviable legs. Monica smiled. From out of nowhere she heard a voice protesting, 'Our women always wear a skirt.' On the day that Monica had appeared in the bright red ski-pants that were all the rage in the fifties, Elizabeth Cornell had frowned her disapproval.

But the outward show of control was the antithesis of her inner self. Even in her wildest days she had taken trouble with her appearance and had kept hidden the depths of her feelings. Although Gerald was outwardly more flamboyant they had shared an ability to conceal or disguise their passions. When Gerald was excited his face might remain impassive but the air crackled around him. Monica had had no idea that the same could be said of herself. Once or twice she had caught people looking back over their shoulders at her as she danced or, shoes off, ran after one of the dogs with a childlike spontaneity.

She sat sideways on the window-seat. Look at me now, she thought, who would take me for anything other than a well-bred, well-heeled middle-aged lady? But the passion was still there, tamped down, maybe, but still smouldering. It was only outwardly she had changed. As tears blurred her eyes the snow disappeared and she saw, not her own garden, but the grounds of Gorstone Manor. There were people on the terrace, drinks in their hands, and the sound of music in the evening air. They were all there; herself and Freddie, Gerald and his family with Olivia looking extra stunning in a floating yellow dress. Luke had been sulky, he had always preferred to shut himself up with the Collinses rather than socialise with the guests. On that occasion he had been made to join the party although he was only five or six. And Grace. She must have been twelve and already

27

turning into a younger replica of Olivia. They were such a beautiful group. Even Freddie had been debonaire and amusing. There were other guests, of course, many of them, but she could no longer recall their names. All she remembered was the dancers spilling out of doors on to the terrace and grass because it was so hot, and herself being whirled around by various men, including her brother. But they had had to give up because they were laughing so much. It had all been so much fun and such a contrast to the role she had had to play as the wife of an officer. But at least it taught me that I could play the part, she thought, and, my God, how much I needed to on occasions.

Monica squinted uncomprehendingly. The sky was indeed blue, but there was snow on the ground. Gorstone and those magic days were no more. She must stop thinking about them.

The percolator was bubbling at last. Monica could hear it, and the slightly bitter aroma of the blend of coffee she bought in a specialist shop in the city filled the room. She wiped her eyes and went to the kitchen where she got out the bone china breakfast cup and saucer decorated with blue flowers. Luke had given it to her for her birthday the year after Freddie died. The undoubtedly beautiful porcelain was a sobering reminder of the state of things: a single cup and saucer. She saw herself as if from afar, sitting drinking coffee in her kitchen like countless other widows. What has happened to me? she wondered. I'm not old. Perhaps it just seems that way sometimes because there's no one left other than Gerald's children. And Luke has drifted away and Grace, so like Olivia, was lost to me eight years ago.

There was no doubting Luke's parentage. He had Gerald's soft, fair hair and stubborn jawline and he even held himself in the same way. After Olivia's departure, when he had gone away to school, she had done all that she supposed was expected of an aunt, for her brother's sake as well as for Luke's. There were food parcels containing cakes and sweets to be shared out with the other boys and trips to the coast followed by dinner in a restaurant on his half-day holidays. Following the parcels and the outings came short, polite notes thanking her. Monica had always known she could not replace his mother but she loved Gerald's child as if he were her own. Luke's letters, written in a childish hand, were still in a box on the top shelf of her walk-in dressing-room along with other precious items. She still did not know if he had taken half as much pleasure from those shared afternoons as she had done.

Naturally, she had expected to see less of Luke as he grew up. The drifting apart had been a gradual occurrence, unlike her rift with Grace. She and Gerald had also seen less of each other after Olivia went away. It was odd, but she had no longer felt quite the same at Gorstone afterwards. It was as if the magnetic force of the place had diminished without Olivia's presence, and Monica's visits became less frequent. She and Gerald knew why this was but they kept their thoughts to themselves.

Then there was the row which had taken place between Gerald and Freddie, the one which she believed Grace might have overheard. Monica had not been a witness to it but Freddie had come home white-faced and with a look of fury which she had rarely seen. It had taken her a long time to realise that she might not have been the focal point of the disagreement but, in view of what happened afterwards, she thought perhaps that she was. Freddie had refused to discuss it.

Everything had changed beyond recognition and she had had to change, too. The inevitable could only be accepted and the best of it made. Which reminded her, it was far too long since Luke had come for dinner. She would ring him later. He always remembered to send a card and a well-chosen gift on her birthday or at Christmas but she really would like to see more of him.

But Grace was the one who worried her. As a child she had been fun and funny, easy in the company of adults and other children, but there was a will of iron beneath the affable exterior. When, at the age of ten, Grace had announced that she was going to become a doctor, no one had disbelieved her. Then, at thirteen, she began to change. She was more withdrawn and secretive and occasionally downright awkward. Monica had recognised the onset of adolescence and was prepared to sit out the storm until her relationship with her niece could be cemented in adulthood. Knowing what some of her friends had gone through with teenage daughters she had pitied Olivia, but then, all of a sudden, Olivia was not there to help Grace through this difficult period.

From the kitchen window Monica logged the blackbird's

movements as it hopped across the lawn then doubled back on itself before disappearing amongst the tangle of the leafless hedge at the side of the house. Twigs shook and a fine spray of snow drifted to the ground. How simple the bird's life seemed compared with her own.

Grace was on her mind a lot recently. Ever since she had read that first report in the newspaper she had felt a sense of danger. It was so unlike her controlled niece to have allowed the situation to develop. The trial was coming up but all Monica knew was what she had read in the press. Luke had little to say on the subject, but that was out of loyalty to his sister, and Olivia with whom she corresponded sporadically knew no more than herself. And there was the real irony, that it was Olivia with whom she still kept in touch. It was all very worrying and she wished now she had not alerted Olivia to what was happening. She might take it into her head to come back and if she did, what then? Does Grace know? Monica thought, not for the first time. Is that why she refuses to have anything to do with me? And would she pass on what she knew to Olivia?

Monica sighed. Grace Elizabeth Cornell, the cumbersome middle name after her paternal grandmother, Monica's mother. She had been a strong woman, too. And it had taken a strong woman to do what Grace had done for Luke, Monica had to admit. Studying for her career and grieving for her father herself, she had somehow kept the boy on his feet and got him through it. Luke's trouble was that he had inherited his father's charm and charisma, along with a certain recklessness, but he lacked the self-discipline which Gerald had applied to his life and of which most people were unaware. He had always known exactly where to draw the line. Except in one thing, she thought, but by then it had been too late. On the other hand it seemed that Grace possessed a little too much self-discipline. Monica wondered if she was ever capable of letting go. She hoped the humour and tenderness which she had displayed as a child and which would be wonderful attributes in her career had not disappeared, but it was a long time since she had seen Grace so she had no idea what she was like. Did she have anyone to lean on, to get her through the trial? Luke had mentioned that her engagement to Matthew was off but as she had never met the man she could not pass judgement. I'm not in a position to pass judgement on anyone, she reminded herself as she poured more coffee and buttered a soft roll which was all that she ate in the mornings.

Breakfast over, Monica walked slowly through the downstairs rooms, the low heels of her leather boots clicking on the woodblock flooring in the hall. She paused to study her face in the mirror, surprised she did not look drawn. Without vanity she was aware that she had worn well, far better than many blondes, who faded into insignificance. Olivia, she thought, will be beautiful still as an old woman. Monica's fair hair was parted slightly to one side. It fell in arcs to just beneath her chin. It was soft although it no longer gleamed as in her youth. Her face was pale, but naturally so, the contours emphasised with blusher, and, she had to admit, she could get away with wearing trousers, unlike many of her contemporaries.

An ornate wrought-iron banister supported a mahogany rail which curved up the carpeted staircase. Monica ran a hand along its polished surface. No child had slid down it, not in her and Freddie's time together. They had had no children, which was a souce of deep regret to Freddie and of complete indifference to Monica. There had always been her brother's family. But Freddie had been right about many things, not least the purchase of the house which had trebled in value and which Monica had gradually come to regard with a little less distaste. There was nothing wrong with it, it was simply that anywhere more than half a mile from Gorstone was too far.

Freddie had been a good husband and a faithful one, she thought, going through to the lounge, a reliable and dependable man who had always stood by her and whom she had mistakenly believed to be rather unexciting until the one time he had allowed his feelings free rein. It startled her that they had almost matched the strength of her own. It was a fanciful idea but Monica wondered if the coronary thrombosis which had killed him had been the direct result of the unexpressed emotions bottled up inside him expanding until they squeezed the life out of him. Or had he simply died of a broken heart?

With the fingers of both hands spread she pushed her hair behind her ears and moved away from the window where she had been standing for some time. The heels of her boots had formed square indentations in the thickness of the pastel Wilton beneath her feet. The robin had appeared, later than usual, and, head on one side, was appraising her through the glass. Her mood lifted. She smiled and moved swiftly to the utility room where she donned a thick coat and scarf and picked up a packet of seed.

The cold air stung her face but it felt clean and purifying in contrast to her thoughts. She shook her head in disbelief. Impossible to imagine Grace attacking a man and then, in turn, terrible things happening to Grace. But the questions which kept ringing in Monica's head were, does she know, and if she does will any of it come out at the trial?

She stood, motionless, her arm outstretched stiffly as the bitterly cold wind penetrated her clothing and she waited for the robin. Action, even as small as feeding the birds, normally relegated thoughts of the past to the back of her mind. Not so on that Saturday morning, knowing that the ordeal Grace was about to face might expose the sham of their lives.

One eye on Monica, the robin pecked at the seed before flying off over the fence to next door's garden.

Monica stamped her boots on the doormat and went inside where she hung up her coat and scarf. She turned and saw the breakfast dishes still on the kitchen table. Something hot spread from her stomach and flowed through her limbs. She lunged forward and picked up Luke's precious gift, hurling the delicate china at the tiled wall where it shattered. The pieces dropped to the floor in slow motion.

Breathing deeply to counteract the racing of her heart, Monica lifted her head, stepped over the broken shards and went into the hall, closing the door behind her.

It was not the cup which she hated but what it represented. Her hand on the banister, she lowered her head and wept. She had destroyed Luke's gift. How could she possibly have done such a thing when she loved him so much and he was all she had left of her brother?

For all her pretences the fires within her burned as hotly as ever.

HARRY

For Harry Jordan Friday nights had once been as predictable as many other nights. He was either on duty or in the pub. The Jolly Porter at the bottom of St David's Hill was the one he used most often and where he stayed long enough for the alcohol to anaesthetise the pain. He rarely got drunk, preferring to achieve that mild form of euphoria where nothing seemed to matter, and his being there delayed his going home. On Wednesdays, whenever possible, he went there to listen to the jazz. Naturally there had been periods of leave but if there was a chance of overtime he took it. If none was available he went to stay with his sister in Okehampton where he suspected he got under her feet although she claimed to be glad of the company and someone to take the children off her hands for an hour or so each day. Their innocence was a refreshing change from what he dealt with at work.

That was how it used to be. It was Friday now but that other life was obsolete. The trial began on Monday and, apart from when he was called to the witness box, matters were out of his hands. Instead of experiencing the anticlimactic lethargy the end of an investigation usually produced, Harry found he could not relax. An hour after he could reasonably have left his desk he was still sitting behind it wondering what Grace was doing. He was certain she would have made for the farmhouse. He thought he knew her well enough to assume that she would not wish to burden anyone with her anxieties. That, of course, had been Grace's problem.

The clock on the wall ticked once for each second. It was a muted, soothing sound and only altered when the minute hand reached the twelve when, for some unknown reason, it gave a clunk. Harry was able to judge the time without the need of a watch but he still looked up on the hour. Nine o'clock, but he couldn't face the pub with its Friday night revellers. No one there knew that his wife had left him. It was eighteen months ago but he was still shaken. Gillian had gone off with one of his

33

colleagues, the man whose position Harry now filled. A nice little irony, that. Had Gillian remained faithful he might still be a sergeant. What he couldn't work out was whether the anger had evaporated in the natural course of events or because of his interest in the Harrington case. On the other hand, did it matter? Yes, he was still shaken, but no longer bitter, miserable and raw.

Initially his emotions had been very close to the surface and he had struggled to keep his temper. This was followed by a period of numbness when he felt empty inside. On those days he would take the car and drive to the Exe and walk along its banks filling his lungs with the sharp air which blew up the estuary as if it might also fill the hiatus within him. At high tide numerous small boats bobbed on its wide surface. During the autumn and winter he watched the waders feeding at the edge of the water, following the ebbing tide as they immersed their long bills deep into the mud, much as the bait diggers, a little behind them, worked away from the shoreline and sank their forks in search of lugworms. Harry had not learned the names of the birds, it was enough to know that their cycle went on uninterrupted, unlike his own. Marriage, a house and kids. That was what he had envisaged for himself. He had managed to acquire the first two but had already lost the former. Many times he had stood by the river looking down towards Dawlish Warren or over to Lympstone Barracks on the opposite bank and wondered if a few turns around the gruelling assault course would bring exhaustion and relief.

The divorce had been messy and acrimonious. Harry did not understand why, when a woman had already done you wrong, she would turn against you as if she had been the injured party. Gillian was not alone in this.

The weather had been too bad for many of those solitary walks this winter but, because of the way things had worked out, Harry would not have had time to take them anyway. The emptiness had been filled although he was not sure with what. He had believed that he had been functioning on two levels, that his private grief had been allowed no room during working hours. He was wrong, many of his colleagues had suffered at his hands, but at least he had been alert enough to spot the name Grace Cornell as PC Cobane tapped it into the computer.

Harry had been baiting a female detective, being deliberately crude because he was hurting and he wanted to hurt back. He couldn't get at Gillian who had moved away with her lover, so any female was game. But, like Gillian, this one had upstaged him. She had let him finish then, with an innocent smile, said quite deliberately, 'I suppose that's the only way someone like you can get your rocks off. Sir.' The 'sir' had been added contemptuously and caused PC Cobane, sitting at his terminal, to try to hide a smirk. He was unsuccessful.

'What's your problem?' Harry had snapped.

Cobane had averted his eyes knowing any sort of reply would lay him open to the inspector's vitriol. They were all aware of the reason for it, they could not help but be.

'What's this?' Harry had indicated the screen, surprising Cobane who had been expecting the worst.

'An affray, sir. A woman by the name of –'

'I can read the bloody name. What happened?'

The young constable had explained how Grace Cornell, a partner in a small GPs' practice, had, without provocation, attacked Carl Roberts in the street. Carl Roberts was blind. A couple who had witnessed the attack from their window had rung the police and a patrol car in the area had arrived pretty quickly. 'According to the report she was incoherent. She was rambling on about letters and being followed. The officers who picked her up thought she was a nutter and had wandered off from somewhere. They brought her in just in case.'

'Any charges?'

'Nope. Roberts wants to let the matter drop. We checked her out, then her brother came to fetch her.'

'The brother's name?'

Cobane did not know. He had had to go and find out. The brother's name was Luke.

'Thanks.' He had not been involved in the investigation into the death of Gerald Cornell, he had been away on a training course at the start, but everyone had heard about it because the name Cornell was well known in Devon and always attracted a lot of press coverage. And the daughter, he recalled, had been at medical school at the time. Then it *was* the same girl. So what, he wondered, had caused Dr Cornell to attack someone when she had spent all those years training to patch them up?

Harry knew all about training. At university he had read law, intending to take up that profession, but something had held him back, some niggling fear of success despite his wish to show his father how wrong he had been. After leaving university he had gone to law school in London then, completing only one year of what was then called Articles, he had walked out, surprising both himself and the firm of solicitors who had taken him on, and joined the police. His degree was still a source of resentment amongst some of his colleagues. But something had led him to the point he had now reached on this bitter January night. Harry was not superstitious nor did he have any faith in fate yet he took comfort from knowing that this was where he was meant to be. Had he not antagonised his father so bullishly, a man he despised for sitting around in his vest and boasting that the only proper way to earn a living was through manual labour, had he not been so determined to shove his father's words down his throat, he would not have stayed on at school to prove that education was not a waste of time. It was thanks to the gently persuasive powers of his mother and teachers that he had been allowed to do so. But would he have arrived here via a different route? It was doubtful. As a teenager, becoming a policeman had not crossed his mind. Had he not gained a university place he would have gone into office work, taken any job as long as it entailed wearing a suit and ensured he did not end up like Frank Jordan. Celia, Harry's mother, was a pacific woman and allowed life to wash over her. Over the years she had become inured to her husband's coarseness and the fact that he didn't bath often enough. A lack of confidence made him aggressive. He had a need to prove to his family that he was a real man doing a real man's work.

Unlike his mother Harry was not prepared to give in and make the best of it. He, too, had something to prove. It saddened him to think that he had not enjoyed university for what it was but had merely used it as a way of hitting back. He rarely saw his parents now. A couple of times a year he took his mother out for a meal but she was always in a hurry to get home. The last time he had paid a visit to the house Frank Jordan had deteriorated further. A paunch hung over his trousers, stretching his vest at the seams, and he was unshaven and stank. What Harry did not fail to notice was the lost look on his father's face as if he had realised, as retirement loomed closer, that there was nothing left for him: no hobbies, no friends, no grandchildren. He had thrown the latter at his son often enough. Harry's sister and family never visited. No wonder Gillian had not been able to stand him. Harry had never blamed her for that.

Gillian worked for a child support agency and had walked into his life one hot summer's afternoon to discuss a case in which several professional teams were involved. She wore the sort of dress of which no mother could disapprove but on her it was sexy. They had gone out for a drink, ostensibly to talk things over although all the necessary discussion had already taken place. They were married within six months, which gave both sets of parents cause for alarm, but to begin with the relationship had strengthened, reaching an apex after approximately three years when Harry acknowledged that the happiness Gillian had found in their marriage had given her a taste for more. She had decided that Inspector Yorke could provide it.

Half-past nine. What on earth was he doing, sitting in his office trying to analyse things he had no chance of under-standing? On the desk in front of him was the transcript of the tapes of the interviews Grace Cornell had given just after her father had died. He still wasn't sure what bearing, if any, they had on Monday's trial, but he decided to go over them again anyway. He skipped the first few sheets which covered the formalities and began to read. Against each line were the initials of the person speaking.

'My father received a telephone call a few minutes after nine o'clock and came to tell me he had to go out. It was snowing heavily and I asked if it was really necessary. He told me it was but that he wouldn't be long.

'Not long after the phone rang again. I was studying because it isn't easy in the daytime with Luke and his friends around and people my father knows in the house. It was a bad line but I heard my father asking me to go and meet him because he was in some sort of difficulty with the car. He gave me directions. They were easy to follow because I know the moors well. I thought the road might have become impassable but it wasn't as bad as I feared and we've all got chains on our wheels. My headlights picked out the car easily, it was parked at the side of the road. I got out but there was no sign of my father and his coat was on the front passenger seat. We've always lived on Dartmoor, none of us would have got out unless we were adequately dressed and I know he wouldn't have left the road in those conditions. His phone wasn't in the car and the battery on mine needed recharging.

'I started to panic. I couldn't go looking for him, it was too dangerous and it would have been foolish to have the rescue teams sent out after me and then to find he'd turned up safely after all. But I had no means of contacting them on his behalf unless I went to the phone box in Princetown or returned home. I thought he might've slipped and fallen into one of those ditches alongside the road. He might've been only yards away, hidden by the snow. I shouted his name. I was crying, I can remember that. I knew I couldn't just leave him but I had to get help. I panicked, I was desperate, I remember running up and down the road shouting, begging him to answer me. That's the last thing I do remember until I woke up in hospital and some-body told me that he was dead.'

Harry was aware of the circumstances but he just wanted to see if the transcript contained any clues to recent events. 'The past is over and done with,' Harrington's first letter had said. Last year, just after Grace had attacked Carl Roberts, he had listened to the tapes themselves; again when Matthew was in hospital and once more during the time that Grace had been missing. Now he was staring at the printed words.

'You seem to have shown little curiosity about where your father was going. Why was that, Miss Cornell?' the interviewing officer had asked.

'My father's personal life is none of my concern.'

'So it was a personal call.'

'I assumed so. An educated guess. It was hardly likely that a business problem would have taken him out at night, not when he can pick up a telephone and ring any of his contacts any-where in the world if necessary.'

Harry chewed the side of his mouth. Grace had been what, twenty? at the time her father had died, yet she had sounded mature and unemotional. When he had first listened to her voice, before he had met her, he imagined she might be mocking the police, that she had something to hide. Now he saw it was her way of distancing herself from pain. She was, and still is, he thought, a very cool customer. He read on.

'Why do you think he went out?'

'My mother left us six years ago and my father is not the sort of man likely to remain celibate. I imagined he was meeting a woman, perhaps one who was married and had got away on some pretext or other, or maybe it was someone who worked until late.'

'Was there any woman in particular?'

'Gorstone Manor is open house to numerous people, obviously some of them are female, but I don't know of anyone who meant more to him than the others. Naturally I can't speak for when I'm away, you'll have to ask Mr and Mrs Collins about that.'

'Why did your mother leave?'

Grace had hesitated before saying that she didn't know, and that she hadn't heard from her since.

'This telephone call you say you received –'

'Which I did receive.' Grace had interrupted very quietly but very firmly. This did not come across on paper but in his head he could still hear her voice over the intermittent bleeps on the tape which were there to prove it had not been tampered with.

'Can you recall your father's exact words?'

'I doubt it, I had no cause to think I would need to.'

'One more thing, Miss Cornell. I can almost accept your lack of curiosity but did you always obey your father's commands as readily as that night?'

When he had heard the soft, seductive laugh its inappropriateness had startled Harry. The written transcription could not convey it or what he took to be the adoration of her father which came over in her voice.

'You did not know my father. There were few people who would not have done anything for him. Particularly . . . me.' Why the pause? Harry wondered. Was it significant or had the reality only just hit her?

After the Carl Roberts incident he had decided that although Gerald Cornell's daughter had shown an amazing lack of curiosity he, Harry Jordan, was suffering from a surfeit of it.

He locked the file away and stretched. Tired and hungry, he

decided there was just time for one drink before he went home, but he would have to hurry. In the men's washroom he splashed water on his face and noticed the dark smudges beneath his eyes as they met their own reflection in the mirror above the basin. His brown hair, two shades lighter than Grace's, was tousled. The lines in his face, especially the arcs from nose to chin, were not signs of age, he was only thirty-four, they were remnants of the months of misery and anger he had endured. His body wasn't bad but he was no great looker and unless he smiled, which was not often enough, he knew he was considered to be ugly. That was something he was helpless to change but he had learned to concentrate on the things which he could.

Later, feeling slightly more optimistic after a pint of bitter and a whisky chaser, he walked home, his collar up against the biting wind. The pavements were clear of snow but slippery with slush which would freeze overnight and make walking hazardous in the morning. There were few people around, most had the sense to stay indoors, but traffic swished along the road, sending filthy spray out from under its wheels. Harry noticed none of this. He was still thinking about Grace. About Grace and her relationship with Harrington. Past and present, he thought, recalling what Ruth Ferrers had told him.

He reached home and fumbled with the front door key. His hands were as numb with cold as his body had once been with unhappiness. The house had a bareness about it since the removal of Gillian's bits and there were still nails sticking out of the wall where her small collection of paintings had hung. These things did not concern Harry; he had never liked the place. It was modern, semi-detached and part of a housing estate. It had been Gillian's choice. He had bought her out some months ago and was now free to sell it. Maybe quite soon he would.

There was half a pizza in the fridge. He warmed it up and poured a whisky then ate in front of the wall-mounted gas fire. In the morning he would go back to the Gerald Cornell file and look at the rest of the statements: Luke's and the Collinses' and Monica's, and, if there was time, all the others which had proved equally useless. The case, if it was one, had never been solved. The Coroner had reluctantly pronounced the verdict of death by misadventure and there had not been a shred of evidence to produce for the Crown Prosecution Service. Yet every copper involved had been dissatisfied with the outcome. However, although it was history, it might have some bearing on the forthcoming trial. Grace certainly believed it did. What concerned him was how Grace would bear up if things went the wrong way. And there was a chance that they would. If the defence lawyers were clever enough they could turn the whole thing around and make Grace seem the guilty party, despite the optimism of the CPS concerning a conviction. They would not have let it go to trial otherwise. Even Ruth Ferrers, Grace's best friend, had admitted that she was concerned about her mental state, as had her partners at the surgery.

He had not known any of these people but it struck him that with the breaking up of the Cornell marriage an awful lot more had been destroyed. Viewed from a distance, he saw that, together, Olivia and Gerald had been like a sun, the others rotating around them like satellites. With Olivia in Italy and Gerald dead a whole solar system had disintegrated, leaving all the survivors scarred.

Harry grinned at his metaphorical line of thought and poured another finger of whisky which he took up to the soulless box of his bedroom, wondering if the time would come when somebody else would share it with him again. Probably not, not here if he really intended to sell. He looked after himself reasonably well, the sheets were clean, but they were icy cold. Harry Jordan fell asleep before his body could register the fact.

GRACE

During the afternoon snow started to fall again. It was heavier now. Large, silent flakes dropped steadily to the ground obscuring the view with their thickness and cutting Grace off from the rest of the world. The room was warm, lit only by the flickering fire as an early dusk descended. Outside there was a deep hush as the snow obliterated everything; from within only the quiet hum of the fridge in the kitchen and the crackling of the fire broke the silence. Grace needed little sleep, like her father five or six hours sufficed, but she had driven herself to the point of exhaustion. Her eyelids drooped and finally closed. When she woke the room was in darkness apart from a few red embers glowing in the grate. She came around slowly. Her mouth tasted horrible. She stretched and got up to switch on the table lamps and repair the fire. It was seven fifteen.

In the kitchen she drank a glass of icy tap water and ran a hand through her hair knowing that she must look a mess but that it didn't matter because at the farmhouse she could be herself. Taking the steak from the fridge she decided to indulge herself with her favourite vegetables. Like a prisoner on the eve of his execution, she thought with a wry smile. The red wine was open to let it breathe, although Anton Roach, the senior partner in the practice who considered himself to be an expert, had said that it should always be decanted. She prepared sprouts and carrots and cauliflower, or broccoli as it was called locally. The florets were yellow, as they should be, and not the startling white which the EU had crazily insisted upon. Grace had been fifteen when she read George Orwell's *1984* and lately, with so many petty restrictions on life, she wondered just how far away the thought police were and was grateful that, for the moment, they could not see into her mind.

This will be a feast, she decided, but looking at the food she wondered if she would be able to eat it all. The carrots had come with their leaves and were encrusted with mud. Judith's brother had grown them and she had proudly claimed they were organic. Grace had seen the brother buying fertiliser; maybe it was organic fertiliser. Once the vegetables were simmering she placed the steak under the grill where it began to spit. Outside the kitchen window the snow continued to fall.

On waking, Olivia had been on her mind although she could not remember dreaming about her. What does she look like? Has she changed at all? she thought. Maybe she had succumbed to too much pasta and become fat and unrecognisable. Olivia had never been vain although she had every reason to be. An image of Harry Jordan came into her head. Perhaps because, in contrast to Olivia, he was far from good-looking. But there was something about his heavy-featured face which she liked. And for a policeman, she thought, he has shown enormous tact and never treated me with anything other than a respect I'm not sure I deserve. She failed to understand what was so compelling about him. He had kissed her once, such an out-of-character act that it had shocked them both. Neither of them had referred to it since. She would see him on Monday because, naturally, Harry would be called to give evidence.

The meal was ready. Grace sat at the kitchen table and tried to concentrate on a play on Radio 4, thinking that other people's dialogue might distract her from the one going on in her head. It is not me who is on trial, she kept reminding herself, but in the eyes of the world it would seem that way, especially in view of what the defendant alleges. She called him that: Lance Harrington, the defendant. It distanced him and made their contact less personal. Whatever the outcome Grace knew she would be damaged in some way and that there was nothing she could do to prevent it.

The play was over. Grace had missed the ending. There was still some food on her plate but she had eaten most of it. The carrots did taste different from those she bought in Exeter, maybe she had maligned Judith's brother. She must leave a note, thanking her. Judith appreciated Grace's need of solitude but might, if she could get through, call in on Sunday.

The dishes were put in the sink to await the morning. Grace found it odd that on the moors she could be so sluttish whereas in the flat everything had to be immaculate. There was no point in analysing it, not when she could not understand the bigger issues and when, like her friends, she had moments of doubt regarding her sanity. Even Ruth doubted it. Grace had seen it in her face. In Judith and Ruth and Fay she had the best friends anyone could wish for, and her partners ran a close second. She had felt mean refusing their offer of dinner but after the conversation with Matthew and with what loomed ahead she had known that normal conversation would have been impossible and that too many questions would have been asked. She would have her fill of those next week. At least Matt now knew there was no going back. She had been stupid to agree to remain friends, the break should have been final.

She smoked her last cigarette of the day and threw the butt in the fire, which she then damped down. The stairs creaked beneath her and a board on the landing groaned. The sounds were ones she had come to know well. There was a small step down into the bathroom. In the days when the toilet was outside it had been a single bedroom and was therefore on the large side. Grace cleaned her teeth and studied her face in the mirror. Some colour had returned and the yellowish tinge which pallor had lent to her olive skin had now disappeared.

She filled a hot water bottle. Like Olivia's her feet were always cold; at least, Olivia's used to be. Maybe she warmed them on Tony's back. Grace remembered him quite clearly. He had always stood out from the crowd of men who had flocked to Gorstone. It was not because he was foreign, many of her father's visitors were from overseas, but because he had a quiet manner and a way of listening to whatever was being said. That he had worshipped Olivia was obvious. His eyes would follow her around a room and he was the first one to jump to his feet to open the door for her. Her father had not objected, Tony was a long-standing family friend, a friend to both of them, and Olivia, who, in turn, worshipped Gerald, would not have dreamed of being unfaithful. But in the end she had been. It still seemed inconceivable. Gerald had been her life; even her children noticed the way her face lit up whenever she saw him, how she could barely refrain from touching him whenever he came near. Tony may have adored Olivia but Olivia idolised Gerald.

And then, six years after her mother had left, on a fine sunny day before Christmas, Grace had asked a question to which her father had not replied. But it did not matter, the silence was answer enough. It was then that everything fell into place. Or so

44

she had thought. She had not known which of her parents she hated most. Too late, she realised how it may have really been.

Grace picked up her novel but Harry Jordan's face floated before her. 'I wish the damn man would leave me alone,' she muttered, turning over to find a more comfortable position. He's ugly, she decided, and what my father would have described as 'too big for himself', the type of man you always felt you would trip over if he was in the same room. It was not that he was clumsy, just that his limbs seemed not to belong to him. Grace had seen people stare at him then look away hurriedly. His features were large and mismatched as if his face had been repaired after an accident, yet she was attracted to their quirkiness. He had said that his wife had left him, perhaps that was why he was sympathetic, because he guessed what she had been going through with Matt on top of everything else. He had mentioned that he had listened to the taped interviews conducted at the time of her father's death but he had not said what he had made of them, nor if he believed any of what he had heard. Harry Jordan does not give much away, she realised.

Grace knew that on Monday, as further proof of her instability, the defence lawyers would bring up the fact that she had attacked a man. A blind man at that, one who was totally innocent of any offence against her. Perhaps it did prove something after all. It certainly proved the state of her mind on that particular day.

She put down the book. It was no good, she had reached page five without taking in a word. Around the time she had received the first letter Grace had told Ruth that she felt sure she was being watched, and that she had noticed the man with the dark glasses and a white stick several times in the vicinity of her flat. Ruth suggested that the letters were making her paranoid but she could not help thinking what a perfect disguise it was. From behind those glasses he could be watching anyone. Dressed in a shapeless mac and wearing an odd straw hat he could easily have been Harrington, the man who had so much power over her, power she had inadvertently given him.

Matt was due at the flat for dinner on the evening it happened. By then the third and last letter had arrived and she had intended telling him about them. This was the same morning

Anton, who knew nothing of what was happening, but who had recognised the state she was in, had called her into his consulting room before surgery began.

'Grace, I feel we ought to talk. Have a seat.' He had paused, his chin in his hand as he paced the floor, wishing he did not have to say what he must. 'Look, a patient asked to speak to me. Apparently you wrote the wrong dosage on his prescription. Luckily the computer in the chemist's picked it up. What's going on, Grace? Are you ill? This isn't like you at all.'

'I'm just tired, Anton,' she had replied, seeing the concern in his face and knowing that she ought to have confided in him.

'I think it's more than that. Don't you trust me enough to tell me what's troubling you?'

Grace had been unable to reply. Of course she trusted him but there was too much at stake to discuss it. Autocratic and cold though he appeared at times, he was a caring man and did not mind that his patients and colleagues alike tittered at the bow-ties he chose to wear. He held himself well and had noticeably smooth narrow hands. His hair was brushed straight back from his high forehead and perched on his nose were rectangular, rimless glasses which he believed gave him added gravitas with the patients. There were times when his irascibility caused friction but he was generally well liked.

'Grace,' he had continued, 'I want you to go home now and I don't expect to see you until you've sorted out whatever it is. Bill and I will cover for you. We can't afford that sort of mistake. Not all prescribing chemists have computers yet. We've all been rather worried about you, you know.'

It was then that Grace felt the first real grip of paranoia. Life was taking unexpected turns; too much was occurring at once. The facade was crumbling. And now her partners were talking about her behind her back. But Grace was already aware that she was making mistakes, that her concentration was letting her down, and she could not afford for that to happen. When, on that Saturday afternoon, Harrington had said, 'You're crazy, Grace. You know that, don't you?' she had experienced real terror. She believed he had worked it out, had finally connected the past with the present. But he had laughed and the moment had passed.

But now the uncertainty returned. Could Harrington have

worked it out? She had lied to the police when she had been questioned eight years ago and she supposed she would have to do so again in court if Harrington's defence counsel brought the matter up. Did Harry Jordan have his suspicions? He must have to have listened to the tapes.

Her mind was jumping from place to place. She had been thinking about Carl Roberts, who had generously decided not to press charges. Anton's suggestion that she take time off had come as a shock and served to emphasise the awful state of her physical and mental health. But Grace had concurred and left the surgery and gone home. Rather than face what was happening and question her state of mind she had started to prepare the meal for the evening. That had been the turning point.

She had run out of black pepper and wanted to buy a decent bottle of wine so she had gone down to the shop on the corner which had a small delicatessen section. A fine drizzle dampened her shoulders as she hurried down the road. By the time she had made her purchases it was raining hard. Head down, a carrier bag in her hand, Grace had walked as fast as possible to avoid a soaking. There, on the corner, unperturbed by the miserable weather, had stood the man she thought to be Lance Harrington, now known to her as Carl Roberts. He was staring up at the flats. She had run at him, screaming, demanding to know what he wanted from her. Acting like a mad woman, she had lashed out at him. He had fallen to the ground, his raincoat muddied in a puddle. Only when his glasses slipped to one side did Grace realise two things. It was not Harrington, and as a doctor, she recognised the clouded pupils of the sightless. She had crouched down, reaching out to help him to his feet, knowing how she must appear to him, how she would appear to anyone watching. He had shaken off her hand roughly as he groped about on the pavement for his glasses.

'Just leave me alone, whoever you are,' he had told her as he struggled to his feet awkwardly. 'You're sick. You need to see a doctor.'

Grace had stood on the pavement, rain dripping down her face, the carrier bag still in her hand, and felt like laughing. That's bloody ironical, I am a doctor, she thought. To try to make amends she had run down the road after him. 'Please wait. I'm sorry. I don't know why I did that,' she had called breathlessly.

When she caught up with him she grabbed his arm to stop him walking off because she wanted to convince him how very sorry she was. But before she could do so a police car had pulled up.

An officer spoke to her but she had been incoherent, hardly aware that she was babbling like an idiot. She had proved herself capable of violence. When she was helped into the back of the car and driven to the police station she had believed herself to be under arrest. Later she saw what the two officers must have been thinking: that she had discharged herself from one of the local psychiatric hospitals. They had given her a towel and as much tea as she could drink while she tried to explain herself. She had received some anonymous letters and was sure she was being watched. Someone had taken notes and suggested that she bring the letters in. Then, after telephoning Luke to ask him to collect her, she had been allowed to leave. Matt's special dinner had been forgotten.

Luke, she recalled, had been a little smug when he arrived, but she guessed he had probably been thinking along the lines that his big sister, who had bailed him out plenty of times, had finally managed to get herself into trouble.

She could not recall the drive back or Matt's presence in the lobby where he had been in conversation with the man on the desk. At least she had been made aware that Carl Roberts only wanted to forget the incident and that little was likely to come of it, although the police, if they chose, could bring charges themselves. A friendly WPC had explained how unlikely this would be. If Roberts was not prepared to go to court their hands were virtually tied; even if subpoenaed, an unwilling witness was of little use to the prosecution. Grace had nodded, uncaring. It was that night she had learned of the existence of a woman called Veronica Beecham, a woman who had inadvertently changed her life. But she would think about Veronica later.

Grace fought for sleep but her mind was reeling. Like probing a raw nerve, her thoughts kept returning to last December.

She was intelligent, but so was Lance Harrington. She had a dreadful feeling she had underestimated him. He had given away so little to the police and there was much he could have said. If he was found not guilty, what then? Would she have to continue spending the rest of her life fearing what he could do to her, what he might even do to her on Monday? Don't torture yourself, she thought. Haven't you had enough years of pain? Hasn't the whole family suffered enough? But there would be more to come if things went wrong. She had to stop thinking of the future.

Tossing and turning, she recalled what happened after she had assaulted Carl Roberts. That same night Matt had dropped his bombshell and on the following one she had experienced her first encounter with Inspector Jordan.

She had answered the door to him in her dressing-gown. Her dark wavy hair was unbrushed and tumbled down her back. In the lounge was a glass and a wine bottle. She had bitten her lip in consternation at the impression she must have given. He must have thought her a slattern.

But the inspector had asked a lot of questions about the letters and seemed to take what Grace told him seriously. Naturally he had been surprised that she had not done anything about them sooner. He had taken them away with him and Grace had not seen them since.

So it's back to Harry Jordan again, she thought, hugging the bedclothes tightly around her and wishing sleep would come and provide some respite from her thoughts.

RUTH

Standing in front of the dusty cheval mirror Ruth Ferrers turned sideways to check that her skirt hung cleanly from her hips. Around her and reflected with her was the clutter of her existence. Half-read books and journals waiting to be read sat in piles, clothes which should have been in the laundry basket were slung on a chair and two empty mugs stood on the chest. Long hanks of silvery blonde hair swung as she turned. Left loose, it softened the strong bones of her face and the lines of her angular body. Because she was tall and wore silky outfits which changed colour with the light she appeared to glide rather than walk. Her hair and clothes flowed palely around her, creating an illusion of glamour although she was actually quite ordinary.

She was dining with friends instead of with Grace and her partners, but she understood Grace's reasons for wanting to be alone. In fifteen minutes the taxi was due to arrive but Ruth no longer felt like going out.

I would like to be alone, too, Ruth thought as she slipped her arms into her coat and picked up her handbag. The taxi tooted outside in the street and she left the house, locking the door behind her, her face tingling in the icy air.

She was grateful that the driver was one of the taciturn breed; he nodded when she gave her destination then ignored her until they reached it. I just hope she's all right, Ruth thought. But Grace had not been all right for a long time.

The complexity of her friend's character was fascinating. She could be witty or sensible, funny or sad, occasionally she took seriously something others found amusing and sometimes her depth of perception was astonishing. When intelligence was called for, Grace provided it; if a party was flagging she enlivened it. Her aura of confidence was tempered by a hint of vulnerability, then just when you thought you had her clocked she would do something totally out of character. And Ruth was in a far better position to assess people than most. At first the changes in Grace had been imperceptible but recently they had increased at an alarming rate. Ruth, who knew her better than anyone, had been frightened by them but had not been able to get her to talk. Her refusal to even mention Lance Harrington's name led Ruth to believe she was in denial. Grace could not have forgotten his part in her past, not when Ruth recalled it so well.

She and Grace had been friends for nine years, real friends, so close that at times their thoughts were almost telepathic. Ruth recalled their first encounter when she had been standing at the bar in the students' union with a group of medics. Grace had approached. She was alone and vaguely aloof but radiated confidence. There were several textbooks under her arm which she had placed on a table, marking her space, before coming to the bar. It was early days, they were all new and finding their feet, unsure of which friendships would develop and who might become a lover. Ruth immediately sensed that neither of those things interested Grace. There was a quiet determination about her which suggested that if they came about, fine, but her reason for being there was to become a doctor. She couldn't help noticing how attractive she was and the way in which the male students looked her up and down. When she ordered her drink it was only her accent which indicated that she was English and not of southern European extraction as Ruth had imagined. Bitter was what they all drank then, an equaliser, even amongst those whose parents augmented their grants generously. Grace had asked for half a pint. Neither of them could remember how or why they had drifted away from the crowd at the bar and sat down at that table in the corner, or what they had talked about.

Together they joined associations and attended parties but they had both continued to work with solid concentration, always a little apart from the others. For Ruth it was a chance to escape the mediocrity of her parents' lives. Lack of money was not the problem, it was the poverty of the Ferrers' outlook which infuriated Ruth. They were not unintelligent people but her father said little, preferring to bury his head in a newspaper whilst her mother gossiped with neighbours in the kitchen. 'For Christ's sake, there's more to life than this,' Ruth had screamed at them during her last year at school.

'Maybe,' her mother had said after her daughter's outburst.

But there had been sadness as well as wariness in her eyes. Ruth would have to learn that life was a mixture of disappointment and contentment. Mrs Ferrers had always worried that her daughter's fervour and endless need for mental stimulation would lead to more of the former than the latter. When she said she had changed her mind about becoming a doctor and wanted to be a psychologist Mrs Ferrers threw up her hands, metaphorically, in elation. Delving into the minds of other people was ideally suited to her daughter's personality and, hopefully, she and her husband would be left in peace. Ruth had never been an easy child.

Gradually Ruth and Grace came to understand that what they had in common was a sense of individuality. Not for them the peer group pressure to conform, consequently they were thrown together. Grace had a far more exotic background. There was a beautiful mother who had run off to Italy with another man, a rich and charming father and a large house run by staff. Ruth envied her on two counts: the proud way in which Grace spoke of Gerald Cornell, and the company of the international businessmen who were drawn to Gorstone Manor and its inhabitants. It was not until a year later that she began to understand how Olivia Cornell's departure had affected her friend, although even then she had no idea how much.

'It really hurt Luke,' Grace would say, or 'He's never got over it.' Ruth began to suspect that Grace was expressing her own feelings in the guise of her brother's. A classic case of projection. It was somewhere around that time that she knew in which direction her future lay. She was aware that beneath necessary social dialogue were hidden layers of pain and confusion and that, unknowingly, what people said was sometimes the opposite of what they really felt.

Wondering how she would stand up to such scrutiny herself, Ruth had undergone two sessions of basic analysis before giving up in disgust and with an inkling that she could do better.

On her first visit to Grace's home she had been left in no doubt about the closeness which existed between Gerald and his daughter. There was genuine warmth and mutual respect which made Grace's behaviour when he died totally incomprehensible. Initially Ruth had put it down to suppressed grief; the loss of both parents prematurely was hard for anyone to assimilate.

Grace had been an adolescent when Olivia left and Gerald was only in his late forties at the time of his death. But Grace had not broken down, and not once, to Ruth's knowledge, had she wept. She had returned to medical school a week after the funeral and taken up her studies as if there had been no interruption. Unimaginable, too, that Grace would sell the beautiful house that was Gorstone Manor, but she had done so and Ruth felt the loss almost as much as her friend.

'I don't want to talk about it,' Grace had said when she returned to Southampton after the funeral, and only a little later than the other students. It was the first time since they had met that any subject had been taboo. Ruth respected her wishes but kept an eye on her, watchful for signs of stress or grief. There were none. After a year, as if Grace had decided that that was long enough to mourn, she had started going to parties again and her laughter returned.

Naturally Ruth had read the newspapers, she knew that there was more to it than the tragic accident Grace refused to speak of, but after a while the fuss died down and Gerald Cornell's death, although never really explained, was forgotten by all except those who had known him or who had been involved in its investigation. Lately, though, Grace had been ambiguous about that period of her life. That she had started to discuss it when there were recent and more important events to worry about had surprised Ruth. She's tough, Ruth thought, but she'll need every ounce of her strength for the coming week.

On reaching their destination the cab driver double parked and Ruth paid him, fumbling in the dim glow of the interior light for coins for a tip. She received a non-committal grunt as she said goodnight and closed the door.

Ruth had always been able to participate rationally in a conversation while her mind roamed freely. It was the way in which she had escaped the mundane dialogues which took place between her parents. The friends she was with did not notice her inattention. By now, she was sure, Grace would have opened a bottle of wine and was probably contemplating the whole mess. Anton Roach, too, must be considering matters, Ruth realised, recalling a conversation when he had tried to claim some of the responsibilty for what had happened to Grace. 'As senior partner I should have suspected something,' he insisted, which was ridiculous when no one else had done so, not even Grace. Or so she said. Would I have known him? Ruth asked herself. Had I seen Harrington would I have recognised him after all this time? I certainly remember him, though. Strange that Grace doesn't.

The food was served and the lively conversation lapsed as they began to eat. It gave Ruth another opportunity to think.

It had been in an Italian restaurant last summer, a week after the attack on Carl Roberts, that Grace had told her about the letters and what she had done. Grace had gone on to explain that Anton did not think her fit for work. 'My God, Grace, why on earth didn't you tell me? At least you'll be safe enough in the flat,' Ruth had added reassuringly, although it was in fact true. Ruth had never known such security as in that luxury block.

Her own security was lax but no burglar would come upstairs once he'd witnessed the shambles that was her home. Ruth's appearance was always immaculate, as were her consulting rooms which were comfortable but plain. Home was where she allowed herself the indulgence of chaos. She and Grace differed greatly here. Grace's flat was tidy, well organised and spotlessly clean even if this was not Grace's own doing. Nothing was ever out of place. Ruth suspected that the order of her domestic arrangements compensated a little for the turmoil of her mind.

When her friends got up to leave Ruth declined the offer of a shared taxi. She was not yet ready to face the empty house from which her latest boyfriend, at her request, had recently departed. Not that she was sorry to see him go. She beckoned a waiter and ordered a malt whisky.

The table was still covered with the debris of their meal. A roll of cigar ash lay next to the ashtray. As she picked it up gently between finger and thumb it disintegrated and floated back on to the tablecloth. 'Madam?' The waiter hesitated before placing the glass on the table. Ruth was frowning in concentration.

Ruth looked up. 'Oh, thanks.' She toyed with the glass, and the golden liquid coated its sides as she recalled Grace's version of Matt's forced confession.

The other diners, noisier now that their stomachs were full and their vocal cords had been lubricated with aperitifs and smooth red Italian wine, were sharing jokes, laughing, and unaware of Ruth's existence. That suited her. I don't want to go home because amongst these people out to enjoy themselves I can pretend that Grace's situation isn't as bad as it seems. It had been in this same restaurant that Ruth had learned of Matt's infidelity.

After Grace's trip to the police station she had returned to her flat, accompanied by Luke, to find Matt waiting anxiously in the foyer. 'We went up in the lift,' Grace had told her. 'I'd done some shopping earlier. Luke was carrying the bag with the wine, Matt had a bunch of roses. I could barely walk. Luke was sort of propping me up. Matt thought I'd been in an accident. I let us into the flat. Matt put the roses on a table and I went to the window. He tried to comfort me but I didn't want to be touched. "Grace," he said, "tell me what's wrong?" I laughed. Can you believe it? I was half hysterical, I suppose. I said much the same to him, that I couldn't believe it, it was no joking matter. Luke had left the room. He'd decided we were in need of the wine I'd bought.

'Honestly, Ruth, how it all came out was ludicrous. I was near to tears by then and I said something along the lines of "How could I?" Matt misheard me. He thought I said, "How could you?" Do you know what he said? He said, "It's over. Forgive me, Grace. It'll never happen again." Oh, he made excuses about not seeing me enough, missing me, that sort of thing. But I didn't understand, not at first. Not until he said there was something about her and he just couldn't help himself.'

Ruth could picture the scene: Grace on her feet, bewildered, repeating the words 'Her? Her?' as she realised what Matt had been saying. Matt, in turn, realising that Grace's distress was not due to her discovery of his affair with Veronica Beecham, a woman with whom he worked.

'Luke was in the doorway holding the glasses and the wine. He called Matt a bastard and said he would see him out. But I wanted to hear what he had to say. Oh, Ruth, it was such a cliché. They went away on a conference together and ended up in the same hotel bedroom. It continued from there.'

Ruth knew how much this had shaken her friend. Whatever her faults, Grace was loyal. Fiercely loyal. It made Matt's behaviour shabbier still.

'I thanked him for being honest,' Grace had said, 'then I handed him back his ring.'

Ruth could imagine the impact of that untheatrical action. There had been no shouting, no recriminations, just one simple, undramatic gesture which told Matt he had lost her. She had agreed to remain friends. Luke showed him out. Poor Grace. She had lost a mother, then a father; she had protected Luke since he was fourteen, found him work, cared for him, and tried to get him to make something of himself. Luke had let her down just as everyone else she had loved had done and then, so had Matt. No wonder she was screwed up.

Studying the other customers Ruth began to try to work out their relationships but found herself thinking of her own instead. The job was fine, she enjoyed it. Invitations came her way regularly. And her emotional life could not be called a mess because she did not have one. There had been men, some of whom had lasted longer than others, and one or two she had imagined she could be happy with. Her failure to settle down had been one of the things discussed over that Italian meal with Grace. It was to her she had looked for a solution because Grace always seemed so much in control. Ironically, it was Grace who had the greater problems.

'Why do I do it, Grace? Why can't I be like you?' Ruth had asked after explaining she had thrown Graham out.

'Why do you do what?' Grace had asked gravely as she crumbled a breadstick between her fingers.

'Have this urge to convince each man I meet that I'm his mother, wife and mistress rolled into one. And don't tell me, I know it's ridiculous when I'm paid to counsel women who have turned themselves into doormats. Anyway, the novelty soon wears off because once they start taking me for granted I show them the door.'

It was not only as a friend that she had sought Grace's advice but as someone who seemed to have it all worked out. Matthew Fielding had come on the scene three years ago and Ruth had noticed the subtle difference in Grace, she had begun to relax a little. But Ruth had been stunned when Grace replied, 'It's no good asking me for advice. I've been an absolute fool,' before going on to explain what had happened and that the wedding was off. Ruth had believed that Matthew would provide the steady, calming influence, the stable point in her life that her friend seemed to need. Tall handsome Matt, gentle, caring Matt, how hard it was to believe that all the time he had been living a double life. But when that blow had struck it had been the least of Grace's worries. Ruth had hoped she would not deal with that particular loss in the same way as she had the others. There was enough scar tissue already. At least, she thought, unaware that Grace had recently decided otherwise, she and Matt are still friends.

A waiter approached, bearing her coat, seconds after the taxi driver put his head around the door and said he'd come for Miss Ferrers. The coat was held at precisely the right angle for Ruth to slip her arms into the sleeves which, considering her height and the shortness of the waiter, was a surprisingly smooth manoeuvre. She opened her bag to pay for her solitary drink.

'Compliments of the house,' the waiter said.

She thanked him, not knowing whether to be flattered or assume that this was the custom with all single females. In the taxi she decided it was no more than good business. They had spent quite a sum of money there that evening, the owner would want to see them back again.

The night was raw. Exhaust fumes hung in the still air and windscreens gathered ice. The branches of the trees which lined the suburban roads glittered with rime. Their branches rose starkly into the night sky as if they had been fossilised and would never bear buds again. But it was warm in the back seat of the taxi. Ruth breathed in the delicious perfume of a previous passenger and wished she knew what it was called.

Her house was in a row of similar brick-built dwellings, each with a tiny front garden and a large one at the back. Fumbling for her keys she dropped them with a metallic clang on the red tiles of the doorstep. As she bent to retrieve them a familiar purring welcomed her home. Against her leg she felt the softness of Tickles whom she had had as a kitten and who had been christened inadvertently by the four-year-old who lived next door. 'Tickles,' he had said, laughing, when she allowed him to hold her. From that moment it had become her name.

The kitten was now a fully grown cat and wound herself between Ruth's legs as she entered the hall, nearly tripping her. A dress still in the dry cleaner's polythene hung over the banister and there was a bag of newspapers ready for recycling at the foot of the stairs.

'God, I really ought to make more effort,' she whispered into the soft fur on Tickles' neck as she picked her up. She had made no plans for the weekend in case Grace needed her and any emergency referrals would be seen by someone else.

Filled with resolution she cleaned her teeth, threw every piece of clothing that was not hung up or in a drawer into the laundry basket and got into bed.

'Grace is as sane as I am,' she told the darkness as she pulled the bedclothes up around her neck before the central heating turned itself off. But Ruth, who loved her dearly, was not certain that she meant it.

The same thought crossed her mind as soon as she awoke. Why had Grace not gone to the police with the letters until after she had attacked Roberts? Why did she behave as though she was the one with something to hide? And why had she not confided in Ruth until after she had received the third letter? That had hurt. 'Know your enemies, Gracie. I do,' it had read. Like the others, it had been posted in Exeter. Ruth had regretted pointing out that as her telephone number was ex-directory the address could not have been gleaned from the telephone book.

Ruth got out of bed and fed Tickles while the kettle boiled but she did not bother to get dressed. When she had accomplished what she set out to do she would shower and make something to eat and listen to some of her jazz CDs. She refused to acknowledge her activity as a ritual cleansing, removing the last traces of Graham, it was simply time the job was done.

She began in the bathroom. By the time she had reached the kitchen, the last room to be tackled, and was suspiciously sniffing the contents of the fridge, the fingers of her rubber gloves had worn through and she ached all over. The house smelled pleasantly of polish and disinfectant. Now might be the time to follow Grace's example and get someone in to make sure it stayed that way.

It seemed a shame to fill the pristine bath with water but Ruth knew that a shower would not relieve her aching joints. She threw the silky white nightie and dressing-gown in which she'd done the cleaning into the laundry basket and sank gratefully into the perfumed water where her loosened hair spread in sodden clumps around her like Ophelia's. Almost seven hours had passed, it was that much nearer Monday. However, there was still tomorrow to get through and although Grace had asked her not to, Ruth very much wanted to telephone just to make sure she was all right.

Once she was dry and warm Ruth set about preparing a meal, a chicken casserole she made from scratch. Unlike Grace she loathed cooking but she did the best she could. As she sliced and chopped, her thoughts took her back to their university days. She ought to have spotted the signals then. People drift in and out of our lives and we disregard them or fail to recognise their potential importance. Until Grace reminded me, I had forgotten him. Now, of course, I can picture him and what happened clearly. 'Some psychologist I've turned out to be,' she muttered, pushing Tickles aside with a slippered foot and slamming the Pyrex dish into the oven.

'And a bloody awful cook I am, too,' she said some time later, addressing the chicken casserole. She ate it anyway. It tasted better than it looked.

Afterwards, with some jazz playing softly and the curtains drawn against the cold night, she dozed on the settee, thinking back to those happy days at Gorstone Manor when life had seemed so simple.

LANCE

It might be Saturday morning, but I'm getting my money's worth – or the taxpayer's money, Lance Harrington thought as he sat in a room set aside for interviews, his arms folded, his feet firmly on the floor.

He had been on remand, awaiting trial since August. Everyone told him how lucky he was, he could have waited an awful lot longer. Luck, he assumed, being relative to your situation. He would have been luckier still not to have been there at all, or never to have met Grace Cornell.

The door clunked open and a warder escorted his solicitor, Brian Conway, into the room. 'I'll be outside if you need me,' he said, as they all did at every visit.

Brian raised his eyebrows and smiled at Lance. 'Thank you,' he said, deadpan, but polite, with his back to the guard. 'I'm sure I'll be fine.'

He sat down and placed his battered briefcase on the table. It had been searched. 'I thought we ought to have one more chat. There won't be time on Monday.'

'Fire away.'

Brian glanced up. From the start Harrington had treated the matter lightly, almost humorously at times. He seemed not to realise the gravity of the charges. Even now there was a quirk to his mouth as though he might smile. Brian Conway was an experienced criminal lawyer and had instructed the best defence counsel possible given that their legal aid resources were not unlimited. He had seen the insides of prisons and courtrooms so often that he felt perfectly at home in them. He had also come across every type of villain (and innocent people who had been charged) but Harrington defeated him by not fitting into any of the patterns he had come to recognise.

Harrington was a handsome man. Big-boned and strong, a ready smile – too ready for his circumstances – thick dark hair and regular features. In his company Brian felt short and podgy, which he was. 'Let's just go through it once more. We don't want any slip-ups on Monday. And if there's anything else you think might be relevant, now is the time to say so.'

'There isn't.'

'And you're quite sure you don't want to change your plea?' He already knew the answer.

'Positive.'

'Look, you know what your chances of acquittal are, the sentence might be lighter if . . .' He hesitated long enough for Lance to interrupt.

'If I plead guilty? Why would it be?' He leaned forward and unfolded his arms. 'Or if I plead insanity.'

Brian had not wanted to bring it up again. 'There's time. We can arrange a psychiatric report.'

'Which will delay the trial. No thanks. Do you think I'm insane?'

'It isn't a question of what I think, it's a question of your defence.' From the start Harrington had claimed he was innocent, had not faltered once when reciting the facts, as unbelievable as they appeared to be. He was an intelligent man but what he said did not make him seem so.

'I've told you, no shrinks. It isn't me who's insane.'

Maybe not, Brian thought, but it's going to be one person's word against another's. And Dr Cornell was beautiful, well spoken and a professional. No matter who was telling the truth she was the one most likely to be believed. It shouldn't work like that but it did. It was the reason he got the little toe-rags to put on a suit or at least not wear jeans for their court appearances.

'She's lying.'

Brian sighed. 'But why would she do that? What can she possibly gain from it?'

Lance met his eyes and shrugged. 'Because she's a woman? Because she wants to see me squirm?' he suggested with a smile.

'Come on, let's stop playing games.'

'Yes. Let's. I've had enough of them to last me a lifetime. All right, I'll tell you what happened one more time then we'll leave it up to the jury to decide.

'I met Grace at university,' he began and ran through the nine years leading up to the present, editing the same bits he had

61

done from the start. 'She's the one who's obsessional, not me. Why doesn't someone get her to see the head doctor?'

Brian Conway, who had heard stranger stories which had proved to be true, knew that the jury, whoever they turned out to be, would find it difficult to believe this one. Grace had studied hard, had followed her career; Harrington had not made the grade. He lived a hand to mouth existence, taking jobs below his capabilities, jobs which kept him close to Grace, a fact that the prosecution would use to their advantage. Why always so close? Why work connected with the medical profession? they would ask. He could almost see the sneer when Harrington answered. Grace was wealthy. Grace had been engaged to be married, had been planning to marry Matthew Fielding, although that had been called off because of his infidelity. It was irrelevant to the case but the defence would use it if they had to, just as they would call her partners to prove she had been going through a period of instability. It was a risk. It could be turned against them. Grace's instability might be put down to the fact that Harrington had been stalking her. Not that he had been, Brian reminded himself, knowing how bleak Harrington's chances were when his own lawyer didn't believe him. Still, as long as he kept declaring his innocence he was entitled to put in a plea of not guilty.

Until recently Harrington had a history of one-night stands. Brian suspected that Anna, his latest girlfriend, was doing him a favour. Harrington badly needed someone to say that he was in a steady relationship, that he did not need to abduct a woman to have sex. Brian had interviewed Anna and been with her during a conference with counsel. She would come across well in the witness box, maybe too well, too rehearsed. 'There's nothing else?'

'No. You know everything there is to know. I realise it's my word against hers, but I'll take my chance. I am not pleading guilty.'

Brian Conway had to be sure. 'No. But are you guilty?'

Lance's eyes darkened. He turned away and did not answer.

Brian went to the grille in the door and summoned the warder then watched as Lance Harrington was led away. There was something all wrong about this case but he had no idea what it was. He had tried, as he always did, but he had already accepted he would lose this one.

Lance sat on the edge of his bunk. He did not feel like socialising. He had adapted to life on remand, but prison would be a different matter. But there was always hope, the jury might believe him and he might not be found guilty.

Of course he hadn't told Conway everything. That was one man who didn't believe him and he could not stretch credulity any further by admitting to the whole truth.

With less than two days to go he both dreaded and looked forward to Monday. The game, if it was one, had got out of hand. He realised that beneath all that had happened lay a hidden agenda, one he had no chance of deciphering.

His own actions had been foolish, ridiculously so in retrospect, but what Grace was doing was dangerous. If ever he got out he would put a stop to it.

Lance lay down and closed his eyes. Which of them would be believed? As Conway had told him, that's what it came down to in the end. Which of them was lying? Or were they both lying? It was up to twelve strangers to decide. Lance knew that whatever happened he would have to stick to his story. He had too much to lose if he changed it now.

He thought back to his university days. How warm Grace had been initially, how loving. And how equal they were then. Oh, Gracie, he thought, if I get out of here things will be very, very different. I shall be the one in charge again.

He looked at his watch and started to count down the minutes until Monday.

OLIVIA

The tall windows leading to the tiny balcony were closed. Through them Olivia could see the curved railings of the wrought-iron balustrade and, across the street, similar buildings to the one she and Tony inhabited. Overhead was a grey, watery sky, the clouds so low they seemed to engulf the city. Below, the rain bounced off the cars. Muffled traffic sounds floated up towards her along with the impatient tooting of horns. It was the Thursday before the trial.

Heavy plush curtains framed Olivia's shapely body as she stood at the window gazing at nothing. She had been out to lunch with an uninteresting group of females who had nothing to do other than shop and gossip. Her leather coat was still draped over the back of a tapestry armchair and she had not bothered to change out of the mustard wool dress with its tortoiseshell buttons she had chosen carefully for the occasion. On her feet were understated brown leather court shoes. Soon it would be dark enough to draw the curtains and cut off the draught for which the apartment was famous. Holidays in Italy had not prepared her for city living. Milan, she realised, was just like anywhere else except perhaps noisier and more chaotic because Milanese drivers seemed to care little about the condition of their vehicles and drove recklessly, often ignoring traffic lights. Tony was away on business although he had offered to postpone the trip. Olivia was far happier with him than she had expected to be but it was a one-sided relationship. Tony adored her, his love was unconditional, yet while she respected and admired him and did her best to please him she had never been able to love him properly.

'Oh, Grace, Grace,' she whispered as she walked away from the windows and sat before the walnut bureau. 'Where are you? What are you doing right now?' Olivia frowned, a single line bisecting her forehead. There were invitations to answer and correspondence to be dealt with. She picked up her fountain pen and tapped it against her pursed lips. How trivial these things were compared with what her daughter had been through. And what was still ahead of her.

Every evening Olivia went down to the kiosk on the corner where she purchased an English newspaper. They were flown over daily and the stallholder always kept one back for her. Grace was never far from her thoughts but it had been a terrible shock to see her name glaring from the page. The article consisted of a few paragraphs somewhere near the middle of the paper. Someone had been stalking her daughter and then tried to abduct her. The reporter had naturally made references to Gerald's death. How they love to dig the dirt, she had thought, biting her lip as she tried not to cry. Tony had suggested she fly back to England immediately but something told Olivia to wait, that she could not just turn up without warning after an absence of fourteen years.

Monica's letter had arrived the following day, during which time Olivia had fought the temptation to catch the next flight to Heathrow. Arriving unexpectedly might do Grace more harm than good. Monica wrote infrequently and had little news of Grace, except on that one occasion. Olivia had written back asking if she would let her know when the trial was to take place.

Olivia had always got on well with Monica. She might be Gerald's sister but what had happened to their marriage had not been her fault. Monica was Olivia's only link with her family.

Pacing back and forth across the carpet which covered the centre of the room but which allowed a border of the polished block flooring to show, Olivia tried to find the words she wanted to write but doubted if they existed. She had written only once to Grace, posting the letter to the surgery. That had been a week after she had learned of the attempted abduction. The reply had been terse and unyielding and did not sound at all like the daughter she had known. But at least she had had a reply. All her other letters had gone unanswered. She had desperately wanted to believe that Grace might have forgiven her.

'Dammit.' Remembering that Angelina had asked to leave early, she realised that unless she was prepared to venture out into the rain again later she must write immediately. Olivia sat down again.

'Dear Grace,' she wrote, feeling her throat tighten. How hard it was to address her daughter as a real mother, from the heart, when all she had written before had been chatty, news, a way of keeping in touch, a way of letting Grace know her existence had not been forgotten and that she was loved. Not once, until recently, had Grace replied.

I may have left this letter too late, it might not reach you until Monday. This is the hardest letter I have had to write, more difficult even than the one I left for you all those years ago. It must have hurt you dreadfully for you not to have wanted to come. I'd like you to know that my leaving was no surprise to your father, he had been expecting it. There is so much you don't know, Grace, so much I want to tell you but it can only be done face to face.

I am flying back for the trial. Please read on, my darling. I do not expect you to feel pleased about it or to want to even see me. I have booked a room at the Great Western Hotel in Exeter. I recall it well. Your father and I had dinner there occasionally.

If you decide you cannot bear to speak to me I will understand and I shall neither appear at the trial nor try to contact you if that is what you want. I will be there for you if you need me, there is no other reason for my journey. Too late, maybe, but it is nonetheless true. As you know I wanted to come before but you wrote and said there was no need. I pray to God I am doing the right thing and that you will at least telephone me at the hotel.

It is fourteen years since I have seen you in the flesh. You are now a woman, and a very beautiful one and we could not have named you more aptly. Both Mrs Collins and Monica have sent me photographs of you over the years. There is a lovely one taken in the grounds of Gorstone on your sixteenth birthday. You are with friends and looking very grown up in a lemon sleeveless dress. Luke is beside you with his unforgettable bemused/sullen/angry expression. He always did hate having his photograph taken. Once I wrote to Anton Roach. Gerald and I knew him in the old days. I had heard, via Monica, that you were working as a GP in Exeter and I wondered if he knew where. It was such a shock when he told me you were with his practice. He assured me that you were given the job on your own merit, not that I needed such an assurance. You always were such a determined little girl. Anton said you are an excellent doctor, along with many other complimentary things, and he enclosed a snapshot taken at another party, this time in an hotel at the surgery's Christmas party. You are in red velvet, an almost medieval dress with a scoop neck and long sleeves which really shows off your slender waist. Anton wrote the names of everyone on the back. One of them was Matt. He's very handsome. I hope he makes you very happy.

Amongst my faults is a bad sense of timing which this letter proves. But when is a good time to make a reappearance? You know where I am staying and I shall be there for a week from Sunday. If I do not hear from you I must accept that there is no room for me in your life but if you would like to meet me or for me to acompany you to the court then you do not know how happy this would make me. The trial, I believe, has been allocated three days.

Whatever you decide I want you to know my thoughts will be with you and whatever you may think I have always loved you and always will.

God bless you, my darling.

Your mother,

It ended with the single word 'Olivia', the looping signature instantly recognisable.

Before she could change her mind, Olivia sealed the envelope and stamped it then, skirting the dark and heavy furniture, went out to the kitchen to find Angelina who was fiddling around with black olives and anchovies, presumably making *tapénade* for Tony who was due back the next day and who loved it although it was a Provençal dish. He always claimed that Italian food was superior to any other.

The kitchen was a work of art but Angelina, who lived in what Olivia could only think of as a tenement block with her husband and four children, took it as a matter of course. Not even at Gorstone Manor had they had so many gadgets and implements. Mrs Collins would have died for such a place in which to prepare food. 'Would you post this for me on your way home, please?' Olivia asked in Italian in which, after so long, she was fluent although Tony teased her that she still spoke it with an English accent.

'Si, si,' Angelina answered brusquely as she stuffed the envelope into her pocket.

Olivia was not offended. Angelina was reliable, she would not forget, and if her answers were abrupt, even rude, it was because her mind was always several stages ahead of her body. There was her own shopping to be done on the way home and her family to look after, and three of her children were boys who were being brought up in the old Italian way which, as far as Olivia could understand, meant they were waited on hand and foot just like their father.

It was Thursday: her flight was booked for Sunday but now that the letter was written she did not think she could wait that long. In fact, it would be unbearable listening to the details of Tony's business trip whilst Grace was so much on her mind. She went back to the lounge, picked up the telephone and asked if there was room on an earlier flight.

Having altered her arrangements Olivia began to shake as the reality hit her. She would be back in England, back in Exeter for the first time since she had left. At least she would have a couple of days there to get used to the idea of seeing Grace again. She prayed that it was possible. Tony would be sorry to miss her when he returned but he would understand, he always did understand because he knew what she had suffered over the years through having lost her children. Tony had been married before but his family had been wiped out in a plane crash and he said it was probably harder for her knowing that Grace and Luke were alive but still out of her reach. He was a good, decent man and deserved a lot more than she had to offer him.

She ate little that evening and, feeling like a schoolgirl, hid the remains of her meal beneath some other rubbish in the bin so as not to offend Angelina. Restless and nervous, she decided to go to bed with a glass of hot milk and whisky and try to read. The morning seemed a long way away. In the bathroom adjoining their bedroom Olivia undressed and studied her figure in the mirrored wall. Her hips were a little heavier these days, so were her breasts, but only a little, she was otherwise slim enough. She let loose the black hair which had been held back in an intricate silver clasp. Above her ears were a few strands of grey; these hairs were thicker than the rest. She reached for cleanser and cotton-wool in the mahogany bathroom cabinet and took off her make-up, then she cleaned her teeth.

Despite their shared use of the bathroom it was impersonal, like those in the hotels in which they stayed. The floor was tiled, with a square drain in the corner beneath the shower. There was no stall, the tiles sloped towards it from the other three corners and the water ran away. Angelina swabbed them daily with her hairy mop and an excess of disinfectant. The bath was big and deep and white, like the basin. White tiles with a black and gold border lined three walls, the fourth was mirrored. Even the towels were white, spotlessly so, and changed daily by Angelina who extravagantly used the hottest setting on the washing-machine to keep them that way. There were no ornaments or plants, only the basic toiletries required by herself and Tony, but that was how she liked it. All that had meant anything to her had been left at Gorstone Manor which she still thought of as home. She wanted no reminders, no replacement objects, just an easing of the pain with which she had lived for so long.

The bedroom was vast in the manner of the rather grand city apartments. To Olivia it had always felt more Venetian than Milanese. Tony had taken the place because of its size and for its central location.

From a drawer in the tallboy Olivia withdrew a lacy night-dress. It was apple green and white. Underwear, negligees and shoes were her passion. The nightdress was flattering, dipping to expose the tops of her breasts and skimming her hips. Putting it on, she caught her fingers in its lace.

In bed, propped against the white broderie anglaise pillows, she took a sip of her drink. Placing the glass on the marble-topped table beside her she saw that the time was ten fifteen. Adjusting to British time, she wondered where Grace was and who, if anyone, she was with.

Her finger was half-way down a page before Olivia removed her reading glasses, realising that she had not been concentrat-ing. All she could see was Gerald's face, the way he had looked at her that last time, with more pity than love. But God, how she had loved him; completely and deeply, so much so that in the end she had had to leave him. Was it possible for anyone to understand that? Would Grace ever believe her? Or Luke? It was

69

unlikely, because the children had idolised their father and had been unable to see his faults and Olivia had not had the heart to disillusion them.

When he had died Olivia had tried to hide her grief from Tony. He had seen that she was suffering, he could not be unaware of it, but he did not know that she still loved Gerald and always would. How kind he was, she thought, taking time away from work to entertain me, making sure I was not left alone to brood. He had offered to go back with her for the funeral but Olivia had decided not to return. She had not been afraid of people's opinions, she had got past that stage years ago. It was Grace and Luke she had been thinking of. No, they would not have been able to cope with her homecoming whilst burying their father.

I might go, she thought as she folded her glasses and slipped them into their case. I just might go to his grave. He can do me no harm now. At least I can say goodbye. But she would not go anywhere near Gorstone Manor. Some years ago Monica had written to say that it had been sold and that the new people seemed to have settled in well, but she, too, felt no desire to go there again. And it had meant as much, if not more, to her than to Olivia.

Perhaps that journalist was right with his headline, perhaps we are a tragic family, Olivia thought before spooning the skin off the milk and swallowing the rest of the lukewarm drink.

She slept until four fifteen. Outside it was still dark and the cold rain continued to slap at the windows but a robe wasn't necessary, the bedroom was over-warm. They had never quite got to grips with the heating system which clanked noisily and seemed to have a perverse mind of its own. In the winter, whichever room they were using always seemed the coldest, apart from the bedroom where they would have preferred less heat.

Olivia opened the wardrobe and stared at her clothes. It was silly to feel so nervous when Grace might not want to see her, but she still wanted to make a good impression, to show her that she had not gone to seed. For travelling she decided upon a caramel wool dress. It was completely plain and very chic. With it would go the brown leather court shoes and the large, brown handbag with a gold clasp. Over this she would wear her camel hair coat with its wide revers. It had no buttons and had to be held together if it was windy but it looked what Gerald would have once called 'the business'.

It had been a harsh winter in England and, according to the newspapers, there was still snow in many areas. Olivia pictured Dartmoor, bleak and uncompromising, its dangers not obvious to the uninitiated. Warm clothes were essential but for a week she would not need to take many.

By five o'clock her case was packed. Leather boots, a couple of suits and some dresses, although no one bothered to change for dinner any more, not even in some of the best hotels. But Olivia needed these things for herself, to boost her own confidence in case she crumpled at the sight of her daughter. Whatever happened she was determined to catch a glimpse of her even if Grace was not aware of her presence.

The hours dragged. Angelina came at eight and was surprised to see Olivia dressed and packed and sipping coffee at the kitchen table. She eyed the espresso machine dubiously, knowing that her employer was in awe of its wild spluttering, but it seemed to be in working order. She had posted the letter, she said.

Olivia thanked her, knowing that she was being scrutinised. Angelina made no secret of it. Her face was pale, she had seen that much herself, and she felt nauseous but she picked at the sweet roll, eating it dry without the rich butter and cherry jam which Angelina placed before her.

She rang for a taxi and arrived at the airport two hours before her flight was due to take off. Here, amongst strangers, she felt better, part of the transient world of travellers. It was a kind of limbo where there was nothing to do but to wait and obey the instructions given over the tannoy. She studied a selection of paperback books but was too on edge to imagine reading one of them and drank more coffee, adding a shot of brandy because she was always a little nervous of flying.

When her flight was finally called her body felt heavy as if she might not be able to drag it to the gate. She could still go home where all was familiar and Tony would be arriving later but all that she had ever loved was ahead of her.

Grace might not receive the letter in time, Olivia thought as she handed over her boarding pass. What then? What then, she comforted herself logically, was that she would receive it on Tuesday or the day after that.

Well-travelled, Olivia stowed the hold-all which contained all she needed in the overhead locker then sat down and idly studied the safety regulations. They were no more reassuring on this journey than on any other. What good was the life jacket when most of the journey was over land? Certainly not much use if they crashed into the Alps. She picked up the duty-free magazine and flicked through it, noticing that no one else seemed anxious. Only when the stewardess came to check that her seat-belt was fastened did her jaw unclamp a little. The pilot wanted to get there safely as did his crew. It was silly to worry. But what if, after all these years and all the journeys she had made during the course of them, this was the one time when something went wrong and she was prevented from seeing Grace? Perhaps it would be poetic justice, Olivia thought. She closed her eyes as the engines roared into life and they began taxiing slowly towards the runway.

'Are you all right?' a stewardess asked, bending over Olivia, having noticed her pallor and her white knuckles as she clenched the arms of her seat. The crew was British, this was the return leg of an outward journey.

'I'm fine, thank you.'

'It should be a smooth flight.'

'Good.' Famous last words, Olivia thought wryly as the pilot instructed the crew to fasten their seat-belts. But it wasn't the flight which was on her mind.

As soon as they touched down Olivia forgot her fears and checked her face in her handbag mirror. There would be no one to meet her but it seemed important that she should look her best on setting foot in England for the first time for so long. When Tony came over on business he always begged her to accompany him but she never had. He, too, she realised, would be on a plane just then, on his way home expecting to find her waiting for him. He had not telephoned last night because he was attending a dinner which was expected to continue until late. He was faithful, Olivia was certain of that but unsure why he should remain so. He was an inch or so taller than her and his dark hair was still thick, although grey now and cut close to his head. His looks were not conventionally handsome but his incongruous blue eyes turned women's heads.

As a businessman he was hard-headed yet as a husband he was gentle and shared none of the views of some of his country-men on the way to treat women. Travel had done that to him, he had seen life all over the world. But maybe he also realised that Olivia would not allow herself to be treated as a chattel or as anything less than an equal.

She had thought of hiring a car and driving down to Devon but it seemed pointless when she could relax on the train and a flight to Exeter would mean going through the same rigmarole again. From Heathrow she took the airport bus to Reading rather than travelling by tube to Paddington. There was only twenty minutes to wait for an inter-city train. How different they were now, each with its new owner's logo on the side. She smiled when she saw that hers was a Great Western, how fitting when that was also the name of the hotel where she would be staying.

There were plenty of seats. She found one with a table and sat down, admiring the green and white livery, charmed further when the man who came to check her ticket stopped to have a few words. In the button hole of his dark green uniform was a pink carnation. Perhaps things would not have changed as much as she had feared in her absence.

The journey passed surprisingly quickly. Through the windows Olivia gaped at the whiteness of the landscape. The low-lying fields of Somerset which flooded in heavy rain were completely covered, and the further west they travelled the thicker the layer of snow.

The train pulled out of Taunton. The next stop was hers. 'I'm home,' she whispered as they slowed through the suburbs of Exeter. The canal came into view on the right before they glided through Exeter St Thomas station and alongside the River Exe. The train stopped. The other alighting passengers were already on their feet, grabbing luggage and carrier bags and coats.

Olivia stood slowly and reached above her head for her camel coat and put it on. She picked up her hold-all from the space behind her seat and walked down the carriage to the door, which was already open. She stepped on to the platform, unable to move and unable to see as the lump in her throat dissolved and tears spilled hotly down her face. Fourteen years of bottled-up emotion seemed to have been unstopped. Her nose was running but Olivia ignored it. People turned to stare then quickly passed by. A girl in a dark red uniform and a clip-board in her hand approached and touched her on the arm. 'Is there anything I can do to help?'

The girl had a kind face but Olivia just wanted her to go away. She shook her head as wave after wave of pain washed over her. 'Thank you, but I'll be all right,' she managed to say.

Icicles dripped from the platform roof. Each night they re-formed and each day they half thawed. Pigeons huddled and cooed in the girders holding up the roof; some made forays on to the platform to search for crumbs.

Olivia began to notice the cold. She sniffed and blew her nose and wiped her eyes, uncaring of the make-up which came away on her tissue. This was not how she had hoped to look but better it had happened now than in front of Grace. She picked up her hold-all, which seemed very heavy all of a sudden, and walked across the concourse and out of the station. A foreshortened bus stood at a stop; it was quite unlike the single and double-deckers she remembered. To her left was the hotel, outwardly un-changed. She walked towards it. Forgetting which way to watch for traffic, she nearly got run over.

It came as a shock to find that little had altered inside as she stood in the warmth of the small foyer. She realised as soon as a puzzled expression crossed the receptionist's face that although she had reserved a room from Sunday she had not let them know she was arriving early, but she was in luck – the hotel was not full.

Room number 10 was on the first floor but Olivia decided she needed a drink first. The bar was to her right. She went in and ordered a glass of wine.

If Grace was at her flat she would be no more than a mile or so away. Olivia wanted to go there, to stand outside and see if she could catch a glimpse of her, but she wasn't sure she was ready to face her yet. Did Grace enjoy periods of solitude in times of trouble as much as she did?

Having finished her drink she made her way up the short flight of stairs. She had a double room with all the usual facili-ties. From the window she could see the station. She kept looking at the name, Exeter St David's, still unable to believe that she was actually there. It seemed silly to have rushed now. It was too late to do more than have a shower and eat dinner and she was tired after her journey. She had no idea how she would occupy herself over the weekend. It would be unbearable to bump into Grace accidentally, especially if she had decided she would rather not meet her mother. This limited her choice of activities. The reunion, if it occurred, must not take place in public.

Olivia ate early, picking at her food before going back up to her room. Memories came flooding back as she had suspected they would. She had averted her eyes from where she had last sat with Gerald on the night he had bought her an orchid and held her hand across the table. She had not been able to get enough of him, even when the children were small, but they had done things together as a family. And then the doubts, the telephone hurriedly put down when she walked into a room, the unexplained absences. Oh, how it had hurt but she had been prepared to put up with it. Only when it was impossible to live with the sickening knowledge of what she suspected did she make the final break. No one else, apart from Tony, knew why that was and he had been there for her, first as a friend, then as a way of escape. But her plans had backfired and she had lost her children for ever.

Tony had been in love with her for years; everybody knew that, but he had never acted upon his feelings because he was Gerald's friend as well as her own. She did not blame him for making his move when she was at her most vulnerable because she, in turn, had been prepared to use him. Now she realised how lucky she was. There would never be the excitement, the lust and the magic she had once known but Tony had given her security and a sort of peace. Until she left she had had no idea how cruel Gerald could be. Olivia had had to learn to let go of her family and settle for a life in Italy.

I did what I believed was best, she told herself just before she fell into a deep sleep. It wasn't good enough, but I will try again now.

GRACE

She sat upright in bed, her eyes wide open in the darkness, one hand automatically reaching for the bedside light which toppled as her fingers struck it. Relief flooded through her as she steadied it and depressed the switch. She was at the farmhouse and she was alone. It was ten past four in the morning. The lamp cast soft shadows but they were not frightening. Grace lay back against the pillows until Lance Harrington's face faded. But she felt sick because she could still feel his hands on her naked body. He had not raped her, he had, in fact, never tried to force himself upon her. But in the dream she had been enjoying it, smiling as he touched her.

She shivered although the bedroom was warm, and got out of bed because movement of any sort was preferable to where her thoughts might lead her.

In the kitchen she sipped tea, her brow furrowed because sometimes it was so hard to differentiate between reality and dreams. 'God, no,' she whispered as sweat broke out beneath her armpits and her hands began to tremble. She felt dirty and scared.

Under the shower she let the pulsing hot water beat on her skin until it was pink and tingled then she dried herself with a towel, scrubbing at her body as if she could rub away her thoughts. Lance Harrington must not be allowed to defile the farmhouse through memory or dreams. Once she was dressed she wandered through each room aimlessly, not knowing how to pass the time until it was light enough to go out. Let it be over with, let next week see the end of it, she prayed silently, knowing that that was impossible.

She thought of Luke, still asleep, his fair hair tousled. Was he tossing and turning, still high on whatever it was he took or sweating out the alcohol? How hard she had tried with him, how dismally she had failed. Together they had searched for the maisonette where he now lived. He had wanted to live with her: Grace had told him it was impossible. Any job he acquired was soon abandoned. Thankfully she had seen to it that before he became of age his money had been invested, but it wouldn't last for ever. Luke was a loser. Even now when Grace needed him he hardly made contact. She knew that he was afraid to, that he couldn't handle his own emotions, let alone hers. And Harry. How did he feel? More than he let on, but how much more? Did he believe her? Did anyone? It was all very well making statements but it would be a different matter in court. The formality alone was intimidating if you were a witness.

How would Lance Harrington stand up to questioning? Back to Lance. Well, it had to be faced. He would answer clearly, of course, and use every ounce of his charisma to charm the jury. But he would be lying. And so would she. One on one, but the balance was tipped in Grace's favour. She was not the person on trial. He would go to prison and then the rest of it would come to light and she would be free for ever. If things went well. Could it be that in a few days' time the past would stop haunting her? Yes, if Harry Jordan had done his homework well. And she believed he had. He was a good man, a decent man, and he was on her side. And if he failed her she had one last recourse.

Dawn broke over the distant hills, preceded by fingers of orange which gradually spread, changed colour and turned the snow pink. The sun began to rise in a clear sky but as Grace filled the washing-up bowl clouds began to form. Pulling on rubber gloves, she got to work on last night's dishes and finished by giving the grill-pan a thorough scouring as the radio played softly in the background.

'Virtue is its own reward,' Mrs Collins used to say. How wrong she could be at times. But at least there wasn't a mess in the kitchen for Judith to clear up.

Ten minutes later, bundled up against the cold, Grace started walking. She went in the opposite direction from the prison. The breeze was behind her as she scrunched through the snow feeling a childish pleasure in leaving her footprints in its unmarred surface. Several cars passed in both directions; the driver of one, a wrinkled farmer, tooted and raised his hand in greeting. Grace waved back although she didn't know him.

In the distance a mound of rock caught her eye. The top of it, smooth and rounded, was dark and stood out. Already, the snow that had fallen last night had begun to melt. The sun was warm on her face and she heard the sound of church bells, their sonorous tones carrying across the vast open spaces. Congregations still gathered in the villages there.

She thought of her partners. Anton would be anticipating his lunch as he ploughed through the *Sunday Times*. He was the only person Grace knew who managed to read the whole paper. Carol would be in the kitchen amongst her gadgetry cooking something fit for a dinner party. It was a wonder Anton kept so trim. Bill and Mary Ryan, both doctors, although Mary was with another practice, would be trying to cope with their four exhuasting boys. At least the oldest would be off to university by the end of the year.

And dear Ruth. Grace pictured her surrounded by her books and unread professional journals or her head in a file as she munched the sandwich which would suffice for her lunch. Tickles wouldn't be far away, she never was. Like me, she doesn't have a man in her life, Grace thought as she turned to make her way back. Since Matt there had been no one and after what had happened male company, other than in friendship, was the last thing she was seeking.

The telephone was ringing as she opened the door. Grace froze. Was it bad news? Was it him? No, Lance couldn't reach her from prison. She let it ring another six times and then it stopped. Lifting the receiver she tapped out 1471 but was told the caller had withheld their number. Harry, then, calling from work. She wished she had picked it up.

There were some herbal teabags in the cupboard. Grace decided they would be better than yet more caffeine. She drank a mug of rosehip and decided that there was little point in lighting a fire when she would be leaving in an hour or so, and little chance that she would be able to relax. Also, the small clouds of the morning had been replaced by a bank of grey ones. It would be more sensible to make an early start. She tidied up and splashed some bleach into the toilet bowl. Then she turned down the central heating and made sure everything was secure. Taking one last look around, as if she might never return, Grace locked the front door, cleared the snow from the car windows and started the engine.

The suburbs of Exeter were dull and grey in the gathering

dusk. Both roads and pavements were wet with a film of muddy slush. Smoke rose from chimneys, breaking up when the breeze disturbed it, but the rise in temperature was noticeable, even in the car. The city centre was almost deserted, only a few dog-walkers and adolescent couples seemed oblivious to the depressing afternoon.

The garage belonging to Grace's flat in the suburbs was beneath the building, which had been constructed on a slope. It was approached by a drive at the side of the block and each resident had their own space. The garage door was activated from inside the car and the back entrance to the flats could only be opened by a special key and a coded card. The metal door clanged shut behind her. Grace parked and, unnecessarily, locked the car. It was a habit acquired from living in a city and carrying drugs when on home visits.

She began walking towards the staircase entrance when she sensed she was not alone. She froze. The hair on the nape of her neck prickled. He was here. She could feel it. Someone was watching her. The keys were in her hand. She felt for the longest one, it was the only weapon she had. The only sounds had been her own footsteps on the concrete floor but out of the corner of her eye she had seen a movement; a slow gliding to the left of her. Inch by inch she turned her head, hardly able to breathe. 'Oh, God. Oh, my God!' The high-pitched laughter of relief echoed as it bounced off the metal of the cars. Backlit by one of the opaque shaded light fittings set high into the wall, her shadow had been thrown sideways and had slithered across the bonnet of the Mortimers' highly polished Rover.

Weak-kneed she made it to the fire door and unlocked it. It was another intimation of her insecurity and nervous state. And had someone actually been there, one of the residents who was entitled to be, what might she have done then? Would she have assaulted someone else?

She took the lift to the second floor. It rode up silently then, like a gentleman, the sliding door allowed her a respectful time to step out into the corridor before closing automatically with a gentle hydraulic hiss.

The building was silent and Grace's footsteps unheard because of the thickness of the carpet. The soundproof doors gave no indication if other residents were at home. At each end of the corridor were fresh flowers arranged in vases on marble-topped tables. Under the concealed lighting they appeared artificial in their perfection. In the time Grace had lived there she had never seen the people who came to change them.

She enjoyed the security of the building but missed the informality there had been at Gorstone with its constant stream of guests, and the comings and goings of the hospital where she had completed her training. At the front was an entry-phone system backed up by the presence of a porter on the desk, usually Joe or Brian who sat and read the tabloids and numerous paperbacks. Their wages came out of the management fees but everyone who lived there could afford them. Both men had taken early retirement from the forces and were a reassuring presence in that they vetted visitors and presented a friendly face if she used the front entrance.

There were eight flats, four to each floor, all of which faced the park. Grace opened the door of her own and stepped inside. The mirror hung on the wall, her one reminder of Gorstone. Had she wanted any of the furniture it would have been too dark and heavy for the modern architecture. Habit made her glance in the mirror. Her face was white and her eyes seemed larger than ever. If I were a patient I'd prescribe myself a good night's sleep, she thought. Her long dark hair shone under the light directly above her and her stomach rumbled because all she had eaten that day was some toast. She needed to adjust to being back in the city before she thought about food.

The plate glass windows of the lounge gave a panoramic view over Exeter. The twin towers of the cathedral were visible above the rooftops in the distance. In the darkness the trees and shrubs in the park had lost their substance and had merged in with the shadows even though snow still clung to their branches.

Grace hung up her coat and undressed. She had changed back into the suit she had worn into work on Friday before leaving the farmhouse earlier. That, too, was hung up. Her blouse and underclothes were tossed into the laundry basket.

In the kitchen with its clear work surfaces and where everything gleamed, she poured some Frascati and savoured the first chill mouthful before taking it into the lounge. She sat in the chair she had bought second-hand and had had re-covered simply because she had loved its shape rather than for any reason of frugality. A white diaphanous curtain hung at the window but the main curtains, the colour of peanut butter, were never drawn. Grace found comfort in the lights of the city.

She had forgotten to check her mail-box. It was attached to the back of the door and whoever was on duty downstairs was responsible for delivering the post to the individual flats. There were several envelopes including one with writing she recognised as Fay's. It was always good to hear from her. She smiled, recalling their university days when life had seemed more simple, consisting of work and exams.

She and Ruth had already become friends when they met Fay, although 'met' was an inaccurate word. She had literally bumped into them as she hurried somewhere or other, late as always. Her books had flown from the satchel she had been carrying and they had stopped to help her pick them up. In those days Fay had mousy hair which curled in clumps and which no hairdresser was able to control. In the third year Fay had cut it with her nail scissors to within an inch of her scalp where it lay like little half moons. It suited her and she had worn it that way ever since. Two stone overweight, Fay had never worried about her looks but they had never deterred the opposite sex. She was always in the company of men who were only too happy to buy her drinks. She was afraid of nothing, not even the first day she was let loose on a ward, and her unladylike laugh could still be heard echoing down the corridors of the London teaching hospital where she was now a registrar. With a disastrous marriage to another doctor behind her she had finally moved in with a bricklayer who was more impressed with her capacity for dry cider and the size of her bosom on which he rested his dusty head at the end of the day than with her ability as a doctor. 'He loves me for all the wrong reasons,' Fay had told Grace over the telephone, 'but who cares. He's terrific.' They had been together for five years and seemed just as happy as at the beginning.

Fay's letter was typically amusing and made Grace smile until she got to the end where Fay mentioned the trial and said that she would be thinking of her. 'I won't ring,' she concluded, 'you might not be up to my inane chatter, but you know where I am if you need me.'

Grace put the letter back in the envelope. Her hand shook. She had been kidding herself that there was nothing important in the post. She had known that the airmail envelope could only be from Olivia. She refilled her wineglass and wondered why she had decided to cook pasta later. Had it been a Freudian reaction to the sight of that envelope?

Not yet ready to read the letter, Grace decided to prepare her meal, relegating all thoughts of her mother to the back of her mind. At one time Harry had asked if one of the other residents could have sent those letters because the postcode had been accurate. Grace had said no, that it was a ludicrous idea. She had described them all. There was Mrs Fortescue who was a harmless old lady with a touch of the Miss Havishams about her with her badly aligned lipstick and a moth-eaten fox fur. She had once mentioned that she was a prison visitor. Grace could not imagine what the inmates must have thought unless her eccentricity gave them something to talk about. On the rare occasions their paths crossed the old lady would pat Grace's arm with her claw-like fingers and tell her what a worthwhile job she was doing.

There was a married couple, in their thirties, both solicitors who worked long hours. Grace rarely saw them and realised they probably saw little of each other. They would have had enough of dictating letters without lowering themselves to sending unsigned ones, she had told Harry.

David Leach, who had asked Grace out and had taken three months to accept that when Grace said no she meant it, was too egocentric to waste his time on spiteful revenge when he could be out chasing other women. The two girls who shared the flat next to his lived such hectic lives they would not have had time to write a note for the milkman let alone anyone else. That only left the Mortimers, a retired couple who, apart from their endless bridge parties, were ordinary enough. One flat had been empty and was still on the market and the last one, directly below Grace's, had recently been purchased and she had not then met the new occupants.

The pasta sauce was ready. Grace returned to the lounge and held Olivia's letter in her hand. It had arrived quickly. Her looped writing was so familiar that Grace could picture her clearly. The thought of all those lost years and how badly she had misjudged Olivia filled her with desolation. One memory came back vividly. Grace had been about four or five and not yet adept at riding her bike without stabilisers. The rooms at Gorstone had been large enough for her to manoeuvre it around indoors, which showed that Olivia cared more for her children having a happy childhood than she did for the furniture. She had ridden into the side of a leather sofa and fallen off the bike, taking with her a small table and a figurine which had rested on it. Naturally it had hit the parquet flooring rather than one of the scatter rugs and smashed beyond repair. Her mother had come in and found her huddled on the floor, holding some of the broken pieces. Olivia was slender but curvy and always wore the same perfume so Grace could always tell when she was in a room or had just left it. She had looked up to see her mother in a cyclamen silk dress, her black hair pulled back and held at the nape in a wooden clasp. There were gold hoops in her ears. Grace remembered because one of them had hit her in the face as Olivia had bent down to pick her up and sit her on her knee to examine her for damage. 'Oh, Grace, you're bubbling,' she had said in her soft, gentle voice. Grace had smiled through the tears, as she had been meant to do. Olivia always said that, never crying. She would catch a tear on her finger and say, 'Go on, burst it,' and Grace would do so. Clambering from her mother's knee she had noticed a small damp patch on the silk dress where her nose had run. Why did I ever think she was no good as a mother? Grace wondered. Then she ripped open the envelope and began to read.

'She's coming back,' she said aloud, her voice catching. 'She's coming home. And just for me. Oh, Olivia, I'm bubbling now.'

HARRY

Harry woke early, his shallow sleep disturbed by the rotating orange lamp of a gritting machine as it flashed across the ceiling. Britain, or at least Devon, had finally caught up with the rest of the world and was taking measures against the extreme weather. The gritting and shovelling and breaking of ice had become routine daily practice.

He peered at the luminous dial of his watch which he wore in bed. Five forty-five. Throwing back the duvet he was shivering before he stood. The heating had not yet come on. In the bathroom he cleaned his teeth to rid his mouth of a dryness which, unusually, wasn't due to alcohol. There was a tickling sensation at the back of his throat. He cursed. So far he had avoided picking up one of the germs which had survived the sub-zero temperatures.

Hurrying downstairs he flicked the boiler switch to the constant setting and filled the kettle. The ugly back garden, half illuminated by a streetlight, was still covered in snow. He had not been out there for months. There was nothing to see, only the creosoted lattice-work fence and the top halves of the houses in the row behind. He was surprised to notice that some of the patchy lawn had reappeared from beneath the snow. The dustbin now stood at the side of the house where it was easier to push out on collection day. The fewer domestic complications he had, the better.

Harry felt a surge of disgust when he opened the fridge. How long was it since he had bothered with proper food? Naturally he ate each day but it was usually a meal from the canteen at work or something cobbled together late at night, augmented by the occasional Indian takeaway. Checking the cupboards he found that many of the packets were out of date, remnants from Gillian's time, things he would never use. He sniffed at a small cellophane envelope containing herbs, more desiccated than dried and scentless now. It went in the bin.

Ten minutes later the cupboard was empty and he found himself staring at the damp cloth in his hand uncomprehendingly. It was ten past six in the morning. Then he smiled. Well, why not?

Fortified with coffee he emptied the other cupboard. There was little storage space in the cramped kitchen. The builders had thrown up as many properties as they could legally cram into the allocated space. If Gillian could see me now, he thought. Not that she would care. Harry stepped back, cursing as he felt the stickiness of spilled sugar beneath his bare feet. Not that I care any more either. He stood frowning at his reflection in the blackness of the window. In a T-shirt and underpants, his night-time attire now that he no longer had a wife, his peculiar face was creased in puzzlement. Since when had he realised that? Since when had his misery and bad-tempered self-pity evaporated and become just a masquerade? With the same cloth he wiped the floor and the sole of his foot then put it back in the washing-up bowl beneath the sink. It was far too early to leave the house so he took his time showering and shaving then made some tea and toast. The supermarkets opened early on Saturdays, he would shop before he went to the station then, on Sunday, his day off, he would spend a quiet day at home. He knew what he would rather be doing but Grace would not wish to see him.

The filthy slush had an icing of grit but Harry still walked with care. The supermarket was already open but there were no queues yet. At the fresh food counters he was served by youths of both sexes wearing white coats and hats. Their faces were almost as pale beneath the harsh, unflattering lighting. In an odd sort of way he was enjoying himself as he filled his basket with meat and vegetables and eggs and milk. He was an adequate cook, it was time he made use of this ability.

Within an hour he had been home and unpacked the groceries and was already on his way to the police station in Heavitree Road. The first part of the journey took him along streets of solid red-brick houses whose front doors opened straight on to the pavement. Gillian had refused to look at any that were on the market at the time of their marriage but Harry would much rather have lived in one than the soulless architecture that was his home.

Nine thirty on a Saturday morning and outwardly there was little activity to behold, and certainly none of the chaos which could be expected by the end of the day. Harry wanted to use this hour or so of relative quiet to study the rest of the statements pertaining to Gerald Cornell's death. Luke Cornell's version was on the top of the files he had pulled yesterday.

At fourteen Luke had come across as immature and his statement was of little relevance. On the night in question he had been watching television with Mr and Mrs Collins. They had turfed him out of their flat at about ten and sent him to his own room.

'I thought Grace was still downstairs studying,' Luke had said. 'She's always studying. Dad was in the library when I last saw him. About half-past ten Maggie, Mrs Collins that is, came in to make sure I was all right and to see if I wanted anything because she was going to have an early night. I woke up again about two o'clock.'

Harry recalled that it had been a female detective who had interviewed Luke. Her voice on the tape had been gentle and full of understanding. The words printed on paper seemed harsh. 'What woke you?' she had asked.

'I don't know. Nothing really. I think I needed to go to the toilet.'

'And you needed to go to Mr and Mrs Collinses' flat to do this?'

'No. I passed Grace's bedroom, the door was open but she wasn't there. Dad wasn't in his room either. I went to the bathroom then I went downstairs. Everything was very quiet, I just felt that no one was at home.'

Harry knew from experience what it was to wake from sleep or to walk into the house and sense, rather than know, that you were alone. On many occasions during the last few months with Gillian he had steeled himself to her absence.

'That's when I went to tell Maggie.'

'What happened next?'

'She came back down with me. She said there would be a note or something, but we couldn't find one, then we went to her flat and she made us a drink. I could see she was worried because they wouldn't both have gone out without telling her, because of me. I was scared when she decided to ring the police.'

'How much later was that?'

'I don't know. Not long, I don't think. She said I must go back to bed because there was no point in us all waiting up.'

It seemed clinical reading the words. During the taped version

Luke had been tearful. Fourteen was a difficult age for any boy, how much worse for one who was motherless and who had just learned that his father was dead?

The Collinses' statements varied little from Luke's, only in that they had been told before the boy that Grace was in hospital and Gerald Cornell was dead. It was Mrs Collins who had volunteered to break the news to his son. The staff at the hospital had already told Grace who had immediately discharged herself and gone home to be with her brother.

There had been no visitors to the house that evening and, cloistered in the self-contained flat with the television on, Luke and the Collinses would not have heard the telephone ringing in Gerald's office. If it had rung.

Harry picked up the next file. Monica Andrews, Gerald's sister. As a close relative she had been questioned extensively for she would have known the family well and might have inside knowledge which would be helpful. Her own financial situation had been investigated although she had never been considered seriously as a suspect in what might or might not have been a murder. But what had seemed to the officers involved to be excessive grief had aroused suspicion. On hearing the news Monica had collapsed and although she had refused her GP's offer of short-term medication she was in a trancelike state throughout her interviews.

Inspector Troy had led the investigation. Harry recalled him vaguely from somewhere in his past. He was a harsh man but had a way with words which cajoled people into saying more than they had intended.

Monica Andrews had stated her name, her address and her relationship with the dead man.

'Were you close, you and your brother?' Troy had begun without preamble.

'Yes, very.'

'When did you last see Mr Cornell?'

'Ten days ago.'

'Ten days? Not that close then.'

'You don't understand . . .'

'Don't I? Try me.'

Harry suddenly recalled where he had met Troy. They had both been involved in a stabbing case. He could almost hear the smugness in the man's voice which witnesses and suspects alike found infuriating.

'You can be exceptionally close without being in each other's pockets. Gerald was a busy man and I've a husband to consider.'

'Yet I understood that you used to be at Gorstone Manor almost every day at one time. What changed that?'

'Olivia.'

'Olivia?' The question had been unnecessary. Troy knew full well to whom Monica Andrews was referring. Harry shook his head. He must forget the nuances of tone as he had heard them on the tapes. What he was looking for was some clue in the words themselves.

'My sister-in-law. Well, ex-sister-in-law.'

'You fell out with her?'

'On the contrary, we got on extremely well. She left Gerald and went to live in Milan with her lover. They eventually married. She hasn't been back to England since. That would be about six or seven years ago.'

Naturally an ex-wife might be expected to have a grievance, especially if she felt the need to move so far from her home and her children. But it had not taken long to ascertain that Olivia Cornell, by that time Mrs Antonio Pisano, could not have been in England at the time because she had been in the Far East accompanying her husband on a business trip. Her passport was stamped accordingly to prove it.

'Why did you stop going to Gorstone Manor?'

'My brother was very much preoccupied with Olivia's decision to leave him. I felt that he needed some time alone. Also, it was mainly Olivia I went to see. We were friends. And the children, of course, until they reached the stage when they were bored in adult company. There was nothing sinister in it, Inspector, the pattern of our lives simply changed, that's all.'

In this instance the written word had more impact than the spoken. Monica's voice had been well modulated and she sounded like a woman who was used to being in control even if that control had temporarily left her at the time of her bereavement. Grace, Harry realised now, had inherited characteristics from her paternal aunt as well as from her parents. Reading on he wondered if there was a certain amount of calculation in Monica's statement. She had ready answers for everything.

The husband, too, had been questioned. Frederick Andrews, to whom his wife referred as Freddie. Public school, ex-services, the whole business. But unlike some he had not lived on his past. When Freddie had come out of the army he had taken a look at the world without the screen of his uniform and rank to protect him and had decided that what it needed was a chain of restaurants somewhere between fast food and the nouvelle cuisine which at that time had taken off in a big way. He had trodden carefully, beginning with one small restaurant which served good but inexpensive food, aimed at the type of customers he wished to attract. Not so cheap that groups of youngsters would fill the place nor so expensive that those who believed the dearer the better would turn up and complain about the wine or compare the place unfavourably with top London restaurants. He refused to take party bookings, the tables seated couples or foursomes. The idea worked and within six years there was a 'Freddie's Bistro' in most West Country resorts.

At the time of Gerald's death this venture had only been in existence for five years; it was still early days so there was the question of Freddie's financial state. If he had been running into difficulties he might have decided that Gerald's wealth would be handy. Monica Andrews had not been included in her brother's will but Freddie might not have been aware of the fact.

'Of course not,' Monica had declared indignantly when it was put to her that her brother had not made provision for her. 'Nor I him. We each had half of what our own father left and that was more than sufficient for anyone. Gerald told me he was leaving everything to his children. Besides, Freddie's doing well and he's got his army pension. And there's my money. He'd come to me if he needed anything, you can be assured of that. But he doesn't. No doubt when you bother to check you'll find out just how well he is doing.'

They had and he was and, on top of that, Monica's own will, which she had offered to show them, left everything to her husband first or, if he predeceased her, to her niece and nephew. She had no children of her own.

What still puzzled Harry was the fact that the lines in the case were blurred. Those in charge had not known what they were dealing with. Given the conditions and the lack of evidence everything seemed to point to an accident, albeit one without explanation. If it hadn't been for the severity of the weather there may have been evidence to find; on the other hand, if the weather had been less inclement Gerald Cornell might still be alive. The only question was, what were both Gerald and his daughter Grace doing out on the moors on such a night?

Money was not the only motive for crime. Troy had demanded an alibi from Monica who was intelligent enough to know why he required one. There was no affront in her calm reply, only sadness. 'How could I ever forget that day? I had been shopping in the afternoon. In Exeter. I met Babs by chance. Barbara Philpotts, an old friend of mine. We hadn't seen each other for ages so I suggested a drink. We went to the Papermakers in Exe Street.'

Harry knew the place, he sometimes used it himself. It was an historical building opposite the weir. In days gone by it was the local for the workers at Headweir Mill who were given tokens to the value of two pints of beer to spend there. The present landlord still had some of those tokens. It was now a wine bar, one wall lined with racks of bottles, another with a blackboard upon which an unusual menu was chalked. Harry read on.

'We shared a bottle of wine and caught up on gossip. Consequently I didn't get home until after seven. In a taxi, of course,' she had added. 'I always treat myself to one into the city and back home when I go in for a day's shopping.'

'And then?'

'Then I prepared a meal and wrote some letters whilst it was cooking. After I'd eaten I listened to the radio and went to bed to read.'

'Where was your husband?'

'At one of the restaurants. He makes random visits, not to check up you understand. He picks the staff himself. He likes them to know he's interested and there if they have any problems. He's out two or three nights a week.'

'So you were alone all evening?'

'I have just said so.'

'What time did your husband return?'

'I've no idea. I was asleep. He would've eaten at the restaurant.'

Harry chewed his lower lip. No alibi. But then why should an innocent person need one? Sighing, he leaned back in his chair. It creaked beneath his weight. Why was he so engrossed with Grace's past? He didn't seriously believe Gerald Cornell's death had anything to do with recent events. The letters Grace had received stated that the past didn't matter. So why bring it up at all? And why had Harrington refused to discuss it? He continued to deny all the charges. And all the time Harry was aware that the only person whose statement might be false was Grace.

According to her partners, and her friend, Ruth Ferrers, Grace had been under pressure before the attempted abduction on that Saturday morning, or, as Anton Roach had put it, 'That young lady has been seriously troubled for some time.' He thought of the assault on Carl Roberts and the desperation which must have provoked it. Yet Harry found it hard to doubt Grace's honesty, even after he had realised the significance of the letters and why she had been so reluctant to show them to anyone. The handwriting was so like her own that Harry wondered if Grace believed that she might, without knowing it, have written them herself.

Rereading the statements was a waste of time. The forthcoming trial concerned Lance Harrington, not her father's death.

Tragic family, the newspapers had labelled the Cornells, and maybe they were. Freddie Andrews was dead, too; a coronary thrombosis had left Monica widowed not long after her brother's death and just as the sale of Gorstone had gone through. From that time onwards the family had drifted apart. It was as if Gorstone Manor was all that had held them together.

Harry reached for the telephone. His large hand shook a little, in fact he was shivering all over and the tickle in his throat had become a rasping pain. Tea and aspirin, he decided, but first more urgent matters claimed his attention. The face of a harassed officer had appeared in the doorway.

The morning passed surprisingly quickly and by lunchtime the fog had begun to clear. Odd that it should have lingered in the city when the forecast had said that the moors were free of it. He thought of Grace, out there somewhere and hopefully enjoying blue skies.

Harry tidied up his desk and went home, parking in the road instead of in his garage at the back. It was daft, but he couldn't face Reg Myers who had the one next to his and who worked on his car every Saturday afternoon all year round and had no conversation unless it concerned oil filters and distributors and leaking brake fluid.

Harry dropped his briefcase on the hall floor and made a mug of tea as he rummaged in a drawer for aspirins. Feed a cold, his mother used to say. Later he would cook his meal, for now he wanted to think.

Since meeting Ruth Ferrers he had started to analyse many of his own actions and he was not unaware of the reason why he had started to clean up the kitchen. What he wanted was an impossibility; he tried not to think about it.

An hour later he poured himself a beer. His throat a little less sore, he walked from room to room surveying his unimaginative house. No amount of redecoration could make it a home. It had to go. He would put it on the market as soon as the trial was over. He had been up a long time, and tiredness and his cold had weakened him. He sat down and closed his eyes merely to rest them. His head ached and his joints felt stiff. This was more than a head cold, probably flu.

The evening after he had seen the name Grace Cornell on PC Cobane's computer screen, Harry had gone to see her. It was late summer then, the trees in the park had been dusty and there was a heavy stillness in the air. He had looked up and seen the silhouette of a woman moving behind a diaphanous curtain and wondered if this was his first sight of Gerald Cornell's daughter.

Getting into the building had been quite a performance. To one side of the front entrance was a row of bells with a small grid in which to speak. Harry had decided against this method of entry and rung the main bell instead although the man on duty behind the desk had already risen and was approaching the plate glass doors. Harry introduced himself and presented his identification and was duly admitted. 'I've come to see Miss Cornell. Is she in?'

'Is she expecting you?'

'No.'

'I'll find out.'

Crafty old buzzard, Harry had thought. The man knew perfectly well that Grace was at home but he could not fault his efficiency. Later he learned the man's name was Joe and they became, if not friendly, then at least on terms which allowed for some polite small talk each time he was there.

Joe had picked up the internal telephone and punched the four digits which would connect him with Grace's flat. His back was turned so Harry hadn't been able to hear what was said.

'You can go up. I told Miss Cornell that I've seen your ID.'

'Cheers.' He had stepped into the lift. Everything was plush and spoke of money. Grace had come into a large inheritance, he knew that from their records, but this was real opulence. The lift doors opened without Harry having felt the ascent. He stepped into a corridor which seemed more appropriate to a four star hotel than a block of flats and walked towards Grace's door. It was not open in expectation of his visit. He had had to ring the bell and he was aware of the spyhole through which he had been observed.

She was smaller than he had expected but his first thought was that he had never seen anyone as beautiful, especially under those circumstances. For several seconds they had appraised each other. The quickly controlled expression which had crossed her pale face registered her shock at this unexpected visit. For the first time in his life Harry wished he was more handsome. He had exhaled deeply, hoping his own surprise at her looks had not shown so clearly. Dressed in a satin robe, her hair wild and unbrushed and with dark shadows beneath her eyes, Grace Cornell was still lovely. He could not imagine what she must look like when at her best.

'Come in,' she had said coldly.

As wide as it was, there was a second or so of confusion in the hallway. She stepped aside to let him pass and to close the door at the same time as Harry reached out to do so. The space seemed to be filled with their bodies. He could feel the heat from Grace's as his hand brushed her shoulder. There was no seductive coyness about Miss Cornell. Her robe was secured at the waist and the revers were high enough that he was not treated to even the slightest hint of cleavage. When she had shown him into the lounge she sat down and crossed her legs but not before taking the precaution of gathering the edges of the robe in both hands and folding them neatly over her knees. Another disappointment.

The room was remarkable for its warmth of colour and the comfort of the furniture. His first thought, as he had stood on the deep carpet the colour of the crust of Devon cream, was that he hoped he hadn't stepped in dog shit.

Grace waved a hand inviting him to be seated. He chose the pale chamois-covered sofa and sank into it rather more quickly than he had intended and wondered if the small twist to Grace's mouth had been a smile at his awkwardness. Having doubly reassured her that there was little chance of charges being brought, he had questioned her about the letters. Almost as if she had been expecting a visit, she indicated the three envelopes on the table next to him.

'Make I take them with me? I'll give you a receipt,' he had said.

'You can burn them for all I care.'

With those weary words he had looked at her closely. Her behaviour the previous day had seemed unlikely in an intelligent and well-respected doctor but he had guessed that here was a woman near the end of her tether. Grace had explained how she had been given indefinite leave and why. She had been quite open about it. 'Oh, God. There's something else you'll have to know. The handwriting. It's mine. Well, not mine, but a damn good likeness.

'I don't expect you to believe me, Inspector. My brother thinks it's a sick joke and that . . .'

Harry had guessed that her sentence would have ended 'and that I wrote them myself.' He remained silent because he had the impression that Grace was more likely to talk if she wasn't pressed. He had been wrong.

'Yesterday,' he had prompted, 'that was all to do with the letters?'

'Yes. When the second one arrived I started to feel really frightened and I'd already got a feeling that I was being watched.' She had shrugged but the robe stayed in place. 'I put it down to paranoia. I'm a doctor, not a super-model or a sportswoman. Why should anyone want to watch me?'

Harry did not answer although he could have given her one very good reason.

'I – well, I know how stupid it was, but I'd seen Mr Roberts outside quite a few times. I thought it was him, you see, watching me. Will you – I mean, is there any way you can let him know how sorry I am?'

Harry understood. It was not unusual for a wrongdoer to feel they could never apologise enough. When he had done a spell with traffic division it was not uncommon for a careless or reckless driver to inundate a victim or his family with letters of apology and to send flowers or gifts when things were better left alone. He chose to ignore the request. 'He recently moved into the area. He was getting his bearings, getting to know the traffic sounds and any hazardous bits of pavement. Have you any idea who wrote the letters?'

'If I had I'd know how to deal with them. Why don't you read them?' Grace had asked in a challenging tone.

He had done so without looking at her. 'And you believe these relate to the time when your father died?'

Her eyes had narrowed, she had not mentioned her father. 'Very astute, Inspector Jordan. To what else can they refer? There's nothing else in my past.'

Harry doubted that statement. 'What does he or she mean about Matt?' There was a reference to him in the second letter. 'Matt isn't right for you, Gracie. You know that and I know that. It's you and me now,' it had said.

'Ah, well.' The smile which accompanied the remark was full of cynicism. 'Matt was my fiancé, until very recently. Until yesterday, in fact.'

No wonder she looked so strained. The man was worthless if he'd left her because of what she'd done. It showed a complete lack of understanding when he should have been supporting her.

'It was nothing to do with Carl Roberts. It was a misunderstanding,' Grace told him, surprising him with what appeared to be telepathic powers. 'Matt knew nothing about the letters. I intended telling him last night.' She had then explained what had occurred and the way in which Matt had been unwittingly forced to confess to his affair with Ronnie Beecham. 'So you see, it was my choice to end it, it was nothing to do with any of this.'

'Could he have written them? Matt?'

'I don't think so. He knows as much about me as anyone but what reason would he have? It could be absolutely anyone.' She had leaned forward, her hands clasped around her knees, and Harry had seen the pleading in her eyes. She wanted him to put things right, to make her life safe again. No crime as such had taken place, the letters were not ostensibly threatening nor were they obscene, and investigating them was certainly not the job of an inspector. Yet, seeing how much they had affected Grace, he had known there was more to it. Not one for crusades he nevertheless saw himself as her lifeline. There could be no harm in making a few unofficial inquiries.

'Look, the detail, the correct postcode and the use of Matt's name suggest it's someone who knows you. Could you make a list? Include everyone, the people with whom you work, your friends and neighbours – well, anyone really with whom you come into contact.

'We'll start from there. It's easier to work outwards, to eliminate the closest first.' He saw the distaste before she turned her head away. Later he realised how much she would have hated putting her partners' and Ruth Ferrers' names amongst the suspects. It hadn't mattered, though, no one on the list was guilty of sending them. It was, ironically, the one person she had failed to include. Now he wondered just why that was.

And what a mixed crew Grace's nearest and dearest had turned out to be. Luke Cornell, acting the part of the playboy without a care in the world and all the time unable to see straight because of his insecurity which was probably the reason he was into drugs. Harry had seen the signs but had decided to let matters lie for a while. Grace could not cope with more strife. The brief lecture Harry had delivered with its threat of imprisonment had shaken the boy a little but he doubted if it had done any good. Luke was just another lost soul who thought that alcohol and dope would alleviate his feeling of alienation from society whereas they only served to increase it. His rudderless existence was a waste of a young life.

Matthew Fielding, the man Grace was to have married, had two sides to him: the loving fiancé and the unfaithful boyfriend. Harry's first encounter with Matt was at the Royal Devon and Exeter Hospital where he had been admitted via Accident and Emergency only two days after Harry had been to see Grace. Upon hearing the name Matthew Fielding and learning that he had been attacked near Grace's flat, he had taken it upon himself to interview him personally. It was too much of a coincidence not to have some relevance to Grace's situation. The death of her father was still unresolved, she had assaulted a stranger in the street, her fiancé, now ex-fiancé, had taken a severe beating a few yards away from her front door and her partners at the practice were concerned about her mental state. Grace seemed to attract violence but so far had remained unscathed herself.

Arriving at the hospital he had found Matthew propped up in bed. His face was bruised and there were stitches in one over-hanging eyebrow. The firm lines of his mouth were blurred, swollen and already discoloured. He was a mess but his boyish good looks were still in evidence. Worse, according to Matt who whispered through his swollen mouth, were his ribs, three of which had been broken, but the doctor had reassured him he had been lucky not to have a damaged spleen or kidneys and that he would make a full recovery.

'What were you doing in the area?' Harry had asked.

'I was going to see Grace. She wasn't expecting me.' The words were just decipherable and caused Matt pain to speak them. 'We'd split . . .'

'Yes. I know. Did you see her?'

Matt shook his head and winced.

'Who did this to you?'

'I don't know. I didn't see them.'

Harry had given him a few minutes' rest. Them. More than one person. Luke Cornell had wanted to throw him out when he admitted to his affair with the Beecham woman. Had he wanted revenge for his sister? Harry doubted it. Luke, whom Harry had questioned about the letters, did not have the build to inflict so much physical damage on someone of Matt's size and, from his brief assessment of him, he doubted if he had the temperament to cause harm, even with the aid of someone else. Luke came across as weak but not vicious and although he wasn't gay there was a certain femininity about his slender body with its long, tapering fingers and the soft fair hair which fell over his fore-head. Naturally the attack might have been random, some thugs after Matthew Fielding's wallet who had been disturbed by the young couple who had come around the corner in time to save him from further harm. According to the couple, they had shouted and the men had run off before they could gain much of an impression of them.

Neither had Matthew Fielding. The first thing he was able to recall was a thump in the kidney region which had winded him sufficiently to cause him to stumble. He had been attacked from behind and had shielded his face with his arms from the lashing feet and therefore seen nothing worth noting.

The same young couple had called an ambulance and Matt had been taken to casualty. His wallet, containing cash and credit cards, was still in his pocket, the expensive watch still on his wrist. No, not random, Harry had thought at the time. But Matthew's attack had taken place five months ago. Since then there had been several others and the men responsible had been arrested and charged. So there was such a thing as coicidence. It was one which had caused Grace added distress.

Just as he was leaving Matthew's bedside an elegant woman had appeared. With her hand at her throat her lips had moved although no sound came from them. She stared at the figure in the bed. 'Oh, my God, Matt,' she finally croaked, hurrying around to the other side. She had kissed his forehead gently and brushed back his hair with an instinctively motherly gesture. 'It's all right. It'll be all right. As soon as they've discharged you you're to come home with us.'

Harry had cleared his throat. 'Mrs Fielding?'

'Yes?' Her voice was sharp. 'Are you a doctor?'

'No. Police. Harry Jordan. Inspector Jordan.'

Joyce Fielding nodded. 'Have you got him, whoever did this to my son?'

'Not yet.' He was fully aware of her scrutiny, of the way in which her eyes had narrowed when she had first really looked at his face. It seemed to have shocked her almost as much as the injured face of her son. Next to the petite woman with the refined accent and immaculate dress sense Harry Jordan had felt loutish and unattractive.

'I wonder if I might have a word with you, Mrs Fielding? Once you've spoken to your son?'

'Of course.'

He had waited outside for twenty minutes and then, as if to prove what an oaf he was, had tactlessly put his foot in it. Joyce Fielding had had no idea that the engagement was off or the reasons why. She had heard nothing about the letters, and the fact that Grace had been given leave from work was also news. Poor Matthew, Harry had thought as he walked the length of the corridor knowing Mrs Fielding's eyes were still upon him. What sort of a grilling will he get now? He guessed that Matthew had said nothing in the hope that the breach would heal itself but from what Harry had observed, he did not think that Grace Cornell would change her mind.

Harry opened his eyes, reached for the remote control gadget and put the television on. The raucous voice of the sports commentator grated on his nerves. He turned it off again. The room was quiet apart from the sound of the occasional car turning into the estate.

His second meeting with Grace had also been at the hospital on that same occasion. He had made it as far as the main entrance and was about to push open the doors when he saw her. She was to his left, studying the direction signs with a worried frown, her lips pursed in concentration. He realised, with an inward smile, that he had not till now seen her dressed. In street clothes she looked entirely different. Her hair was held back neatly and the russet wool coat swung at the hem where it covered the tops of her boots as she turned to walk down the corridor.

'Grace! Miss Cornell!' he had called after her. She was still frowning when she turned to face him but she stood quite still until he had reached her. 'Mrs Fielding's with Matthew. Can we have a word?' He indicated one of the seats against the wall but Grace had remained standing. Her face was paler than before. 'Were you expecting him?' Tactlessly he had put his immediate suspicions into words.

'Pardon?'

'Matthew said he was on his way to visit you when it happened.'

'I don't know what's happened, only that his mother rang me and said he'd been admitted to hospital. How is he?'

'He'll live.' Harry did not like the fact that she cared.

Grace shook her head. 'Please, I don't understand any of this.'

'Someone attacked Matthew, not far from your flat. He doesn't know who it was and he's lucky it wasn't worse.'

'I see.' Grace's voice had been so low he had had to bend forward to hear her. Her hands were clasped tightly in front of her. She had no handbag, only a bunch of keys gripped between her fingers. 'I thought he was ill, I didn't realise . . . I suppose you think I did this too.'

It was not a question so Harry did not answer. 'I don't know what's going on, Miss Cornell, but I intend to find out. Do you know anything at all about this?'

'How can you ask that? I might not be engaged to Matt now but I'd never wish him any harm.'

He had looked away. Those huge eyes did things to his

99

insides. Grace understood as little as he did himself, and she was frightened – but whether of herself, the past or the person responsible for attacking Matthew, he had no idea. All he knew at that moment was that, whatever was in her eyes, it wasn't madness even if she was beginning to believe it herself. He never found out what had been said during her bedside visit to Matthew but she did not change her mind about marrying him, the relationship was off.

Harry went to the kitchen and got another can of beer from the fridge. It was now completely dark. He switched on the overhead spotlights and one of the bulbs blew. He got a spare from the cupboard under the stairs and stood on a chair to replace it, wondering how it was that no amount of light could cheer the place up. Grace's lounge had such a warm, welcoming feeling without any obvious reason for it; or none that he could see. He sipped his beer. It tasted strange, as had the first one. He sipped again. It was slightly metallic. He checked the heating. It was on full yet he was still cold. Tentatively he pressed the glands at the side of his throat between finger and thumb. They were painful. He was definitely going down with something. He had run out of aspirin but there was a bottle of paracetamol in the drawer beside the sink. He swallowed two in the hope of staving off whatever it was until after Monday.

A flurry of snow caught his eye. Big white flakes settled on the window ledge and hit the glass. He looked up through the narrow gap between the house and the back fence. The clouds were heavy, low in the sky, as if the weight of the precipitation they carried was dragging them down. We're in for another blizzard, he thought. But his forecasting was way out. A few more flakes fell then it stopped.

'Feed a cold.' Harry heard his mother's words again and intended doing just that. He studied the shopping he had bought and put together a meal. There were two thick gammon steaks to grill with tomatoes, oven chips for convenience and fresh sprouts and carrots. He surprised himself by getting the timing right although he could hardly taste the food.

He washed up and made tea. The rawness of his throat had worsened so he decided that the sensible thing to do was to get into bed where he would be warm and stay there until the morning. He might even read for a while. It was a long time since he had had the chance to get to grips with a novel. But once under the bedclothes he found himself unable to concentrate on anything other than the people he had come to know in the months since meeting Grace.

Monica Andrews he had found cold at first, until he realised she was desperately worried about her niece, although she would not say why. But there had been something under the surface, some other anxiety.

'These are very different days from when Gorstone Manor was in full swing,' she had told him with a sigh. 'Very different. Do you know, there were times when our feet didn't touch the ground. Dinners and card games and drinks parties and outings, you name it. I often wonder what's happened to all those people. Of course, it was Olivia and Gerald's doing. They had allure, both of them, people came to Gorstone like moths to a candle as they say. I think Grace has that quality too.'

'Why did you lose touch with her?' Harry had asked.

'I'm not sure. She leads a busy life, you know how it is. She used to confide in me such a lot. Luke told me about Matthew, about the engagement being off, then his attack. I never met him, of course.'

By the time Harry got around to visiting Monica, Matthew had been discharged from hospital and was recovering at his parents' house. After the meeting Harry realised how evasive Monica's answers had been, not at all like the transcripts of the tapes where she had been self-assured and articulate.

Harry was aware that his unexpected call had flustered Monica, although he had been amused at the way in which she watched the blackbird whilst she spoke, and impressed with the tea trolley upon which stood a silver teapot and water jug and a plate of cakes. She had apologised because they were not home-made. During her brief absence from the room he had noticed the lack of personal bits and pieces. There were no family photographs or ornaments which had sentimental value as far as he could see. The few that there were had been chosen with the decor in mind. He had wondered why that should be. But there were numerous books and an open one which lay on the settee where she had been sitting.

In that lovely room, with autumn sunshine streaming through the windows, he had felt a chill, a sense of something unresolved, and he had wondered what was going on beneath Monica Andrews' unruffled performance. Her efficiency and control seemed at odds with what he guessed to be an under-lying ardent nature.

'One of my friends,' Monica had said with a smile when she saw Harry following her eyes to the blackbird. 'Are you interested in nature, Inspector?'

He was not sure if he was being mocked. 'I sometimes take a walk along the Exe and watch the waders in the winter.'

'Indeed. They're so much easier to identify than other birds, don't you find? They don't fly off the minute someone approaches, they just carry on plodding about in the mud as if you're of no consequence, unless you get too close.

'I've had a thought, Inspector. It couldn't be this Ronnie woman whom Matt was seeing who sent the letters, could it? Females can do strange things if they're thwarted.'

Harry had thought she might be speaking from experience. 'We are, to coin a phrase, investigating every angle. I believe you lost your husband some time ago?' It was not Freddie in whom he was interested but he had decided to let Monica bring up Gerald's name and had thought that the mention of death might provoke it.

'Yes. I never really loved him, you know, but I liked and admired him tremendously. I think that's important in a marriage. He was a good and faithful man and not many can say that about their spouses. Are you married, Inspector?'

'I was.'

'Ah. I'm sorry.'

Lying in bed, slightly feverish, Harry remembered an unreadable expression on her face, a sort of knowledgeable moue. He had not known what to make of it. In the end the subject of Gerald Cornell and his death had not arisen. Monica, he realised, had seen to that.

Harry read a couple of chapters of a novel then put down the book. He pulled the duvet up around his ears, swallowed painfully and closed his eyes. Tomorrow he would go over Harrington's statement. He and Grace might have written theirs in tandem. They only differed in one respect. It was the crucial point upon which the trial would be conducted.

Harry slept from nine thirty until eight the next morning, waking only once to find himself grasping at nothing. He had dreamed he was reaching for Grace's hand.

OLIVIA

'It's so damned cold.' Olivia shivered and folded her arms beneath her breasts as she stared out of the hotel window. Snow still lay on the ground but the room was centrally heated, pleasantly warm. The chill came from within, from the fear that her daughter would choose to ignore her presence. A long, lonely Sunday lay ahead. Yesterday she had bought small, amusing gifts, but nothing which might imply she was trying to buy the affection of her children. Today she might take a walk, remind herself of her old haunts, look at the cathedral, she could even remember its full name – the Cathedral Church of St Peter in Exeter – strange, that, when Tony teased her about her lack of interest in Italian churches. Olivia was too ashamed to admit that she was of the view that if you'd seen one ornate monument, you'd seen them all. The opera was different, she enjoyed that and the shopping and one or two of the museums, but she'd never been able to build up any enthusiasm for places of worship or religious artifacts. As a child she had attended the church in Shillingford St George with her parents. In those days she supposed she had beliefs, or at least she didn't question those promulgated by the Church. With Gerald she had attended services in one or other of the nearby villages, taking pleasure in the familiarity of the responses and the hymns even after she had convinced herself that there was no God.

Tony knew none of this and would have laughed at her lack of faith because his Roman Catholic upbringing had left him no room for doubt. He may no longer attend mass or go to confession but he still believed in the doctrines of his Church. Dear Tony. If only she could love him completely the way she had Gerald. Perhaps she was what they called a one man woman. Her financial, mental and physical needs were taken care of, she was greedy to want more, but there were times when she could have given up her advantages just to feel what she had experienced during those nights with Gerald. Tony was no Latin lover. Stupidly, she had believed the myth and had expected hot breath

103

against her neck and urgent and demanding passion. Tony was slow and gentle and considerate and it was ridiculous to acknowledge that, although sex with him was occasionally better than it had been with Gerald, it was her dead husband's face she sometimes pictured when they lay together between the cool sheets in the high wooden bed.

> Blow, blow, thou winter wind,
> Thou art not so unkind
> As man's ingratitude . . .

How apt the quotation, considering the weather and her own feelings. Where was it from . . .? Shakespeare, naturally, because he was always going on about infidelity and ungrateful kin. *As You Like It*, of course. She had once had a small part in a school production which she had played rather sulkily because she had imagined she was good enough to have been picked for Rosalind. But she had had the advantage of having less to do on stage and therefore more time to flirt with one of the sixth form boys who was helping with the scenery and with whom she had believed herself to be in love. Oh, how little she knew then. There had only ever been one love.

Through the window Olivia saw one or two cars pull into the hotel's parking spaces below her. Each time her heart beat faster but none of the drivers was Grace. At irregular intervals buses stopped outside the station, disgorging few passengers out into the bitter January morning and taking on fewer still. A couple with a baby in a pushchair and two heavy-looking suitcases trudged towards the station concourse. If only she could be out there, just walking, amongst other people, anything to take her mind off tomorrow and the possibility of seeing one or both of her children.

But she had decided she would not leave the hotel after all. Impossible to know if Grace had yet received her letter but she could not take the chance again as she had done yesterday of bumping into her. How much more conspicuous she would be in the quiet Sunday streets. There was also the chance that Grace might ring or decide to turn up without telephoning first. If Olivia wasn't there it could appear that she did not care enough to wait for her call.

Breakfast was over long ago. Going down to the dining-room and ordering food she knew she would be unable to eat had passed an hour away. When the waitress refilled her coffee cup Olivia had taken it through to the bar where she smoked a cigarette and glanced at the Sunday papers which lay on a table for guests to read. No news, no matter how sensational, could be more important than the reason she had come home.

As soon as she woke she had showered and washed her long hair, wanting to look her best at all times. Now she wondered whether a bath would dissolve the cold in her bones and pass away another half an hour. No, she thought with panic, I might not hear the telephone. The waiting was agony but she had to acknowledge the fact that the whole week might go by without Grace getting in touch. If that happens, Olivia vowed, then I must accept that my daughter is lost to me for ever. There were so many things she wanted to say to her, so many things she wanted to hear from Grace, but she was already steeling herself for the worst.

Unsure how the licensing laws which had been introduced after she had left England applied, she decided to go downstairs and see if the bar was open.

Making her way along the red-carpeted corridor which smelled of the roast lunches being prepared in the kitchen, she stopped to examine the paintings on the wall and felt quite certain they had been there on her last visit to the hotel. It was eleven forty-five. The girl behind the reception desk explained politely that the bar would be open at twelve but she could sit there and wait or order a pot of coffee.

'I'm expecting a telephone call. My name's Olivia Pisano. Can you let me know if someone rings?'

'Of course, Mrs Pisano. I'll be here for the next couple of hours.'

'Thank you.'

Already awash with coffee which tasted nothing like the espresso to which she had become accustomed, Olivia decided to wait until she could have a proper drink. The barman had pulled up the shutters and was filling an ice bucket. He glanced up as Olivia entered and saw the room key which she had placed on the round table. 'You're a resident?' he asked with a smile.

105

'What? Oh, yes.'

He looked at his watch and winked. 'Won't be a mo.'

But by the time he was ready to serve her there was less than a minute to go before the official opening time.

She made two gins and a bottle of low calorie tonic water last until one thirty. Lunch was still being served but she couldn't face more food. All she could see was her daughter as a little girl and then as an adult as she had looked in the photograph Anton had sent her. She might have gone away for the weekend, Olivia thought. Perhaps she's staying with friends. And there was the farmhouse which Grace had mentioned in her terse reply to Olivia's letter. If the roads were passable she may have gone there and if so she would not have received Saturday's post. Her optimism was short-lived because there was the more realistic possibility that Grace had read the letter and thrown it in the bin, or screwed it up without even opening it.

The shock at receiving a reply to her first letter had not diminished. She had cried with joy, then with disappointment at the coldness of the tone, believing it would have been better if Grace had not written at all than in that unfeeling manner. At least her dreams would have remained intact.

How did it feel, my darling? she asked herself, remembering that although she might be suffering Grace had been through worse. Olivia was not able to picture her beautiful daughter threatened and terrified by a man who had been stalking her.

Olivia wondered how Luke had coped over the years. Apart from Monica there was no one else but Grace to look out for him. Had he known about the stalker? Had Grace confided in him? One letter from Monica had said that she saw less of Luke now but that on each visit he looked more and more like Gerald. For that reason only, Olivia dreaded setting eyes on him. She was not sure how it would affect her.

And Monica? Yes, I'll be glad to see her again, we used to have such fun together. But those times could never be recaptured, too much had happened to all of them since then.

Olivia looked up with a broad smile as a figure approached her table and blocked the light from the window.

'Are you eating with us today?' A plumpish blonde with a pretty face smiled back at Olivia. In her hand was a menu, bound in imitation leather.

'No. Yes. Yes, thank you. I think I will.' She took the menu and bowed her head as if to study it because tears of disappointment had filled her eyes. She had been certain the girl had come to say that Grace was on the line. 'Could I just have a salad and half a bottle of the house dry white wine, please?'

'Certainly, madam. Ham, cheese or beef?'

'Oh, ham, I think.' It doesn't matter, I won't eat it, she thought, as she followed the girl to the dining-room, but the idea of going back to her solitary room was unbearable.

'I'll be in the restaurant if that phone call comes,' she told the girl on reception as she passed the desk.

The girl nodded, understanding that Mrs Pisano was extremely anxious not to miss the call she was expecting. Wrongly, she assumed it would be from a man.

But it didn't come. For the rest of the afternoon Olivia lay on the bed staring at the ceiling. Sometimes when she looked at her watch only minutes had passed, at others, she was surprised to see that half an hour had gone by.

But whatever the outcome she knew that she had had to come, that at least Grace would know she was there.

The streetlights flickered on as darkness descended over the city whose streets she had known so well. Now and then, when the wind changed direction, she was able to hear the hiss of the brakes of an inter-city train as it pulled up alongside a platform. Outside, life still went on.

She did not bother to go down for dinner, enough food had been wasted for one day. At ten o'clock she picked up the telephone beside the bed and dialled the number of the Milan apartment. Never before had she been so relieved to hear Tony's voice. They chatted, discussing his trip and her flight but making no mention of why she was in England. Tony knew, of course, but he also knew his wife well enough to realise she could not bear to give voice to her anxieties for fear they would turn out to be justified. And obviously, if Grace had been in touch she would have said so at once.

'When you come home we will have a long talk, my darling,' he said quietly in Italian. 'I think there is so much you haven't told me.'

'Yes, we'll do that. Tony. Goodnight.' Olivia replaced the receiver. She would talk to him, he deserved that much, but she wasn't sure what there was to say. There were so many things she did not know or understand herself.

There, in the hotel room, not so many miles from the place where she had been most happy, it suddenly occurred to her how well Tony and Gerald had known one other. Perhaps she had been a fool to imagine her second husband knew little about the personal life of her first. Olivia had run to Tony when she was desperate because he was an easy man in whom to confide and one whose help could be relied upon. Maybe Gerald had treated him equally as a confidant. Surely men confided in one another as frequently as women did? Maybe now, after all this time, she would learn of the woman who had usurped her in Gerald's affections. Maybe that was what Tony wanted to discuss.

She lay in bed, her arms on the bedclothes, her hair flowing over the pillow, and breathed deeply, in and out, counting the breaths to clear her mind for sleep. But every time she closed her eyes she saw Grace hurtling around Gorstone on her bike or tucked up in bed with her thumb in her mouth, and Luke, with his soft blond hair, who had trailed around after her, gripping the hem of her dresses. The tears rolled down the sides of her cheekbones and welled beneath her ears, wetting the pillow. She would allow herself this one night of grief, she would permit the pictures to come and then, tomorrow, she would find the strength she might need if everything went the way she hoped it would.

It was after two before Olivia drifted off to sleep but she woke again at six, exhausted and heavy with dreams.

HARRY

Sleep did not seem to have done him much good. Heavy-limbed and sneezing, Harry threw back the bedclothes and pulled on yesterday's clothes, adding an extra jumper. Downstairs he made coffee and swallowed two more paracetamols. It was years since he had been ill and he cursed that it had to happen now.

Without thinking, he lit a cigarette. It tasted foul so he stubbed it out. Harry didn't smoke much, unlike his father who chain-smoked. He thought of him with bitterness. If only once in his life Frank Jordan could have said well done, or let him know he was proud of him in some way . . . But it was not in the man's character. Discontented himself, he begrudged anyone else any form of success or happiness.

And Gillian, what was she doing now? Curled up next to her husband, her second husband, Harry's ex-friend, or cheerfully making their breakfast? The guilt remained. His guilt. Everything that happened to him was his fault. It had been ingrained in him since the time he could walk. If he fell over it was because he was clumsy, if he quarrelled with a friend it was because he was unlikeable, if girls weren't interested it was because he was ugly. Strange that even that was down to him. He had had no say in the genes he was born with. When Gill was unfaithful he believed it was because he had given too much time to work and had not paid her enough attention or, to quote his father, because he hadn't 'given her a regular seeing to'. He had, in his crude way, offered to do the job for him himself. This was Frank Jordan's creed, the litany to which he had subjected his son on a daily basis until he had left home. Although Harry had come to realise that his father's bullying and apportionment of blame to others when things went wrong with his own life were due to inadequacy, they had left their scars. The lack of sensitivity his father had shown around the time of the divorce was typical. It was his mother he had gone to see to break the news but it was raining that day. A continuous downpour had meant that Frank was home from work early because the site at which he was employed at the time had turned into a quagmire. Harry would never forget the smirk of pleasurable spite on his face when he learned what had happened.

His guilt was something he believed he would carry with him for the rest of his life. Despite the cruelty of his father's words there had been some truth in them. Gill had been left alone too often and sometimes, even when he desired her badly, he had been too tired to perform properly or at all. She had tried, he had to give her that. But in the end she had left him for a man who was little different from himself.

And Grace? He sipped the coffee, which was strong and very hot. Had it been the same with her and Matt? Matthew Fielding had said so. If so it was something they had in common: too great a dedication to their jobs. Oddly, the idea cheered him.

Had he and Gill had children no doubt he would have been planning something exciting to do with them on a Sunday. He had watched single or remarried fathers, even in this weather, with their bundled-up offspring as they tried to entertain them for their day of access when they probably would rather have been at home watching television or playing with their friends. Gill was pregnant now. Someone at the station had mentioned it, with what motive, Harry neither knew nor cared. The news hadn't hurt as much as he'd feared.

He ate some scrambled eggs and toast and felt marginally better as the paracetamol began to take effect. He showered in the poky bathroom, dressed in clean clothes and went down to the shop for the paper, which he read in front of the fire.

Wrapped up warmly he walked to the station. More snow had melted since his earlier trip to the newsagent's.

Harry sat at his desk surrounded by every piece of information relating to Grace Cornell and the trial. To the left were files pertaining to her father's death, to the right were the more recent ones. Harry fingered the file which contained Lance Harrington's view of events. The Crown Prosecution Service had been satisfied that there was enough evidence for a trial to take place. But to his mind there were still things which did not add up. The discrepancies worried Harry because he cared about Grace far more than he wanted to admit. He shook his head, the matter was out of his hands. What he was doing was a waste of time, only a jury could decide Lance Harrington's fate. Even so, he opened the file.

110

'When did you first meet Dr Cornell?' Harry had asked. The answer had shaken him.

'Nine years ago, at university,'

Grace had not mentioned this. When questioned, she claimed she had forgotten him, had not recognised him. Strange when Ruth Ferrers could recall him. Harry had come to know and like Ruth and respected her for her unwavering friendship with Grace. In fact, if it had not been for Ruth no one would have known that she had been in danger.

On the Saturday of the attempted abduction Ruth had rung the station and, knowing he had met Grace, asked to speak to Harry personally. Coolly, but insistently, Ruth had stated that Grace had arranged to meet her for lunch but had not turned up, neither had she got in touch, which was totally out of character. 'We were due to meet at twelve thirty,' she said. It was one thirty when Ruth rang because Grace had still not made contact. 'I've tried the flat and the farmhouse several times. She would never cancel without letting me know. I know her, Inspector, and I know the strain she's been under because of those damn letters. You've got to look for her before that man harms her.'

Harry had taken her at her word and started looking for her immediately. She had not been hard to find.

Prior to this he had spoken to everyone at the surgery. Because he was convinced that the author of the letters was someone close to Grace it was the logical place to begin. He had arrived at an inconvenient time. Evening surgery was about to begin and the girl on the desk looked flustered. Her name badge told him she was called Nicky. In front of her was a lumpy-looking bag. 'Can you come back later? Or you can wait, if you prefer?' She had looked over his shoulder and grinned with relief. 'I thought you'd forgotten us,' she said to a man wearing leathers. Outside the sky was a clear blue, a perfect August evening. The waiting-room windows were flung open and birdsong could be heard from the small garden surrounding the building. Backlit, and all in black, the man seemed almost menacing until he approached the desk and grinned. He was about thirty, good-looking, and he winked at Nicky.

'Sorry, love. It was the traffic. I took a short cut, but that was even worse.'

'Never mind, you're here now.' She had handed him the bag.

'Blood samples and specimens,' Nicky had told Harry, seeing the question in his face. 'They're collected daily and taken to the path lab for analysis. The results come back by post.'

Grace had not listed such a person when he had asked her for the names of everyone she knew and worked with.

Harry had decided to wait until Anton Roach was free rather than have to come back later. 'Sorry to have kept you waiting,' Anton had said as he stretched out a hand. 'We'll use my room, it's more private.'

A few disconsolate patients read the notices on the walls or flicked through old copies of magazines. Harry sympathised, he had felt the same way during the time he had waited.

Anton's room was modern and clinical and there was a computer terminal on his desk. 'How may I help you?' he had asked, pulling out a seat for Harry.

'We're trying to locate a person who might be stalking Dr Cornell. I understand you've given her some time off and the reason for it, which is understandable.'

'And they deem it worthwhile to send an inspector? Be frank with me, it's a little more important than that if you're here.' Anton had removed his glasses and polished them on a navy and white spotted handkerchief which matched his bow-tie. 'It was obvious to me that Grace has problems. However, she chose not to confide them.'

'We know she's been the recipient of some disturbing letters.'

'Grace? Good God, she didn't say anything. No wonder her mind wasn't on the job. Anonymous, I take it?'

'Yes. We don't know if she's in any danger but we can't afford to take chances.'

'Quite. But I still don't see how any of us can help.'

'Excuse my bluntness, but is there any internal rivalry? Personal dislikes, anything that might add to the picture? What I'm trying to say is do you know any reason why anyone would want to upset Dr Cornell to this extent?'

Anton had laughed. 'Absolutely none. We're a small practice and we all get on well. Naturally, if you wish to question the other people who work here, you may do so.'

'Thank you. A patient, maybe?'

Anton had thought about this before answering. He did not know that Ruth Ferrers had suggested this possibility to Harry but he did know about transference, it had happened to him on

112

more than one occasion. A patient could become just as hooked on a nurse or a doctor as sometimes occurred with psychiatrists. It might be someone whom she had treated recently, or even further back. Which widened the field enormously.

'Not that she's mentioned. And believe me, she would have done. I've always encouraged discussion of such things, that way we can try to prevent matters getting out of hand. If any patient shows signs of developing such traits we hand them over to another partner without further ado. Excuse me a second, I've just remembered something.' Anton had picked up the telephone and tapped out three digits. 'Nicky, have the samples been collected yet?'

Harry had not been able to hear the answer.

'Yes, I forgot. All right, I'll drop if off myself on my way home. My memory doesn't improve with age,' Anton had continued, replacing the receiver and turning back to Harry. 'Our despatch rider comes at varying times, depending on traffic. I've just missed him.' He had shaken his head. 'Look, I find it hard to believe this is happening to Grace.'

'That's what everyone says and why we're taking this seriously. What's the name of your despatch rider?'

'Harrington. Lance Harrington.'

Harry had taken Grace's list out of his pocket. The name, as he had already guessed, was not on it. He had specifically asked for the names of *everyone* she knew, however insignificant they were in her life. 'How long has he been coming here?'

'Oh, about three or four months, I believe. He seems reliable.'

'I'd like to speak to him. May I have his address?'

'I'm afraid I don't have it. He's employed by the health authority, not by us individually.'

'Thank you for your time.'

Anton had been amazed at how fast the awkward-looking man had risen from his seat and left the room without knocking anything over.

Harry knew they must speak to Harrington; they couldn't afford to ignore anyone, however trivial their role in Grace's life. And Harrington had a connection with the surgery. When Ruth reported Grace's disappearance both Harrington and the surgery had sprung to mind. Although what had come out afterwards made Harry doubt every word Grace had ever spoken.

As soon as Ruth hung up, Harry had telephoned everyone

connected with Grace. Matt, by then out of hospital and convalescing with his parents, had not heard from her, neither had her brother, Luke. There seemed to be few other people in Grace's life apart from a friend in London who had been on duty all night and had no idea where Grace might be.

It was Luke who had let Harry and a female detective into the flat. He and Grace each held the other's spare key. There were no signs that Grace had made preparations for a trip. As far as Luke could tell no clothes were missing and her cosmetics were still on the bathroom shelf. 'The thing is,' Luke had said, 'if she's at the farmhouse she wouldn't have taken anything. She keeps clothes there.' But Grace wasn't at the farmhouse, they had tried that number repeatedly.

As he had known it would be, a telephone call to Monica Andrews had also proved fruitless, but by then anything had been worth a try. In the end it was chance which led them to Grace.

God, I've had enough of this, Harry decided. The room was stuffy and made his throat tickle. It was time to take a walk.

Outside the snow had almost disappeared. There were little piles of slush at the sides of the road and a shiny wetness everywhere. He sniffed and blew his nose, knowing that it must be bright red. With his thick overcoat buttoned and a scarf wrapped around his neck he walked towards the city centre wishing he had worn the fur-lined gloves which Gill had given him. What a bloody gloomy afternoon, he thought.

He found himself in the cathedral close before he had any idea of where he was going. Grace had once told him that she sometimes sat there if she wanted a few minutes' peace. Ignoring the wetness and the state of his health, Harry chose a bench and sat down with his back to the historical facade of Eland's tea-shop and Hansons next door but where he could take in the beauty of the cathedral with its square towers and the many small spires on the lower roofs. No other person was in sight. The grass surrounding the cathedral had little strips of snow around the borders but was otherwise a lush green.

Evensong did not commence for another two hours. He wondered how big a congregation attended the service. For now, there was an eerie silence, unbroken by voices or footsteps or the sound of traffic.

He felt the dampness which had penetrated his clothing and

114

cursed himself for his stupidity. But he had been thinking of Grace and any possible feelings he might have for her. The idea scared him. He had vowed that he would never commit himself to any woman again. He had adored Gill. He had, in the clichéd words of his mother who could not understand why Gill had left her son, worshipped the ground she walked on. And all the time he had believed that she knew this, that his love for her must be so obvious it did not need spelling out constantly. He had been wrong. Or she had not loved him as much in return. He could not, would not, suffer another such loss. Besides, Dr Grace Cornell could not possibly have any interest in a divorced copper some six years older than herself, a man with whom she appeared to have little in common. And yet there had been occasions when he believed that she might have, occasions when he caught her watching him or when she smiled that slow smile or when he made her laugh. That had been the best thing in all this, the return of her laughter for which he liked to think he had been partially responsible.

After Gill left he had been virtually celibate and with little desire for sex. There had been a couple of casual relationships with no strings attached on either side but they had soon petered out. So why did he keep picturing Grace's face?

'Is it just sex?' he wondered, as he stood gazing up at the cathedral. He realised that he was no longer alone and that he had spoken aloud. An old man, his shape disguised beneath layers of clothing stuffed with newspapers, was staring at him. His bloodshot eyes suggested the reason for his homeless state, as did the bottle neck which was poking out of the greasy topcoat pocket. Harry stared at the man, trying to imagine how anyone could survive in these conditions through the night. Perhaps he had some sort of a squat or maybe he stayed in a hostel. Did this man walk around as riddled with guilt as he did, and Grace and Luke? Oh, yes, he knew they felt it, too, he saw it in their eyes. Monica Andrews too, although what she had to feel guilty about was beyond him. Maybe it was a Cornell idiosyncrasy or perhaps it was the natural human state.

The old man held out his hand. He wore gloves which had once been pink, a woman's gloves, but he could no longer afford the price of pride. His voice was a croak, his words slightly slurred. Harry dug into the pocket of his jacket, an awkward movement with the bulk of his own coat over it. The man took the coins, eyeing Harry suspiciously when he looked into his dirty woollen palm and saw two of them, both pounds. He shuffled away without a thank you, looking back once over his shoulder as if he was afraid that Harry would change his mind and ask for the money back.

I can't allow myself to have these feelings, Harry was thinking as he came out into the High Street and began to retrace his steps. If the man points the finger at Grace during the trial, if he really does know something about her past, then it is a dangerous and stupid game I'm playing. But so far he wouldn't talk; not to the police, not to anyone except his lawyer. All the accused was prepared to say was that he had known Grace since their university days and that she had been a willing participant in what had taken place during the time she was with him. 'It was her idea,' he had insisted.

What puzzled Harry was why the man seemed so unconcerned. The charge was serious. Did Harrington honestly expect to be believed in court? Would the jury accept that Grace, professional, rich and beautiful, could have allowed herself to be fooled into such a position? No wonder Grace wore that haunted look.

But if Harrington did know something to Grace's disadvantage, something which would show her to be as unstable as the defence hoped to prove, he was undoubtedly saving it for the courtroom when its impact would be greater and could do most harm. What worried Harry most was the fact that Harrington had known Grace in the days before her father died. But it all now depended on the jury. And Grace is not the one on trial, he reminded himself.

Harry turned into the first pub he came to that was open all day and ordered a whisky mac for medicinal purposes. It warmed him immediately and eased his throat. After a second his head swam. He needed to go home and have something to eat. He looked at his watch. Five thirty. Yes, a meal and another early night. There were now less than seventeen hours to go.

GRACE

Grace undressed, knowing there was little chance of sleep. The trial was tomorrow. Just as at the farmhouse, memories came flooding back. Not distant memories, she had had enough of those. She recalled the day she had first viewed the flat. It was brand new and therefore empty. Sunlight had streamed in through the south-facing bedroom window which had given her the idea to continue the theme. She had chosen buttermilk paint for the walls, a pale gold carpet and a sunny yellow and white duvet cover and matching curtains. The furnishings were sparse but effective. A built-in wardrobe lined one wall but the antique pine bed had taken her and Luke two hours to assemble because Grace had not realised it did not come already made up. A chest of drawers matched the bed. On the wall were three delicate Japanese prints which bore no resemblance to anything that had been hung at Gorstone Manor.

Her needs in the flat were taken care of by Jackie who cleaned for several of the residents. They had agreed it was simpler to vet only one person and it also made life more convenient for Jackie. In her spare time she wrote unpublished poetry and had once showed a piece to Grace who had not had the heart to tell her why it would probably remain unpublished.

She sat, head in hands, on the edge of the bed, unwilling to get into it, because now the trial was so nearly upon her she wished it was not so. The hem of her nightdress rested on her bare feet and her hair hung down over her shoulders touching her face. She noticed neither sensation. How could she have not sensed that her mother was nearby? How could she have been so cruel as to write that clinical, cynical letter in reply to Olivia's first one? Because I was in a state of shock, she thought, because after missing and wanting to see her for so long I did not know how to deal with my feelings. Although her hand had hovered over the telephone several times during the evening she had not been able to bring herself to ring the hotel. It was too late to do so now. Olivia would probably be asleep. Has she done this, given

117

me this additional shock to help take my mind off tomorrow? Grace wondered. It was the sort of thing Olivia would do. When they were children she had distracted Grace and Luke from minor catastrophes by such tactics.

Grace got up and walked to the dressing-table. She picked up her brush and drew it through her hair until static crackled. The action was soothing. Scenarios of their reunion ran through her head although she was not yet entirely sure if there would be one, if she could really go through with it.

Had Harry Jordan told her about the trial, or Monica? Maybe her mother still took an English newspaper and learned of it through its pages. It had shocked her to the core to learn that Olivia and her aunt still kept in touch.

And what of Harry? Was there a chance he had made contact with Olivia in order to nose around in the past? Was that his fascination with her, Grace, that she might be a murderess? For there was no doubt the fascination was there. But the kiss which had startled them both had been genuine, if unreferred to since.

Grace sighed. Everything she had taken for granted had disappeared. Once so confident and lacking in self-doubt, she had simply reached out and attained her goals. Now, intelligence and logic seemed to have flown out of the window. At least her friends and partners had eventually come to believe her, to see that she was not suffering from paranoid delusions, that the man responsible for her condition had been living in their midst and was now facing trial for his actions.

Harrington had behaved oddly. Alone with Grace he could have done whatever he wanted to her, but he hadn't. Instead he had appeared overawed with what was happening, puzzled by it. It was Ruth upon whom she had relied to contact the police when she didn't turn up as arranged.

Grace slid into bed. Weariness had finally overcome her. Are you asleep, Olivia? she asked silently. Are you thinking of me? The bedside clocked ticked comfortably. Its hands showed twelve forty-five. Today, she thought, I shall see my mother again. But not before the trial began, that would be impossible to cope with. Sometime during the past half-hour Grace had come to the unconscious decision that she could not let Olivia return to Italy without seeing her.

It was odd that following her father's death, and even at his funeral, she had not shed one tear yet a letter from her mother had opened the floodgates.

Will Luke come to the trial? she wondered. Poor aimless Luke who drank and smoked too much and who took who knew what substances. And it was beginning to show. Maggie Collins had done her best to be a substitute mother. After Gorstone was sold, Grace had taken on that role. She had seen him through school, got a financial adviser to invest his money and helped him to choose the maisonette where he now lived alone. It was modern and masculine and, like Grace, he had hung the second mirror of the pair which used to be at Gorstone in his hallway.

She had tried to make him take responsibility for his own life but it seemed she had failed. Grace had sublimated her feelings, Luke went out of his way to alleviate his. In their different ways they had both failed.

Only once had he discussed Olivia with her. He had come to the flat for dinner and drunk too much wine. 'It was my fault she left,' he had said. 'I was clumsy and I cried a lot. I must've driven her mad.' Grace had finally persuaded him that this was not so, that Olivia had loved him more than he could possibly realise.

'Then why did she go?'

'I don't know,' she had answered quietly, because to tell the truth would have been impossible. She could understand why Luke thought that way. After Olivia left, Gerald had told them she had gone to live with Tony because she no longer loved them. It was a lie, one that Grace had initially believed.

Luke had talked of the times their mother had taken them into Exeter. 'Do you remember the history lessons?'

Grace had smiled. 'Isca. Built by the Romans in 80 AD. You never forget things you learn early.' Olivia had insisted they knew something of the city other than where the cinema and shops were.

Luke had gone quiet. 'What're you thinking?' Grace had asked him.

'I was thinking about Northernhay Gardens and Rougemen Castle, actually.' He had swept back his hair with that boyish gesture and looked as though he might cry. 'Do you remember the day I took a tumble by the war memorial?'

119

Grace hadn't because Luke often tripped over his own feet. 'No. Tell me about it.'

'There's nothing to tell, really. I just remembered how, whenever I fell over, she'd kneel down next to me and hold me and how she would play with my hair. She always wore the same perfume. I can never smell it without remembering her. She can't have been all bad, Grace, not when I can recall things like that.'

'She wasn't bad, Luke, she was unhappy.'

'Maybe.' He had grinned then. It altered his face totally. 'You made me cry in those gardens, too.'

'I did?' Her eyes had opened wide in surprise.

'After she'd gone you carried on where she'd left off. When Dad dropped us off one day, I suppose it must've been during the holidays, you made me read that plaque on the wall at the entrance to the gardens.'

'The one with the names of the last three women in England to be executed for witchcraft?' Some of the things she had told him must have sunk in. It was a pity they didn't now.

'Yes. I know they were only tried at the Gatehouse, it was out at Heavitree they were hanged, but I always imagined them being hanged right there. It used to terrify me. Every time we went there I imagined I could see their ghosts.'

'Why do you hate her?' Grace had asked later, making the most of a rare opportunity to discuss Olivia.

'Because of what she's made me.'

Grace had become angry then. She was tired of his self-pity. 'It's up to each of us to make what we can of ourselves. It's no good blaming someone else, Luke.'

'But you're different, Grace. Even when Dad died you didn't show any emotion.'

Oh, God, not that again, she had thought. But Luke had changed the subject and she had gone to make coffee.

Impossible though it had seemed, Grace fell asleep and slept dreamlessly. Emotion had exhausted her and crying had reduced the level of tension with which she had become accustomed to living.

She got out of bed with Harry on her mind. He was a good policeman, one who had a need to get at the truth. But what was

120

the truth? There were several different versions of it in Grace's head.

She had set the alarm clock needlessly because she woke before it went off. It was dark and across the road in the park everything seemed blacker still now that the grass and shrubs had lost their covering of snow. Where would she be in the spring? Was there a chance of life ever becoming normal?

The fridge rumbled into life as she opened its door and felt the chill on her bare legs. Everything gleamed and comforted her; only the primary colours of the bowls and jugs on a shelf brightened up an otherwise austere room. But Grace did not like clutter in the space in which she cooked. She had never cooked for Harry. For some reason she found herself wondering what sort of food he enjoyed, apart from the take-away curries they had shared.

Water was running through the coffee machine but unless she wanted to faint midway through the proceedings she must force down some food, and it would not be long before Ruth arrived. She had promised to drive Grace to court. Oh, God – Luke, she thought. I must warn him. If Olivia broke her promise and turned up at court she had no idea what it might do to him if he was there too.

Luke's voice was thick with sleep and she could picture his sad, boyish face as he answered. 'Is anything wrong?'

'No. Luke, look, there's something I've got to tell you.' Grace explained, adding that she had not read the letter until late last night when it was too late to phone him.

Luke reacted as if what he had heard was of no importance. 'Why are you telling me?'

'You had to know. She's here, Luke, in Exeter,' Grace added, hoping to make the situation perfectly clear. 'She says we can get in touch with her at the hotel, if we want to. She's here because of the trial.'

'Her support's a few years too late, wouldn't you say?' His bitterness was unmistakable but Grace did not blame him. She had been bitter herself for many years. But she was not up to dealing with her brother on top of everything else.

'I suppose you've already spoken to her?'

Grace heard the resentment in his voice and understood it.

121

Olivia had not written to Luke. 'No, but I think I will. Not this morning, though. We could do it together if you like?'

'No. But it's up to you what you do, Grace. I'll see you later.'

'Bye, Luke.' The intercom buzzed as she replaced the receiver. Grace spoke into it and told Ruth to come on up. She was early but that was typical of her kindness. She would have known Grace would already be up.

Ruth wafted in on a cloud of Chanel No. 5. She was dressed in a fake fur coat and hat and wore black gloves, looking just as if she had landed at Heathrow and was about to take a press call. Grace could not help smiling. If there was an opportunity to be dramatic, Ruth never failed to take it. Her lips were the same shocking pink as her nails and as she unbuttoned her coat Grace saw the cerise suit beneath it.

'You certainly look cheerful,' Grace said, kissing her cheek.

'And you look as if you've had some sleep.'

'I did. Coffee?'

'When do I ever say no? And these. Muffins.' Ruth placed a bag on the table.

'They're still warm. You didn't make them yourself?'

Ruth raised an eyebrow and grinned. '*Moi*?'

'Well, no, I didn't really think so.'

'The baker at the end of my road was open.'

As Grace picked at hers she told Ruth about the letter from Olivia. Her reaction was disappointing. Grace had expected all sorts of psychological wisdom and advice but all Ruth said was, 'Will you see her?'

'Yes. I'd like to.'

'It's a big decision. Can you bear to go to court not having contacted her?'

'I wouldn't get through the day if I did so. I'd just be thinking about what we'd said and how she looked.'

'Does Luke know?' Ruth was spreading her second muffin thickly with butter.

'I told him just now.' Grace shrugged. 'He's still so very bitter.'

Ruth nodded. It was time to change the subject. 'What're you going to wear?'

'Does it matter?'

'Of course it matters. A suit, I think. Something smart but not too doctorish or you'll come across as hard or frumpy. Something feminine without being sexy. The last impression you want to convey is that of a prick-teaser, which is what *he* wants the jury to believe. How about the slub silk mustard one? Wear a white blouse underneath if the jacket's cut too low.'

Grace concurred because she had not given her clothes any thought. Ruth had made her realise how important they might be.

'Go on, hurry up and get dressed. I'll rinse these dishes.'

The offer to do so showed Grace the depth of her concern. Ruth would leave a week's worth of crockery in the sink if there were still enough plates from which to eat.

Ten minutes before they were due to leave the trembling started. Grace's whole body shook. 'I'd forgotten, Ruth,' she said. 'I'd forgotten I'd have to face him again today. I'll have to see him, to listen to his voice again. I don't think I can bear it.'

'You won't be there all the time, you know that. Pull yourself together, Grace, don't let the bastard see that he's won.'

Ruth took her arm and checked that Grace had her keys and that the door was locked behind them. They went down in the lift to the front entrance and as they passed the desk Joe gave a thumbs-up sign. Ruth kept a firm hold on Grace as if she was afraid she might decide to run off. At last they were on their way and joined the rush-hour traffic as it headed towards the city centre.

Ruth parked and locked the car while Grace leant on the bonnet, her legs hardly able to hold her up.

'Deep breaths, girl, we're nearly there.' With a grip of iron Ruth almost dragged her across the road.

At the entrance to the court Grace lifted her head, removed Ruth's hand from her arm and fixed a smile on her face. 'Right,' she said. 'Here we go. This is it.'

THE TRIAL

Grace's apparent calmness fooled everyone apart from Ruth who, with one hand on her arm, was within her aura of tension. They had both overlooked the fact that more than one case would be heard, that other people with other problems would be milling around anxiously. It was not difficult to guess at the roles of the participants. Witnesses and potential jurors wore their best clothes and serious faces and seemed uncertain how to behave. They shuffled and coughed but were mainly silent. Those in the legal profession – the clerks of the court, solicitors and barristers – moved briskly amongst the assembled crowd with a pre-occupied air. One or two stood in last-minute consultations.

Harry Jordan had arrived early. He raised a hand when Ruth and Grace entered the foyer but dropped it quickly because they had just encountered Anton Roach and had not seen him. But he had to smile at Ruth's appearance, she certainly knew how to turn heads. Grace was lovely in a different, understated way and he would have liked to have told her so, to help boost her confidence for what was to come. He watched the expression on her face turn from confusion to pleasure as she stepped around Anton and embraced a plump female with short cropped hair and a large smiling mouth.

'Fay! How wonderful.' Grace shook her head in disbelief.

'I hoped you'd make it,' Ruth said with a grin as she hugged the warm bulk of her friend and smelled with nostalgia pepper-mints and Johnson's Baby Lotion.

'When Ruth rang me I knew I'd have to come,' Fay said, studying Grace as she spoke. She felt sickened by what she saw. Her friend's beauty had not diminished but the suggestion of tragedy which had been intriguing during their university days now clung to her like something solid. Grace is ill, she thought, and if, as Ruth says, she has no recollection of Lance Harrington then something's very wrong.

Fay was introduced to Anton who politely inquired about her work then resumed his previous posture, his hands in the pockets of his suit trousers as he rocked backwards and forwards on his heels, not quite sure what he was doing there.

Ruth and Fay were quietly exchanging news when Grace finally noticed Harry. He was standing alone, looking in her direction. She smiled tentatively, unsure whether they were allowed to converse before they had given evidence.

Tanya Gregory was the Crown Prosecutor. She seemed too young to have completed university let alone have become a qualified barrister. In conference with Grace, she had gone through the procedure very carefully and advised her as to what she was likely to be asked by the defence but Grace had not taken it in properly. Tanya had fine ginger hair tied back in a pony tail and a rash of freckles beneath gooseberry eyes. She was thin and intense and Grace hoped that meant she was hungry for success.

'You're exactly as I pictured you,' Fay was saying to Anton while Ruth went to find the Ladies.

'Ah, good,' Anton replied, smoothing back his hair and tweaking his bow-tie as he wondered just how Grace had described him to her old friend. But he stopped thinking about himself when he saw Matthew Fielding across the lobby. He wondered if he was to be called as a witness, and, if so, for which side? For Grace's sake he was glad Matt made no effort to join them.

Ruth returned and they stood in awkward silence until the moment which Grace had been dreading arrived. Their case had been called. Doors opened and people began to move. Fay, not being a witness, was able to enter the courtroom. She had promised to tell Grace everything that went on.

As the crowd thinned Grace glanced around nervously but there was no sign of Olivia. Her mouth was dry and she wondered it she would be able to speak at all when the time came.

Nothing seemed to happen for ages. Grace wished she could hear Tanya Gregory's summary to the jury of how she intended presenting the case. But Fay wouldn't let her down, she had a good memory and would be able to repeat almost everything she heard.

The press would be present, Grace had steeled herself to that. She and her family had been public property via their hands before.

After Ruth's telephone call on that Saturday it was not long before Harry found Grace and Harrington at the surgery and all his thoughts were thrown into confusion. Despite her protests he had insisted that she had a medical check-up. Reporters had gathered and hung around outside the hospital whilst she was being examined. How they found out she was there she had no idea. Later, each article published had described her as the daughter of Gerald Cornell who had died in mysterious circumstances. She had been shown out of the hospital via a staff entrance. Then the reporters had camped outside her flat until they realised that they had been tricked, that Harry had had an unmarked car concealed in the garage with a plain-clothes officer at the wheel. He had driven Grace to the farmhouse. She had felt a fool sitting beside him, her hair tucked up under a scarf, but it had worked, they were not noticed and had not been followed. Luke had promised to collect her whenever she wanted to return. She had stayed on the moors for a fortnight, able to enjoy the tail end of the summer because her brain had ceased to function in any capacity other than in keeping her body alive.

Then, one morning, she had woken up knowing that it was time to return to the real world. It was a similar feeling to the one she had experienced after her father's death. Grace allowed herself far less time for recovery than she did her patients.

Luke had collected her on Sunday lunchtime and she had returned to work on Monday morning. The following day a freelance reporter had turned up at the surgery. Grace had been horrified, not expecting to be bothered at work. She had fled into Anton's room before he had a chance to speak to her.

Anton, true to his word that he would deal with such a situation if it arose, had stormed out into the waiting area and let rip, leaving the reporter in no doubt as to his views on the callousness and lack of respect for privacy being displayed. 'There are sick people here,' he had roared. 'This is a health centre, not a fucking circus.' The reporter had left, scowling at Grace who had stood, open-mouthed, behind Anton.

The morning dragged to an end and the court emptied for the lunch recess. 'It was all legal toing and froing,' Fay said. 'Setting the scene, if you like. Come on, I'll buy you both lunch.'

The Crown Court was adjacent to the castle and there were

several pubs nearby. True to form, Fay ordered a pint of cider and a ham roll. Ruth had a whisky and Grace asked for a white wine and a large splash of soda. She did not want to make a bad impression by breathing alcohol over the defence lawyer if she was called that afternoon.

Fay said she had been impressed with the barrister's opening speech. 'I'll tell you something, Tanya Gregory may be diminutive but she's damn good,' she stated decisively. The gown and wig, which ought to have swamped her, somehow added to her presence and her voice was clear and authoritative. 'If anyone can get him sent down, she will.'

Grace nodded. She had felt much the same thing in Tanya's presence.

Neither Grace nor Ruth ate anything. Grace's stomach was in knots anticipating what the afternoon might hold. The fifty minutes they spent in the pub seemed more like fifteen. Ruth grinned. 'Come on, let's go. The first day's always the worst,' she added as if court appearances were an everyday occurence for her.

Fay bit her lip and tried not to look over her shoulder when Grace was called as the first witness for the prosecution. She looked at the jury instead, trying to gauge their impression of Grace. It was impossible. Tugging at her corduroy skirt which stretched tightly across her heavy thighs she took a deep breath and silently wished Grace luck.

Grace walked straight to the witness box without looking left or right, hoping it was not obvious to everyone that she was on the verge of hysterical laughter. The hushed atmosphere, broken only by a few rustlings, and the regalia which she had always loved as part of English tradition, suddenly seemed ludicrous. She dared not even glance at the judge because she knew she would start giggling and, without having opened her mouth, would have proved she was crazy. But once she was facing the court and taking the oath it no longer seemed so funny. Her voice was a croak. She cleared her throat, knowing that she had to give a performance, just as the lawyers would do. Tanya Gregory approached and gave her a small smile of reassurance, invisible to the jurors. It helps, Grace thought, this stating my name and address. It confirms who I am and allows me a few seconds to adapt to my surroundings.

'Dr Cornell, I'd like to start with the events which led up to Saturday 29th August last year. Would you please tell the court what they were?'

Grace began to speak, wishing that she could read the minds of the jury. 'For a week or so I had the feeling that I was being watched. It was only a feeling, I had no proof.' Her words were chosen carefully, she wanted to sound believable, not paranoid. 'I ignored it until anonymous letters started to arrive. There were three of them.'

There was a pause as the exhibits were handed around the court and the jurors were able to see for themselves what they contained.

'Why did you wait so long before showing them to anyone?'

Grace swallowed. 'Because the handwriting was so like my own I thought no one would believe I hadn't written them myself.'

'Did you write them?'

'No. I did not.'

'What finally made you hand them over to the police?'

Grace had been expecting this. Harry Jordan had told her that it was far better for the prosecution to bring up the assault on Carl Roberts and make light of it than allow Harrington's defence to make much of it.

'I was obviously more anxious than I had allowed myself to believe. I started making mistakes at work. My partners, quite rightly, suggested that I took some leave.' She went on to explain the circumstances of her attack on the blind man.

'Yes. That's quite understandable.'

'Objection, your honour. That's not for counsel to decide.'

Tanya smiled. The opposition might be on his feet and the objection sustained but the words had been spoken and would remain in the memory of the jurors, more so because they had been told to disregard them.

Tanya hesitated. She and her team had toyed with the idea of bringing Matthew Fielding into the case but had decided that it might confuse the issue, especially as the break-up of the engagement was not directly involved. 'Will you please tell the court what you were doing at the surgery on the day the defendant tried to abduct you?'

'I had arranged to meet a friend at twelve thirty, for lunch, but

128

as I'd been off for a week and had decided to return to work on the Monday, I thought I'd call in. There had been no more letters and because I knew the police were making investigations I felt much better about it. I realise now it was stupid of me not to have gone to the police sooner.' There was a small nod of recognition from Tanya. Grace Cornell was doing all right. She was coming across as entirely credible. 'There were a couple of patients I'd been particularly concerned about and I just wanted to see what had been done for them in my absence. I also hoped to speak to one of my partners to let them know I would be back on Monday.'

'Were you expecting to see either of them there?'

'We have an emergency surgery which finishes at twelve. It was ten past when I arrived but the place was empty. It must've been a quiet morning.'

'I see. Could you not have rung one of them at home?'

'I intended to as soon as I got home later that day. But I hoped Dr Roach would be there because I knew how much better I looked and I wanted him to see for himself that I was ready to return.'

'What happened next, Dr Cornell?'

'I was sitting at my desk trying to find something on the computer when the doorbell rang. I assumed that a patient had seen my car and hoped for a quick consultation. I almost didn't go to the door but then I thought it might save someone a trip to casualty.' Grace paused and bowed her head. 'It wasn't a patient. It was Lance Harrington.' Saying the name made her feel sick.

'Dr Cornell, would you explain his function at the surgery?'

Grace nodded and did so.

'Was it his practice to collect on Saturdays?'

'No. Any samples we took then would be stored in the fridge until Monday.'

'But you let him in?'

'I saw no reason not to. I thought he might have left something he needed at the desk by mistake. And, besides, it wasn't as if he was a stranger.' It was true and everyone knew that Harrington had collected from the surgery for several months. But Grace thought she had sounded as if they were on familiar terms. And if her own barrister was taking this line what chance did she have with the defence when cross-examined? Tanya Gregory had warned her what to expect and maybe this was her way of preparing her for worse.

'What happened next?'

Grace leaned forward, anxious to get this bit right. A curtain of dark hair hid her face from the jury, some of whom were also leaning forward. 'I asked him what he wanted but he didn't answer. He pushed me back into the waiting-room. He just kept walking towards me. We ended up in Anton's room. When he did speak . . .' She inhaled deeply and continued, her voice stronger. 'When he did speak I knew it was him who had written the letters.'

'What did he say?'

'He said, "You've always wanted this, haven't you, Gracie? You've always wanted to be alone with me." No one calls me Gracie, except my father and whoever wrote those letters.' Grace knew her mistake. She should not have mentioned her father. She hurried on. 'He wanted to talk, he said. I let him, I thought it was the best course of action. He must've talked for over an hour. He wanted me to go with him. When I refused he grabbed me and tried to drag me out. I struggled but I stumbled and hit my head on the desk and lost consciousness. The next thing I knew the police had arrived.'

'Could anyone have seen this man enter the surgery?'

'Not unless they were in the car-park.'

'Could you describe the building to us?'

Grace did so, explaining that it wasn't a modern health centre but a conversion from a large house. There was a high privet hedge in the front with a wide gateway leading to the drive which swept around the side where part of the garden had been tarmacked over for use as a car-park. There was even an old conservatory on the side which was used for the mother and toddler group. The inside bore no resemblance to the original house, the consulting rooms were up to date and served by technology and the practice nurses had rooms as good as anywhere. The only alteration to the outside of the building had been the addition of a wheelchair ramp.

'So the surgery isn't overlooked at all?'

'No. There's a hedge at the back, too, shielding us from the properties behind.'

130

'Thank you.'

Grace could not see why any of this was relevant but perhaps Tanya wanted to prove that Harrington had picked his spot with care.

'And at any other time did the defendant touch you?'

'No.'

'That's fine. Thank you, Dr Cornell. No more questions, your honour.'

Grace watched as the defence lawyer stood up. His smile was wide; friendly and disingenuous. It terrified her. She knew nothing of him other than that his name was Alan Lamberton.

'Just now you told the court that Mr Harrington was no stranger to you and that was why you let him into the surgery. But you've known him longer than the short time he's been coming there. You were at Southampton University together so you've known him, what? roughly nine years?'

'I didn't realise until recently it was the same person. I didn't recognise him.'

'Mr Harrington failed to complete his training, but you ended up working at the same hospital as him one year after you completed yours. He was an assistant in the pathology lab.'

'I didn't . . .' But this time her words were drowned by the barrister's.

'You met again far more recently when my client was employed to pay daily visits to your surgery. I find it highly unlikely that you could forget a man with whom, it appears, you kept in contact through your work over the years.'

Grace didn't bother to reply, to say that she rarely saw him. She had been warned to expect this. Harry Jordan had warned her.

'You claim that the defendant wrote those anonymous letters, letters which are remarkable in their similarity to your own handwriting. We shall hear what the experts have to say later but for now can you tell me how – if you had no contact with him – it was possible for him to have copied it so accurately?'

'I don't know.'

He made her tell the story again but unlike the prosecution, who wanted to stress to the jury that this was a professional woman, a woman who had been wronged, he did not once allow her her professional title. 'Is it likely that a man you have known for most of your adult life, and with whom you have worked, should suddenly, after nine years and without, you claim, any provocation or encouragement, take it into his head to try to abduct you? Come, Miss Cornell, surely it's more likely that you did encourage him and that maybe you panicked when things went too far? I am not saying Mr Harrington is blameless, he has admitted he enjoyed your company and was attracted to you, but he also said he had misread the signals, that he truly believed you were interested in him. My client also admits that he does not have a problem finding girlfriends, so why, then, should he have behaved in the manner in which you have alleged?'

Grace remained silent, her head held high. It was all she could do for the moment. Surely no one would believe she had encouraged him.

'Miss Cornell?'

'I don't know.'

'You don't know.' He sighed dramatically. 'Let us return to your days at Southampton. We have reason to believe that you not only knew the defendant, but that you actually went out with him. Is that true?'

Recalling two conversations simultaneously, one with Ruth and a more recent one with Judith, Grace decided the time had come for a carefully calculated risk. She had to admit the truth. 'Until my friend, Ruth Ferrers, mentioned it I'd completely forgotten it. He meant nothing to me, I went out with several fellow students.'

Tanya Gregory put her head in her hands. Grace had come across as uncaring and promiscuous.

'I see.' Lamberton turned his back to her and smiled broadly at the court in general. 'I have to say I find it hard to believe that you could have forgotten him, Miss Cornell. How many people called Lance do you know? It is not that common a name.'

'We didn't know him by that name then. He preferred to be called Larry.' Grace stared at the man in front of her. She knew what she had done. She had just let everybody down. By remembering his nickname she had admitted she had not forgotten him. It was his word against hers and one of them had to be believed. For the moment he had the upper hand.

Alan Lamberton could have made her look even more of a fool

but he seemed satisfied to leave it at that. He turned to the jury and raised both palms a little, as if to say, 'Can you believe this woman?' It was enough to influence them, and Grace knew it.

She had been dismissed which meant she could leave the court or, if she preferred, remain to watch the remainder of the proceedings. Catching Fay's eye she went to sit by her.

'You were fine,' Fay said as Grace sank down. She squeezed her hand and wondered if Grace knew how much damage she had done. Harry Jordan was the next to be sworn in. Fay liked the look of him and hoped some of the damage could be repaired.

There were no surprises in Harry Jordan's evidence. In a husky voice, the remnants of flu in evidence, he stated the facts and answered questions without embellishment.

Miss Ruth Ferrers had alerted the police when she believed Dr Cornell to be missing. 'We made some inquiries in view of the fact of the anonymous letters Dr Cornell had received.'

'And how did you come to find Dr Cornell?' Tanya asked.

'By telephoning anyone she might be with then realising there was one other place she might be, which was the surgery.'

'What happened when you arrived?'

'We saw her car and rang the bell. The defendant let us in.'

'Just like that? He made no attempt to escape?'

'No. He did not.'

'How did he seem?' Tanya knew this was a weakness in their case but she might be able to use it to advantage.

'His face was white and he was shaking. When we asked what had happened he was unable to answer.'

'He said nothing at all?'

'Only that he didn't understand what was happening and that we had come just in time as he was trying to revive Dr Cornell.'

'In your opinion did he appear mentally disturbed?'

'Objection.'

Tanya had known it was coming before she asked the question but had hoped to sow some seeds of doubt as to Harrington's sanity.

The rest of her questions concerned the facts of the incident and she asked more than were necessary in order to divert the jury from Harrington's actions.

'And Dr Cornell, did she say anything?' Tanya, like any good barrister, tried to ask only the questions to which she already knew the answer.

'No. She didn't speak at all. She seemed to be in shock and –'

'Objection, your honour.' Alan Lamberton was on his feet, but to his surprise the objection was overruled. The judge pointed out that the police were trained in first aid, would recognise the signs and be able to act accordingly.

'Please continue, Inspector Jordan.' Tanya was gratified to have won a minor victory.

'Dr Cornell had a small head wound which had stopped bleeding but she was dazed and unsteady on her feet. We took her to hospital immediately, rather than wait for the paramedics.'

'Thank you.'

That was it, Harry was free to go. A witness from the hospital followed him.

Grace, taking it all in, realised that most of the first day would be taken up with re-creating the scene, that nothing crucial would happen until tomorrow at least. But for her, the worst was over. She had said her bit, no matter how badly, and it was now up to everyone else.

Ruth was called to the witness box. She had removed her hat and coat, and her cerise suit was eye-catching as she walked through the doors and down the centre aisle, her hair flowing down her back. Grace listened dispassionately as her best friend depicted her behaviour over the past few months. The woman she was describing sounded crazy.

Tanya Gregory took pains to point out that although Miss Ferrers was a fully qualified psychologist she was not giving evidence in a professional capacity. Dr Cornell had neither consulted her nor been treated by her.

The court heard that Grace was a caring doctor and a loyal friend, but the defence, when it was their turn to question Ruth, wanted to know why, in that case, Miss Cornell had not confided in her. 'You've been close friends for nine years, you say you were aware something was wrong, could you not have persuaded her to talk to you, to tell you what was troubling her?'

Ruth spotted the trick. No specific incident had been referred to. Did they know that Grace had recently begun talking about her father's death? 'If Grace was one of my clients I would have done. As a friend, it was out of the question. We respect each other's privacy and, besides, no one can make Grace do anything unless she wants to.' Oh, shit, Ruth thought. By trying to defend her I've only succeeded in doing the opposite. She knew she could not have said anything better in Harrington's favour.

'Were you aware of the relationship between Miss Cornell and Lance Harrington at Southampton?'

'It wasn't exactly a relationship.'

'My apologies, Miss Ferrers, I use the term in the literal sense. You were aware that they knew each other as students?'

'Yes.'

'I see. Yet you recall this more clearly than Miss Cornell who, it is understood, actually went out with him.'

It was not a question but a carefully worded statement for the jury's benefit.

'Grace had more important things to think about than a love-sick admirer,' Ruth said loudly, annoyed by the attitude of her cross-examiner, exactly as he had intended her to be.

'Such as?'

'Her career. Also, her father died around that time.'

'Ah, yes. Her father.'

He already knew, Ruth thought, but he had to make me say it. But to her surprise he left it there.

Ruth stepped down, her face red with anger, and joined Grace and Fay. 'I'm so sorry,' she whispered.

Grace squeezed her hand, just as Fay had squeezed her own. It didn't matter because everything taking place in the courtroom no longer seemed to be relevant. It was as if she had left her body and was watching herself.

Anton Roach, as Grace's senior partner, was sworn in. He spoke of Grace's dedication as a doctor and how highly her patients thought of her, but, he admitted ruefully, her work had slipped lately and she appeared to have been under considerable pressure. 'No. As far as I'm aware she didn't confide in anyone at the surgery. Certainly not in me,' he concluded.

Anton wondered what had been achieved by his brief testimony. Grace's non-communication could be taken two ways, serving both the defence and the prosecution.

Not once during the afternoon's proceedings had Grace looked towards the dock but she was aware of Harrington's eyes on her for most of the time. She did not wish to see the expression in them because she knew what he thought of her.

As soon as they were outside the courtroom Ruth grabbed Grace's arm. 'Come on,' she said.

'Where're we going?' Grace shivered. It was dark and, after the warmth of the court, chilly outside.

'To Anton's. Carol's expecting us all. Fay, too.'

'Ruth, you know I can't. I have to speak to Olivia.' Although she had not dared to think about it, knowing that her mother was in the same city had been at the back of her mind all day.

'Grace, take my advice, ring her from Anton's. Do it with friends around you. Take my word for it, you're in no state to meet her tonight, you'll only blow it.'

Grace nodded, Ruth was right. What difference did it make where she telephoned from?

Lights blazed from the Roach household and several other vehicles were already parked in the sweeping drive. Carol came to the door and kissed the two women she knew before shaking hands with Fay whom she had not met. Shocked at Grace's appearance she said nothing but merely hoped she would not collapse. Ruth had warned her about Olivia, especially in view of the fact that Carol and Anton had known the Cornells in the days of Gorstone Manor, although not intimately. The poor girl's shattered, Carol thought as she led them through to the lounge where Anton was pouring drinks.

Carol had once been a stunner but had gained weight and become motherly. In compensation she had lost some of the acidity of her wit and become more comfortable to be with. Knowing that her guests would not have had time to dress for dinner she had simply touched up her make-up and sprayed perfume on her wrists. She felt quite at home in the crêpe trouser suit she had worn all day. It had adapted its shape to her

136

contours. 'What would you like to drink, Grace? I think we've got almost everything.'

Grace had not been expecting what appeared to be a party. Apart from Carol and Anton there was herself, Ruth and Fay. And standing by the chimney breast was Harry Jordan with Luke beside him. Harry, she decided, looked unwell. His nose was red and his eyes were rheumy and his voice had been croaky in court. Luke had not made it to court. For Grace's sake Harry had gone to collect him and insisted that he put in an appearance that evening. 'She'll be hurt enough that you weren't there earlier,' he had told him. 'Now get off your arse and come with me. Mrs Roach is expecting you.' Shame faced, Luke had done so. Only later did Harry realise what he had been afraid of, that he might have seen his mother at court.

Luke, too, was shocked when he saw Grace. She looked ill and thin. He apologised, saying he couldn't face it, but Grace saw by his bloodshot eyes the real reason he had not made it that morning.

'How's it going?' he asked.

Grace shrugged. She neither knew nor cared any longer. The fact that she seemed to be in a world of her own terrified Luke.

'Very badly,' Harry whispered, then shook his head to warn Luke to leave it at that. Harry would have been flattered if he had known that Grace, unable to face the present, was thinking about an evening several weeks previously when he had turned up at her flat with an Indian take-away. He never arrived empty-handed and rarely without warning. That night was an exception. He suspected Grace was becoming too optimistic, that she imagined just because there would be a court case that was the end of the matter. 'You must understand, Grace,' he had explained after she had expressed her gratitude for the food which told him that this was another occasion on which she had neglected to feed herself, 'this isn't about truth, it's about proving whether, with admissible evidence, he really intended to take you hostage. As long as he continues to profess his innocence it's the defence's job to get him off even if they believe he's guilty. And he's denying everything. They'll set out to make it seem that you were in some way involved. They can't do it any other way, they can't argue that you fabricated the whole thing because it was us who found you with him. We know it happened, they know it happened, but they'll want to convince the jury it happened in a different way. The DPP thinks there's a case to answer, at least that's one thing in our favour.'

Harry had waved his fork to emphasise his points and had dropped rice on the carpet. He had blushed when he saw Grace had noticed, although he could not decipher her enigmatic smile.

On that occasion Grace had thought of him as ungainly and awkward, but she also recognised what a solace his presence provided. Her thoughts were very similar as he approached her now from the far side of the lounge, but Carol intercepted him and got to her first.

'Ruth said you've got a phone call to make. Use the line in our bedroom, it's more private.' She smiled her encouragement and almost pushed Grace towards the door. The rest of the group pretended not to notice her leaving.

With a thudding heart and heavy legs she walked up the stairs and along the landing to the main bedroom. It was a large room with a high ceiling. The bed was covered with an apple green satin eiderdown. Grace sat on the edge of it and nearly slid off the slippery material. Her hand shook so much as she reached for the telephone extension that she misdialled and had to try again. Voices carried up the stairs but whatever they were saying had become a buzzing in her head. 'Mrs Pisano, please,' she managed to croak. She held her breath, expecting to hear Olivia speak.

'Mrs Pisano has left.' The room span and Grace felt sick. She's gone, she thought, she didn't want to see me after all. She couldn't even wait one day.

'But she's left a contact number. Is that her daughter?'

'Yes. I'm Grace Cornell.' Automatically she wrote down the number and thanked the hotel receptionist. Oh, God, it's Monica's number, she thought with despair as her stomach churned. But to speak to Olivia she would have to dial it. It was answered on the fourth ring.

'Hello?'

'It's Grace.'

'I rather thought it might be. I expect you want to speak to your mother? How are you, Grace?'

138

'I'm fine, thank you.' Why else would I be ringing? she thought. What reason could I possibly have for wanting to speak to you? There were background noises then silence.

'Grace?' It was Olivia's voice.

But Grace couldn't speak. Her body shuddered as she pressed her lips together tightly and the tears rolled down her face.

'Hello? Is there anyone there?'

'Yes. It's me. It's Grace.' She spoke so quietly she was not sure if Olivia had heard her.

'Oh, Grace.'

There was a silence which Olivia had to break. She was terrified that Grace might hang up. 'For two supposedly intelligent people this isn't much of a dialogue,' she said. Then they were both talking at once and Grace was laughing and Olivia was crying. 'You're bubbling,' Grace said, 'I can tell,' and she found herself laughing harder. I'm hysterical, she thought. If the jury could see me now there wouldn't be any need for the trial to continue. It would be me they considered insane enough to lock up.

'Where're you ringing from, Grace?'

'From Anton's. Ruth is here, and Fay.' Suddenly the years were a barrier between them. Olivia had not met either of Grace's friends. 'Luke's here, too.'

'Luke?'

'Yes. But he isn't quite ready to speak to you yet.'

'No. I understand.' Olivia, guessing what her daughter had already been through, realised that it would be too much to expect Grace to see her that evening but her pleasure when Grace asked if she could buy her dinner the following night was almost unbearable.

'There's nothing I'd like more, my darling. Except it'll be my treat. You just say where you want to go.' She decided against mentioning the second day of the trial. Now she knew she would see Grace it seemed inappropriate that their first meeting should be amongst other people, many of them strangers.

The arrangements were made and Grace went downstairs looking and feeling more carefree than she had done for a long time. It was noticeable to her friends who had no need to ask the outcome of the conversation. Only Ruth came over and hugged her. 'I'm so pleased,' she said. 'How do you feel?'

'I don't know. I can't explain. It's like a sort of limbo because I haven't read the script. I'm not sure how I'm supposed to react.'

'There aren't any set ways. Anyway, I'll tell you how you feel.'

Grace smiled. 'I thought you might.'

'You're worried about the trial but you don't care any more. Because you're going to see your mother you know you can cope with anything. And you can't wait to get away from all of us and cry with joy.'

'Oh, Ruth.' Grace sniffed. 'How can you always see straight through me?'

'Because I care. What about Luke?' Ruth nodded in his direction. His expression was surly.

'He knows, but he refuses to have anything to do with her.'

'Ah, well. Maybe in time.'

Carol came over to say that dinner was ready. They went across the hall to the dining-room where the linen was starched and the silver and glasses sparkled. Their hostess was in her element as she produced three perfectly cooked courses followed by cheese. 'You make it all seem so effortless,' Fay commented as she shook her head in bewilderment. 'I can't even synchronise egg on toast.'

Anton had poured the wines and produced champagne to go with the pudding. Grace ate little, but enough to satisfy Harry who had been watching her. It was the first time he had seen her so relaxed and therefore even more beautiful. Despite the trial, some inner happiness made her glow.

Carol, flushed with pleasure, said to Fay who had cleared her plate and taken a second helping of almost everything, 'You can come to dinner any time.'

'If only!' Fay replied through a mouthful of biscuit and ripe Stilton.

They sat around the dinner table until ten o'clock. Anton's face was pink and his hair was sticking up. It amused Grace, who had never seen him look anything other than immaculate. 'I think I'd better get Grace home,' Ruth whispered to Carol, noticing how quiet her friend had become.

'Are you all right to drive?'

'Yes, unfortunately.' She had forgone most of the wine. 'Can I give you a lift, Fay?'

'No. I'll get a cab. I'm going the other way.' She had booked into a hotel and would be travelling back to London on the first train in the morning.

'I can't thank you enough for coming,' Grace told her.

'I just wish it could have been the last day. We'd have had even more to celebrate then.' Fay did not notice Harry's doubtful frown.

Carol and Anton watched them depart from the doorstep, Grace and Ruth together, then Harry, Luke and Fay who had agreed to share a taxi. Harry would collect his car in the morning, he said. Neither he nor Luke had had much chance to speak to Grace but he hoped that their presence had shown her they cared.

'She's heading for a breakdown,' Carol said when she and Anton were alone. 'How has she been at work?'

'Hiding it well, whatever it is. And it's more than the trial. Anyway, it was a superb meal and they all enjoyed it. Shall we go up?'

Carol turned off all the downstairs lights and shut the door on the mess in the kitchen. The dishwasher would deal with the worst of it in the morning.

Ruth dropped Grace off outside her flat but did not go in. 'You need to be alone,' she said. 'I'll give you a ring tomorrow morning before I go to work.'

Whoever was on desk duty was either in the lavatory or doing his rounds. Grace slipped into the lift, thankful that she did not have to answer any well-meant questions. In the quietness of her flat the events of the day replayed themselves, more vivid now than when they were real. She had spotted Matt that morning, although she had pretended not to. It would have been impossible under those circumstances to make small talk with the man who should have, by now, been her husband. The last time she had seen him was when he was in hospital and she had passed the stage of thinking, I must tell Matt this or that. I did miss him, she thought, but was it the idea of him or the man himself I yearned for? And it was at the hospital that she had run into Harry Jordan for a second time, not knowing then how much a part of her life he was to become. It was some weeks before

141

Grace realised that not all his visits to the flat were necessary, that he saw her as a woman as well as a victim. But underneath she still suspected he was out to prove that she had killed Gerald Cornell, that she was guilty of patricide. If Harrington was imprisoned there was nothing else Harry would need to do for her and they would lose touch. She wasn't sure how she felt about that.

Dropping her coat on to a chair, Grace checked the telephone for messages but there were none, then she went to the mail-box. There was a letter from Harvey from America. They had continued to keep in touch. He had remembered the date of the trial and written to wish her luck. 'I'll keep you to your promise,' he ended. 'When it's over you're to come and stay with me. At my expense, if you wish, but as long as you come.'

Grace thought about it. Yes, she decided. It'll be good to get away from everything and everyone I know and to be spoiled by that lovely old gentleman. He had also mentioned the possibility of her finding work in America but Grace had given this little thought.

She read the letter in the hall. Glancing up, she saw her own tired face in the mirror which had so often reflected Olivia's. She ran a hand through her hair and decided to have a bath. Being in the court had made her feel dirty although she was aware it was mental rather than physical. Hopefully the lines around my eyes will disappear after I've slept, she thought, only caring because she wanted to look her best for Olivia.

She back lay in the hot water and went over the past months. Her only immediate worry was that she had misjudged things, that what she most hoped for would elude her again.

But tomorrow is another day, tomorrow I shall see Olivia, my mother, she thought as she closed her eyes.

The Roaches' dinner invitation had surprised Harry but he guessed that Ruth Ferrers had had something to do with it. He was certain she knew how he felt about Grace.

The taxi had dropped him off last. Expecting to want to fall into bed, he was surprised to discover his tiredness had evaporated and his throat felt a little better. It was late but he wanted to speak to Grace, to ask about Olivia and to make sure she was all right. Grace, he thought, does not know what a bad start this trial's got off to.

He made a hot lemon drink and switched off the overhead light which was making his eyes ache. He was thinking about the time she was interviewed after they had first found her. The hospital had not kept her long and she had insisted on going to the police station and making a statement at once. He had struggled not to take her in his arms and hug her with relief.

'Did you suspect it was him?' he had asked her.

'No. I did not.' Grace's face had been pinched and white with indignation.

'How long have you known him?'

'Since he started coming to the practice.'

'That's not what he says.'

'I don't give a shit what he says.'

Her responses were genuine, he was certain of that. 'How does he know so much about you?'

'I don't know.'

Grace had sounded close to despair with that answer. 'All right, let's for the moment assume he asked around and found out for himself. Have you ever done or said anything which he might have misconstrued as a come-on?'

'Dear God! What is this?'

Harry had bowed his head. It had needed to be asked but he hated himself for doing so. At the same time he had not wanted someone else to be the one to ask, someone who might, deep down, believe Harrington's story. 'Don't be offended, Dr Cornell.' Dr Cornell because this was official, the interview was being taped. 'If this comes to court you'll be asked a lot worse and a lot more personal questions than the ones we intend putting to you today. I understand what you've been through but this is necessary, believe me.'

'*If* it comes to court? You mean there's a chance it won't? After what he's done?'

'The decision isn't mine. It's up to the Crown Prosecution Service to decide if there's sufficient evidence. Harrington is continuing to deny his part in it.'

'And you believe him.' It was a statement.

'No! No, I don't,' he had added more quietly. Grace had looked at him then with a spark of hope in her eyes. He knew

143

that this was the first time she understood he was on her side. With a sigh she explained once more the sequence of events leading up to that afternoon.

'What happened between the time Harrington rang the bell and we arrived, Dr Cornell?'

'Oh, we played Scrabble and shared a few jokes,' she had answered with a dangerous sweetness.

'Your statement is being recorded.'

'So you told me, to which I replied that I understood the procedure. What do you think we did? He talked. On and on and on. I sat there on Anton's chair with no choice but to listen to him. I was terrified of antagonising him.'

'Talked about what?'

'About his feelings for me, and, supposedly, mine for him. He kept saying we were meant to be together, that sort of sickening rubbish.'

'Did he touch you, other than pushing you into the room and when you struggled?' Harry hated asking and dreaded the questions which would follow if Harrington had done so.

'No. Not once.'

Harry admired her honesty. 'Was there anything, no matter how trivial it may seem, that he said regarding your past and how he knows about it?'

'No. Nothing he couldn't have found out quite easily anyway, or by following me. The letters . . .?' Her eyes had been full of hope. Harry had had to look away again.

'He claims that you wrote them yourself. That it was all part of one of your games. You liked to be the victim and –'

'Don't!' Grace was on her feet. 'Don't say it. That's what the jury will think, too, *if* it comes to court, isn't it?'

'Dr Cornell, Grace . . . please, sit down and let me explain something.' Reluctantly she had done so. 'This isn't over yet. We've been making investigations. To start with, you came to us about the letters.' But not until after she had attacked a man, Harry had reminded himself. 'You expressed your fears which we took seriously. It was apparent you were under stress and that you genuinely felt in danger. Your best friend, Ruth Ferrers, also believed it, and strongly enough for her to ring us only an hour after you were supposed to meet her. I don't imagine any

144

court'll think you went to that much trouble for the sake of a game.'

'Will you tell them that?'

'If I'm asked.' He had known he would not be asked, and he could not express any personal views, but Grace had been in desperate need of reassurance.

'Thank you.'

They had been interrupted at that point. PC Cobane had apologised for the intrusion but said there was something the inspector ought to see. Following Harrington's statement they had made inquiries as to its veracity. A fax had been received stating that Lance Harrington had been a student at Southampton University at the same time as Grace but he had not lasted the course. It was the first anyone knew of it, except possibly Grace. 'That far back,' Harry had muttered. They had already discovered that the man had worked in the path lab of the hospital where Grace had completed her training.

Until then they had believed Harrington relevant only to her recent past, now it seemed he had known her from way back. Neither Grace nor Harry had paid enough attention to him. Grace had left him off her list because she had not considered him to be one of the surgery staff or of any importance in her life. She had only included the names of her family and friends and the people with whom she worked directly. But he had been there, in the background, for nine years. Why had Grace pretended otherwise? He had asked her.

'I didn't know it was the same person. I certainly didn't recognise him. He's put on weight and looks quite different now.'

The police had spoken to the hospital, the staff in the path lab, the people at the surgery and the other doctors from whom he collected samples. No one had a bad word to say against him.

Harrington had been clever because it always came down to his word against Grace's. Now it was simply a question of what the jury would believe. Surely having seen Grace they would be on her side. Harrington, yet to stand in the witness box, was tall and strong and running to fat. In a way he could be considered good-looking even though his lips were too full and his chin too fleshy. There was nothing particularly strange about him, nothing which cried out stalker or pervert. And he could be so plausible. Not once had he changed his story and throughout every interview he had remained calm and polite. Grace, he had said, was a very mixed-up lady. 'Still, she always has been. She likes her bit of fun, but I really didn't think she'd take things this far,' he'd added sadly.

And yet the DPP had given the go-ahead for the trial. They agreed that the circumstantial evidence, the fact of Harrington having been in the same three places as Grace, was more than a coincidence especially as, when questioned, no one she had worked with recalled her being friendly with or even acknowledging the existence of the man. They had seen the photographic evidence of her head wound. They had had sight of the letters which experts would later comment upon and had read the statements from her colleagues which expressed their professional opinion of her state of mind. And Grace's own statement had added weight, she had sworn that she could not recall Harrington prior to his starting at the surgery. The case, surprisingly, had been allowed to go ahead.

But Harry, sitting on his own settee nursing a cold, was aware how damaging Grace's appearance in the witness box had been.

He struggled to his feet and went to the telephone. What's that woman done to me? he wondered, knowing that to hear her voice would do more for him than any amount of aspirin and hot lemon.

The outlook from the lounge window was very different with the absence of snow. The resilient grass was emerald, thriving on the moisture of the thaw. Right now, Monica thought, Grace will be in court and despite everything, I wish her well. She wished she and her niece could have remained friends, but if, as she suspected, Grace had discovered the truth there would never be any chance of that.

Having tidied the kitchen Monica pulled on boots and an old jacket and went outside to loosen the soil between the plants in the herbaceous borders. The frost had broken it up and the soil was damp so the work would be easy. It was a pleasure to be doing something physical, something to distract her from what she feared might happen if Olivia really decided to come.

In the early afternoon she soaked in the bath, using the hot water to relieve the ache in her back and her joints. She dressed carefully, dried her hair so it lay in smooth curves to her chin then applied fresh make-up. Although she would have done so anyway, instinct told her that she might be receiving a visitor. It had always been there, the ability to guess at what anyone connected with Gerald might take it into their heads to do.

A steady drizzle had begun to fall. Monica switched on one of the table lamps to dispel the gloom. Her hand shook and the lamp tilted before righting itself. She felt unusually on edge. There were some personal letters she had intended to reply to but she knew if she attempted to write them now they would sound stilted. Three times she checked her appearance before sitting down with the daily newspaper. She was ashamed to acknowledge the significance of the number three with its associations with Judas Iscariot. She waited for the telephone to ring as if the call had been pre-arranged.

At ten past five Monica poured a large gin and tonic. It was an hour earlier than her strict regime dictated but she knew she would need it. After only one sip the phone rang. 'Oh, God,' she said. Her knees felt wobbly as she went to answer it.

The gin and tonic rippled in the glass and ice chinked against its side when she heard the soft voice asking if that was Monica.

'It's me, Olivia. I was going to write, but there wasn't time. I'm in Exeter. I had to come, Monica, I'm sure you can understand that.'

'Of course I can.' She had known. She had expected this. All day she had been no further than the garden because she felt certain this call was coming. When Olivia had written to say she was thinking of returning to England for the trial, Monica imagined she would change her mind when the time actually came, knowing it might do more harm than good. The last thing Grace needed was another shock.

'How did it go today? The trial?' Olivia asked. 'How was Grace?'

'I wasn't there.' Monica placed her glass on the mahogany table upon which the telephone rested as she came to a decision. 'Look, cancel your room and come and stay with me. God

147

knows, I could do with some company and there's an awful lot we have to talk about.'

'Are you sure?'

'I'm positive. Get a taxi and come right over. You can join me for supper.' She replaced the receiver and exhaled deeply. 'What the hell have I done now?' she asked the empty room, feeling the hotness of tears on her face. Hearing Olivia's voice again had wiped out the years. For a second she had believed that Gerald was still alive and Gorstone Manor still belonged to the family. She controlled the rage which filled her body. Nothing was Olivia's fault, nor that of her daughter. She must stay calm. She must not upset the status quo, such as it was.

She swallowed more gin as she realised that Olivia would leave a message at the hotel letting Grace know where she could be contacted, and Grace would ring Monica. Would she be able to cope with that? Yes, she decided, I've always coped before. All those years of living a lie and she had played her part faultlessly. If it had to continue, then so be it. Besides, it was by no means certain Grace did know. And then, knowing that within the hour she would see her ex-sister-in-law, she fought to subdue the memories of Gorstone Manor and tried to decide what to cook for their supper.

She had promised Olivia food but would either of them be able to eat if she cooked it? She cannot possibly know what went on, Monica reassured herself as she opened the fridge to take stock of its contents. If she did she would never, ever have agreed to come here.

But when Monica heard the rumble of the diesel engine as the taxi drew up in the drive, she gripped the edge of the kitchen sink and prayed she would not faint. 'Fourteen years,' she muttered. 'And now it seems like yesterday.'

Grace sat in her chair by the window. She had allowed herself to be tied in knots by Alan Lamberton. What sort of impression had she made on the jury? She had been aware of their intent gaze at they listened to her testimony. And then she had had to face the dinner at Anton's. It had been a kind thought, the action of true friends, but she had not felt like socialising. But the telephone conversation with Olivia, short though it was, had made up for everything else.

Luke had refrained from asking her what had been said, and if their mother was only staying for a week it was doubtful he would change his mind about seeing her.

And Harry. How surprised Grace had been to see him at Anton's. He had made several attempts to speak to her but had been thwarted each time. She was glad, she had not wished to discuss the trial. There was no point in analysing it, the jury would draw their own conclusions and come to their decision one way or another. Harry had not spoken up in her defence but she knew that it was not his place to do so. It was nobody's place to do so. It's not me who is on trial, she reminded herself yet again.

She had imagined that once the trial had started and the waiting was over, sleep would come easily. Instead she found she was more on edge than ever, jittery and over-tired, but she could not face going to bed. I need to hear another human voice, she thought, despite her earlier wish to be alone. Luke would still be up, he kept very late hours. She dialled his number.

'Luke, I wish you'd talk to me, you know, the way you used to? You hardly said a word to me tonight.'

'I wouldn't have wished any of this on you, Grace, you know that, don't you?'

'Yes, I do know, but I wasn't talking about the trial. Won't you reconsider about Olivia? She's really desperate to see you.'

'You didn't mention it earlier. Besides, for someone who's desperate she's waited rather a long time to make the effort. And, Grace, we both know she wouldn't be here at all if it wasn't for the trial. It's hardly the most flattering statement she's ever made.'

Grace saw how it must appear to Luke and knew that he was right, but Luke did not know all the circumstances. He will never know them, she thought, no one must ever know them.

'I can't do it, Grace. I don't want to see her.'

'You're sure?'

'Yes.'

Although he did not sound it, Grace did not push the point. She felt he had the right to know that she was seeing Olivia the next day and told him so. 'She's left the Great Western Hotel. She's staying with Monica now. I spoke to her there.'

'But you haven't had anything to do with Monica for ages, although I've never understood why. There're things you don't discuss with me, too, you know.'

'We're not meeting at Monica's,' Grace said, ignoring his last comment.

'You were always more forgiving than me.'

'Oh, I don't think so, Luke. Will you just promise to think about seeing her?'

'Maybe. Goodnight, Grace.'

She hung up, knowing that trying to insist upon anything where Luke was concerned was a waste of breath. He was stubborn and it would only make him more averse to it.

It was eleven thirty. Feeling almost as dissolute as her brother was inclined to be, Grace poured a glass of wine and wondered if she would be considered alcoholic as well as insane if her detractors could see her. Her eyes were on the kitchen telephone extension which hung on the wall next to the fridge freezer. She felt a sudden desire for company, someone there with her whom she could trust. But who was there any more? Once Matthew would have fulfilled that role, but Matthew was a thing of the past.

When, as if in answer to her wishes, the phone rang, its purr shattered the silence of the night and Grace jumped. Her glass fell as she attempted to place it on the worktop, too near to the edge. Red wine dribbled across the surface and on to the floor. A chunk of glass shaped like half a tulip had broken off neatly. Grace stepped back, away from the stickiness because she was not wearing slippers, and reached for the receiver.

'Hello?' There was a note of panic in her voice as she thought that Olivia might have changed her mind and was ringing to say so. Her next thought was that it was Luke who had changed his mind.

'Grace? It's me. Harry Jordan.'

He had once told her he rarely went to bed until one but she had no idea he would ring her so late. Her stomach muscles tightened, half in pleasure, half in apprehension.

'I know it's late but I thought I'd . . . Oh, are you alone?'

'Yes, I am.'

'Ah. I imagined you'd prefer to be.'

Is that how he sees me? she thought. As a solitary person? Well, ten out of ten for observation, Inspector Jordan, but is he expecting me to invite him over?

'I just wondered if you felt the need to talk about it? You avoided the subject of the trial at Anton's.'

Grace was startled to find that she did want to discuss it, that she would very much like the reassurance of his big, awkward body and his now familiar face. She did not know when she had started to think of him in those terms until she recalled that one kiss which still made her blush.

'I was pleased to see you eat something tonight,' he said to fill the silence.

'Well, Carol's a marvellous cook.'

'Yes, but you must keep it up because you've lost enough weight as it is.'

Grace nearly laughed. He sounded as though he really cared.

'I'm sorry. I didn't mean to sound dictatorial. I meant to offer advice, but you, Grace Cornell, are a very hard woman to advise and I am not the most tactful of people. Have you ever let down your shield, I wonder?'

'What's that supposed to mean?'

'You know perfectly well what it means. What're you hiding from, Grace? And don't tell me it's just to do with Harrington. There's a brick wall surrounding you three feet thick.'

How dare he? she thought. He has no conception of what the past has done to me. Be careful. The warning voice sounded in her head. 'I suppose you think that because you kissed me once it gives you the right to speak to me however you like. How typical of a man.' Why on earth did I say that? Grace wondered. He'll know I was thinking about it now.

'Other men have kissed you too,' he reminded her cruelly. 'I suppose it's all the same to you.'

'You bastard.' She slammed the wall-phone back on to its cradle but not very accurately because the receiver slipped off and dangled on its coiled lead, knocking rhythmically against the side of the fridge. She felt impotent with anger before recognising it was a better feeling than self-pity or anxiety. Perhaps Harry had annoyed her deliberately. Surely he would not have been so callous otherwise, knowing that the trial would last at least another two days.

Avoiding the broken wineglass and the mess, Grace paced the kitchen. Matt had accused her of the same thing. But I can't help it, really I can't. It's the only way to get through life.

Grace swore as a tiny, unseen sliver of glass pierced the sole of her foot. She hopped to the bathroom, a wad of kitchen roll under the cut. 'Why is it that whenever Harry and I start getting – well, let's say getting close to holding an ordinary conversation, we end up arguing?' she asked herself.

And then she pictured Matt's face as it had looked that morning; solemn yet handsome and once so dear to her. She still missed him but only because he had been so much a part of her life that his disappearance had left a gap. She had loved him, she had no doubts on that score, but she was uncertain if she had loved him enough. Not enough to forgive him, certainly, and not enough to want him back now, she realised.

The telephone remained silent. Any decent human being would have rung back to apologise, she thought. This is surely madness. I am trying to think about Matt, the man I was going to marry, and Harry Jordan comes into my head again.

Her foot bathed, doused in Dettol and protected by a strip of plaster, Grace put on her slippers and went back to pick up the broken glass. As she wiped the floor she noticed that the whiter band around her finger where her engagement ring had once been worn had reverted to the same colour as the rest of her flesh. It seemed like an omen that that part of her life was finally over.

Far from sleep she replaced the glass of wine she had spilled with another and took it through to the lounge, wishing that it was Friday night and she was already at the farmhouse, just as she had been after she made her statement and that officer had driven her down there.

Anton had been marvellous in his own peculiar way. He didn't mention her absence or what had occurred during it. All he had said was, 'Two weeks' holiday. No arguments. You know where I am if you want to talk.'

Bill Ryan had behaved a little strangely until he could no longer refrain from asking her what it had felt like to be held at someone's mercy. 'I don't want to talk about it,' Grace had told

him, sensing his interest was more prurient than well inten-
tioned.

Sandy, one of the practice nurses and a good friend to Grace,
had fussed over her. She did not ask questions, she simply
demanded to know every detail, bringing cups of coffee at far
too frequent intervals even by Grace's standards when she
thought of something else she wanted to know.

But how kind people had been. Once she was back at work
Judith had telephoned almost on a daily basis to begin with, and
Ruth had become like a second skin. She was able to deal with
it best, allowing Grace to talk or not, depending upon her mood
at the time. She had offered no explanations, no recriminations
and no platitudes. Her comfort came in the form of her presence
and her acceptance of everything that was said.

Matt, too, had tried to re-establish contact but it was too late.
His idea of helping was to offer to buy Grace a meal or to take
her to the cinema. But these distractions would not have worked
and, despite Matt's desperate attempts to get her back, Grace
knew with certainty that it was over and it would have been
unfair to give him hope.

Time passed and things settled down at work. Grace was no
longer a freak and the newspapers stopped mentioning her
name as soon as the next thing came along. She couldn't remember what it was, some MP up to something sordid, more than
likely. Some other poor sod had to be put through the wringer,
judged and sentenced by one or another journalist, before I was
off the hook, she thought.

Then came Christmas which she spent with Luke. They had
both tried to make the best of it but it was a miserable time.
Grace wished she had been on call and suspected that Luke
would rather have been with his friends who had gone skiing.

Grace had cooked a goose and all the trimmings but they
hadn't bothered with a tree or a cake. They were both relieved
when it was over. Since the days at Gorstone Christmas had
never been the same. And how Olivia had relished it. For weeks
she would be chivvying Mrs Collins in the kitchen. Poor Mrs
Collins, who then went up to their flat to arrange their own
celebrations. Every year they were invited to join the family but
they always refused. Grace guessed that they were glad to get
away from them all for a few days. Olivia supervised, Maggie

Collins cooked and between them they did a magnificent job. Olivia saw to the mincemeat personally. She made it herself. It was rich and delicious. Luke had once made himself sick by eating seven mince pies smothered in rich clotted cream in one go. The flowers and one of the trees were also Olivia's responsibility. As children they had taken no part in decorating the one in the drawing-room. Olivia would shut herself away and turn a six foot spruce into something magical. The other tree, in the hall, was the one Grace and Luke were allowed to decorate. They were also responsible for the table decorations; they constructed these from fir cones and holly and glitter which ended up everywhere but where it should and which Mrs Collins would still be hoovering out of the rugs weeks later. If the house was full throughout the year it was overflowing at Christmas. One party ran into the next for both adults and children.

What will next Christmas hold? Grace wondered. And where will I be? The answer to that depended upon the outcome of the trial. And if Harrington was convicted how long would he get?

The telephone rang again. Grace could hardly believe it. Time seemed to mean nothing to people that evening. It was Joe, who was on duty downstairs. 'Dr Cornell, Inspector Jordan is here to see you.'

'Shit,' she said, unable to stop herself. Joe pretended not to have heard. 'All right. Send him up.'

She ran to the bathroom to check her face. It was devoid of make-up and she was wearing her nightclothes. Static snapped as she brushed her hair and lifted it away from her head to give it extra body. With a quick slurp of mouthwash Grace wondered just what she was doing as she went to answer the door.

Letting him in, she heard herself snapping, 'Oh, take that expression off your face.' They were hardly welcoming words after her rapid preparation but Harry looked so contrite, which she had not expected.

He handed her a plastic carrier. 'A peace offering. I found an all-night garage for the chocolates, the wine's from my rack. And I meant what I said, about your losing weight.'

'Way beyond the call of duty, Inspector, worrying about a witness's figure. But thanks for the wine and the chocolates. Are you all right? Your voice doesn't sound right.'

'Just a cold.' He made no further comment but followed Grace to the kitchen hoping he was to be invited to share the wine. Grace did not look in the least tired although she was undressed, ready for bed.

'Well, open it then.'

Harry was shocked at Grace's abruptness. He had never known her to be rude. 'Of course, if you want me to.'

They sat at the kitchen table. To an onlooker they might have been two old friends but there was a tension between them.

Grace broke the silence. 'I'm sorry, Harry. I'm a bit jumpy. I made a fool of myself today. The jury'll already think I'm half-way to being sectioned under the Mental Health Act.'

'You had little choice in the matter. Lamberton's a clever bastard, and I did warn you, Grace. At least you answered the questions truthfully. That's all anyone can do.' Even if your unexpected recovery from amnesia means Harrington goes free. He did not need to tell her, he saw by Grace's face she knew what she had done.

Like herself, Harry had elected to stay on after he had given evidence. 'They twisted my answers.'

'That's what they're paid to do.'

'Do you still believe me, Harry?'

'Yes.' But doubts were creeping in. There were so many things Grace refused to talk about. He watched her take a sip of wine, deliberately avoiding eye contact. Even now, he thought, even now she's holding back.

Grace saw anew how unlike Matt Harry was, and not just physically. Inspector Jordan, she realised, was somewhat fright-ening at times. But he had been hurt. He must have been if what he had told her about his wife running off with a colleague was true. In the months she had known him he had not mentioned any other women.

'Look, Grace, if Harrington does know something about your past don't you think you'd better tell me?'

'What good will it do? It's not up to you any longer.' He won't be beaten, she thought, he's determined to prove I killed my father, or, if not me, then whoever did.

'But think about it, supposing he does have information, we might be able to solve the mystery of your father's death.'

So there we have it, in words at last, Grace thought. He's using

155

me, and this trial, as a way of gaining glory. 'You mean as seen in the films when someone comes rushing into the court waving a piece of paper containing the vital piece of missing evidence? Oh, grow up, Harry. You've done your duty. You found me, you arrested Harrington. Your duty stops with the trial.' Her disappointment in him made her want to weep. She had been fooling herself for all these months. His interest was not in her, it was in a case which had long been forgotten by most people.

'Christ! Don't you ever give up?' He pushed back his chair and stood up, running both hands through his hair in exasperation.

'More to the point, Inspector, don't you?' Grace did not see it coming. Furious, she was totally unprepared for the firm grip on her arms and the even firmer kiss which followed, a repeat of that previous occasion. For a split second Grace responded. Then, pushing at his chest, she said, 'Let go of me. I suppose you think a bottle of wine justifies that. No doubt if you took me out for a meal you'd expect me to go to bed with you.'

'There's nothing I'd like better. Food, or no food.'

Grace was stunned into silence. He had spoken calmly and without the passion of a minute earlier but she knew that he meant it. It made her feel ashamed of her behaviour although she was aware that he tended to bring out the worst in her. Near to tears she bit her lip. Why was she always so lachrymose lately? She had done enough crying over the past months.

'I apologise, Grace. I had no intention of upsetting you.' He turned to leave.

'No, wait, Harry. It's not you. I'm seeing my mother tomorrow, it's really unsettled me.'

'Your mother?'

She sat down and stared up at him. His nose appeared more crooked from below and the two lines which ran from his nostrils to the corners of his mouth more deeply etched. There was an expression of incomprehension on his face until he asked, 'You mean she's actually here?' He was aware that Grace had rung her from Anton's house but he had assumed the call had been made to Italy.

'Yes. And to be honest, it scares me more than the trial. I didn't realise just how long I've waited for this.'

'Then I'm really pleased for you. And you might finally discover that you do need someone. I just hope your mother can penetrate that wall.'

Grace was tempted to throw her wine in his face but knew she would appear ridiculous. 'You bastard,' she muttered instead. She was still standing in the kitchen with the glass in her hand when Harry left, closing the front door quietly behind him. 'Need? Do I need people?' she muttered. 'I'm a doctor, people need me. Luke needs me, and I once thought that Matt did too.' But she knew that she would not allow herself the luxury of becoming dependent upon anybody. It was too much of a risk. Even Matt's infidelity had not devastated her because deep down she had known that a little of the blame had been hers. There had been other things on her mind but she should not have shut him out. She had been going to marry him after all. I held back, even with Matt, she realised. Would it be the same with Olivia? Her hand was on her mouth. She could still feel Harry's kiss. Her eyes were heavy and her head ached. It was almost 2 a.m. Without some sleep she would be a wreck in the morning.

I have friends, a brother whom I love despite the way he is and my work, she thought. I don't need anyone else. Especially not Harry Jordan. But as she got into bed she had to admit that his kiss had aroused her.

Ruth had known that the fake fur and the cerise suit of the previous day had been over the top but it had helped draw some of the attention away from Grace. The outfit had certainly raised Harry Jordan's eyebrows.

Before dressing for work she rang Grace as promised and tried to keep the grin out of her voice when she heard what Harry had done. Good for him, she thought as she hung up, that's just what Grace needs. Even though she doesn't realise how much she cares for him.

She was now running late. Fingering her more formal suits which hung in a row in her wardrobe, Ruth could not make up her mind which to wear. It would, of course, depend on which blouses were clean. She sighed. Her spell of spring cleaning had done little to change her sloppy ways. Already there were clothes all over the room. Not the oyster or the charcoal pinstripe. She felt the need for something more cheerful and finally picked an emerald pencil-line skirt with a split at the back, down one side of which ran a row of white buttons. With it went a green and white striped blouse and an emerald silk cardigan. She twisted her hair into a French pleat and checked the back with the aid of two mirrors.

Tickles mewed from the rumpled bed. Ruth smiled. 'I can't possibly shake the duvet with you on top of it,' she said, as if she needed an excuse for not doing so.

Downstairs she put on her coat and picked up her bag. When she opened the front door there was no need to brace herself against the cold. The snow had disappeared and the sun shone. It was the mildest day since the end of the autumn. 'At last,' she said, almost tripping over Tickles who had fled down the stairs in her wake and slid out just as she was about to shut the door. Holding it open, she was ignored. Ruth shrugged. The cat would survive and there was a magnetic flap on the back door if she wanted to go back inside.

Ruth glanced at the car then at the sky. She'd walk. She set off, wondering if Harry would turn up at court that day. He had taken some time off and she suspected it was to be with Grace, but after last night he might not want to face her. As she made her way down the hill towards her consulting rooms she realised that Harry was in love with Grace even if neither of them knew it.

Before her first patient arrived Ruth familiarised herself with the file. Yesterday had been traumatic, her patients' worries temporarily forgotten. What will today hold for Grace? How would she stand up to listening to Harrington's evidence? 'Don't go, Grace,' Ruth had said that morning. 'You can't change anything by being there.'

'I have to be there,' Grace had replied. 'I have to hear what he says.'

'I'm sorry I can't come with you, but I'll be thinking about you.' And she would. Ruth hoped it would not interfere with her work.

As she settled the client into a chair Matt's face came into her head. He might be called to give evidence today. If he was asked about Grace ending their engagement he would have to mention that the letters had precipitated their break-up – and that, surely,

158

would prove that Grace could not have written them. The second one had warned her not to trust Matt but she had known nothing of Veronica Beecham until that fateful evening . . .

'Well, Elizabeth, how've you been since I last saw you? Have you felt able to discuss any of the things we've talked about with your husband yet?' Ruth asked as she picked up her fountain pen ready to make notes.

Tanya Gregory had decided to call Matthew Fielding as a witness. The fact that Grace had broken off the engagement only days prior to the interlude with Harrington at the surgery would add weight to what Grace had said about being frightened and confused. Matt had loved Grace, maybe still did, and did not come across as vindictive.

The way things were going it seemed unlikely Matthew, let alone Harrington, would make it to the witness box that day. An interminably long time had been spent with the two hand-writing experts, one for each side. Their individual evidence was, as Tanya had anticipated, inconclusive. Neither man could say with total certainty whether Grace or some other person had written the letters. Alan Lamberton made much of this, asking how, in that case, if the writing was so very like Miss Cornell's, the defendant could have copied it so accurately. Naturally, they did not know.

Tanya had already pointed out that Harrington had daily access to the histology forms written and signed by Grace and therefore every opportunity to have learned to copy her writing.

Tanya was wrong about Matt. He was sworn in as the last witness of the day and looked very nervous.

'Did you have any idea that Dr Cornell was about to end your engagement?' Tanya began.

'None whatsoever.'

From the well of the courtroom. Grace stared at Matt. Why didn't he admit the reason for it? Was this his form of revenge? she wondered.

'Mr Fielding, Mr Harrington claims that Dr Cornell invited him to the surgery which implies she knew him well. Did she ever mention Mr Harrington to you?'

'No.'

'I see. But surely it would be natural to mention the name of someone with whom she came into contact regularly?'

'Dr Cornell is not secretive, nor is she a liar,' Matt said loudly and firmly. 'Grace is the most honest person I know. And she would mostly have been taking surgery when he came to collect. It was entirely my fault that the engagement ended. I had been seeing another woman.'

Grace sensed, rather than heard, the small ripple which ran round the courtroom. Thank you, Matt, she thought, surprised at his indignation on her behalf.

'Mr Fielding, may I –'

'Dr Cornell works hard and she's well respected, but that man –' Everyone was really taking notice now, their eyes following the direction of Matt's accusatory finger.

'Mr Fielding, you must only answer the questions put to you,' the judge intervened.

Alan Lamberton decided he had no questions. The ones he had planned were now obsolete. Fielding was on Grace Cornell's side.

The court rose and the judge departed. People began to file out. Grace tried to find Matt to thank him, but he had already disappeared. She felt a sense of anticlimax. Harrington had not yet been sworn in. She would have to go through it all again tomorrow. She dreaded it but knew that she must forget about it when there was still the evening to look forward to. Strangely, it filled her with an equal mixture of dread and pleasure.

She walked to the car with her coat unbuttoned. The air was fresh on her face and stars littered the sky overhead. Grace felt strangely becalmed. It was the first time for years her heart was not thudding in her chest.

Olivia had rung Monica from the telephone in her hotel room. She replaced the receiver and wondered why on earth she had accepted the invitation to stay so readily. Despite the passage of time and all that the intervening years had brought, there had been no awkwardness between them. Once they had shared many things in common, until the time Olivia had been unable to stand it any more and the close bond between them had loosened. There were so many things she wanted to know and it would help to talk to Monica about Grace before she met her child who was now a woman – if she was able to meet her.

She packed her case and went downstairs, apologetically asking for her bill and explaining that her plans had changed again.

How familiar everything looked as the taxi cruised through the city streets, the streetlights flashing intermittently across its bonnet. Within fifteen minutes they had reached the outskirts, the residential area where Monica lived. Even in the dark the gardens looked damp and the soil gleamed; the rich, red Devon soil. She thought of Gorstone and smelled the earth as if she was there. Soon the daffodils she had planted randomly beneath the trees in the lawn would be pushing up through the grass. They would have multiplied tenfold by now.

The last time Olivia had seen Monica Freddie had been alive. They had lived at the lodge then and the house where Monica now lived, bought as an investment, had been let to an elderly couple. Olivia had only seen it once when she went with her sister-in-law to view it. The restaurants had been sold off after Freddie's death. Monica had no interest in them. But she had sold them individually because, she had told Olivia, she thought Freddie would have preferred it that way. It would give more than one person a chance to make something of himself. It was odd that she had considered his feelings more after his death than she had done when he was around to appreciate it. But Olivia understood the convoluted workings of the bereaved mind.

I just can't get used to this weather, she thought, unaware that the temperature was little different from that in Milan and that the coldness came from within. Even though it was much milder she was grateful for her coat. The taxi pulled in. She had arrived. Her mouth was dry as she paid the driver and handed him a tip. She walked up the drive, her gloved finger hesitating only a second before she rang the bell, unaware that Monica had heard the cab and had been standing motionless in the hall, prepared for the moment when she must open the door.

Olivia was not sure what to expect. Perhaps Monica had turned into an old and frail woman. She certainly hadn't antici- pated such little change in her ex-sister-in-law's appearance. She gazed at her with wide eyes. 'My God, you haven't changed at all.'

Monica was shaking her head and smiling. 'I can't believe it. Neither have you.'

But we have changed, Olivia thought, only not drastically physically. We're older, that's all. Mentally was another matter.

Monica took Olivia's case and placed it on one of the hard-backed chairs which flanked the half-moon table containing a telephone extension and a bowl of flowers. 'A drink? I need one even if you don't. And I have to admit, it won't be my first today, either. I poured one just before you telephoned. I somehow thought you might contact me. Gin and tonic?'

'You remembered. Oh, Monica, I just can't believe I'm here.' They were standing in the lounge staring at one another, unable to believe so many years had passed. It might have been yesterday they had last met. Olivia did not know whether to laugh or to cry. She took her drink and sipped it, glad of the glass to hide behind. Her throat tightened when she thought of the happy times they had shared in their youth and the way things had turned out.

Monica feels the same, she thought, seeing the other woman's eyes fill with tears. Or are we simply sentimental old fools? 'It's so good of you, Monica. I was amazed when you kept writing. I thought – well, I thought you'd blame me for everything. I know how close to Gerald you were.'

'No. I never blamed you. Gerald was greedy. Any other man would have been more than happy to have you as a wife. I think my brother's problem was that he always had too much yet thought he didn't have enough. Does that make sense?'

Olivia nodded and sat down. She felt weak. Being face to face with Gerald's sister was very different from reading the occasional letter written by her. 'We were so young then. Oh, Monica, nothing's ever hurt so much since.'

'I know. Time does that to you, mellows you and makes you less sensitive to pain.' She paused. 'Most of the time, anyway.' It was too soon to talk of the past; Monica changed the subject. 'I've prepared a meal for us, nothing complicated but the veget-ables are all fresh. You always did insist upon that, I recall.'

'Yes, mostly for the children's sake, but Gerald and I loved them too.' Gerald and I. It was years since she had coupled their names.

'They're survivors in their different ways, your children.' Monica knew she had to bring the subject up but how could she tell Olivia that she had had nothing to do with Grace for a long time?

'How is the trial going?'

'I don't know. Has Grace agreed to see you?'

Olivia leant her head against the back of the sofa and sighed. 'She hasn't been in touch yet. I hope you don't mind but I've left your number with the hotel receptionist.' She hesitated before saying, 'Tell me about the time when Gerald died, Monica. I never really knew what happened.'

Monica looked away as the painful memories returned. 'There isn't a lot to say. I understood the Italian police informed you at the time.'

'Yes. But I always supposed it was their way of checking up on me. We were long divorced by then but they didn't seem satisfied with the circumstances surrounding his death.'

'I think it's best forgotten, Olivia. Gerald had an accident. It was as simple as that, although, naturally, people love a scandal and some tried to read more into it.'

'Please? I really need to know.'

Monica sighed. 'I doubt if I know any more than you do. Grace went out to meet him. Gerald had rung for some reason, something to do with the car, I believe, but all she found was the car itself. Luckily a passing motorist found Grace or she, too, might have died from exposure.'

'It was exposure?'

'That's what the post-mortem said. Gerald's body was found in a narrow ravine. It seems he lost his footing and fell and hit his head, but not hard enough to kill him. It was snowing hard, his body would soon have been covered.'

'I still don't understand, Gerald was meticulous about servicing the car. And why on earth would he have gone out without his coat? I read that he'd done so in the paper.'

'I've no idea,' Monica replied, more sharply than she intended. 'And I don't suppose we'll even know.'

Olivia realised that the discussion was at an end and she did not want to spoil the friendship which had, despite the circumstances, survived so many years, by pursuing the matter. But she would, if given the chance, ask Grace.

'I think I'd better see to the food.' As Monica stood the telephone rang. She walked gracefully to the table against the wall near the window. Making calls in the daytime she could watch the birds or look at the garden. 'It's for you. It's Grace!' Monica handed her the receiver then left the room.

Olivia was puzzled. Monica had been brusque with Grace. She felt a restriction in her chest as differing emotions fought for supremacy. 'Grace?' she said tentatively in case her daughter had decided to hang up. 'Hello? Is there anyone there?' Tears filled her eyes. Grace had changed her mind, she wasn't going to speak.

'Yes. It's me. It's Grace,' she heard her daughter say in a voice so like her own.

'Oh, Grace.' Olivia smiled into the following silence. It was filled with a tension she had to break. 'For two supposedly intelligent people this isn't much of a dialogue,' she said. And the ice was broken. They were talking over one another but not caring. Olivia felt wetness on the hand which held the phone and realised that she was crying.

'You're bubbling,' Grace said, which, because of the memories the phrase evoked, made her cry harder. Then suddenly it was all right. Olivia had no idea how long they talked for but Monica was tactful enough to stay out of the room. Tomorrow she would see her daughter. It made her feel weak with joy.

Monica reappeared, opening the door quietly and listening, checking that Olivia had finished the call. 'I think you need another drink. Will she see you?'

'Yes.'

'I'm glad.' She refilled their glasses. 'Come with me, you must be starving.'

Olivia was. For the first time in days she was ready to eat.

Over the meal they talked of Freddie's restaurants and Gorstone and what they had been doing in the years since they last saw each other. But Olivia noticed that each time she brought up the subject of Grace and the trial, Monica tried to change it. Something is very wrong, she thought, but she could not offend Monica, whose hospitality she was accepting, by

164

asking what it was. Olivia contented herself with hearing about Luke.

'He's never settled down,' Monica said, shaking her head. 'He acts like some sort of playboy and I'm not certain he mixes with the right kind of friends. Grace did her best, I have to give her that, but he has his father's waywardness without the self-discipline. At least he's managed to keep out of trouble.'

The sadness Olivia felt showed in her face. It was her fault: had she not left, Luke would have turned out a better man.

To her surprise Monica reached across the kitchen table where they had decided to eat and held her hand. 'Don't, Olivia. There was nothing you could've done. It was always Luke's destiny. Everyone tried with him, his school, Gerald and Grace, and, of course, Mr and Mrs Collins. Don't have any regrets, it's far too late for that for all of us.'

Unsure what Monica, who had had a happy marriage, meant by that Olivia kept the conversation to more cheerful topics. 'I thought I'd gone native, you know, until the train pulled in at Exeter. I didn't realise how homesick I was nor how much I still miss Gorstone.'

'We all do. It's a part of us. But it's in the past. I must admit I was surprised when Grace bought that farmhouse on Dart-moor, it's so near the manor yet Luke says she never goes near the manor or wants to set eyes on it again.'

Luke says. Clearly Monica saw very little, if anything, of Grace these days.

'Shall we finish the wine? I'll get us some cheese. We ought to eat a bit more if we're not to get sloshed.'

Olivia smiled. It was the word they had all used in the old days. She watched Monica as she crossed the room. Her own Italian clothes were stylishly cut but Monica was just as well turned out. Gerald's mother's influence, she realised. Mrs Cornell senior set very high standards which her family was expected to keep. It was a blessing that Gerald's parents were dead when she decided to leave because they would never have got over the ordeal of a divorce even though it had become common practice years before. 'Do you ever get lonely, Monica, here in this house by yourself?'

Monica placed their glasses on the table and pursed her lips. 'No. Not lonely. I got used to it about a year after Freddie died.

I don't think I could live with anyone again. One can become very selfish living alone.

'You're different, Olivia. I've always sensed that you need someone important in your life. I was very surprised when it turned out to be Tony. I mean, we all knew you were friends, but . . .' She stopped. How can I possibly sit here and pass judgement? she asked herself. 'I'm sorry, that was rude of me. Anyway, it was obvious that he worshipped you.'

'It doesn't matter. Really, it doesn't. I don't expect anyone to understand what I did.' How could she say that no one could replace Gerald, not even Tony who had been so very good to her, who had, in fact, made it possible to make the break? 'Tony's a good man and he loves me.'

'But does he make you happy?'

'As far as I shall ever be. And he allows me my own life.'

'Well, there. We're both selfish. I'll just stack the dishwasher then we'll have coffee.'

'Monica, would you mind if I didn't? I feel exhausted.'

'Of course not. I've made up the spare room next to mine. Come on, I'll show you where it is. Look,' she continued as they went upstairs, 'if you like we could drive there tomorrow, to Gorstone, and have a peep at the outside.'

Olivia hesitated before saying, 'Thank you, I think I would like that.' Once Monica had gone back downstairs Olivia stood in the window and stared into the distance where the lights of the city glowed orange. Somewhere down there was Grace. I hope she's not alone tonight, Olivia thought as she made use of the adjoining bathroom.

Within seconds of getting into bed she was asleep. Now that she knew she would see Grace she felt truly relaxed. It was the first time she had done so in fourteen years.

In the morning Monica went through her usual routine of feeding the birds. Olivia watched from a safe distance from inside the bay window of the lounge in order not to frighten them.

'There. Shall we go now?'

They wrapped up warmly and Monica drove them out of Exeter and towards Dartmoor. As the road began to wind and rise and the hills seemed to surround them even though they were still at a distance, both women wondered whether they

166

would be able to bear the memories the sight of Gorstone Manor would evoke. Last night they had talked but still so much had been left unsaid. As if reading Olivia's mind, knowing that to drive right up to the gates might upset them both, Monica pulled on to the verge as soon as the chimneys and roof of Gorstone became visible.

The years fell away. Olivia pictured herself in the garden along with the ghosts of their friends. She recalled the glittering parties, the Christmases and the children's parties, the school-children who had come to stay and would be grown men and women now, perhaps even with children of their own. And Gerald. Gorstone was nothing without him. Gerald laughing, Gerald stroking her hair, Gerald in bed with her telling her how much he loved her. And all of it a lie. She shook her head. Not quite a lie but not what she had believed either.

'Olivia?'

'I'm all right. I'm sorry, Monica.' She reached into her handbag and produced a tissue. 'I didn't expect it to hit me so hard. I thought the years would have softened the memories.' And if a distant sighting of Gorstone could produce this effect how would she feel later when she saw Grace?

'We shouldn't have come. It was a bad idea.' Monica started the engine.

'Just drive past the gates,' Olivia said. She wanted one final glimpse of the past then she must put it behind her for ever.

They slowed by the open gates. 'They need painting,' Olivia commented.

Monica smiled for the first time that day. 'They always did. They rusted every year. You obviously never noticed.'

There were many things she had not noticed until it was too late.

They spent an idle afternoon reading in front of the fire – in Olivia's case, trying to read. 'Olivia, the taxi's ordered, will you stop worrying.'

Every few minutes she had been glancing at the clock, willing time to pass more quickly. The seconds ticked by until ten minutes before Olivia was due to leave. Suddenly there hardly seemed time to renew her lipstick and spray on some perfume. Shaking with nerves she told Monica she had no idea what time she would be back but she'd ring anyway.

167

'Thank you.' Monica realised that the meeting might not go as well as Olivia hoped, that too many years might have passed to heal the rift. But she also knew there were things which Grace might say which would change everything. It was Monica's turn to worry.

Olivia took in every detail of the drive to Grace's flat where they had arranged to meet. The flats themselves were built between large, older houses but somehow did not look out of place. She mounted the two steps at the front of the building wondering how to get in. Did she press the buzzer of Grace's entry-phone or did the man she could see through the glass doors come to let her in? He was approaching her. She decided to wait. 'Good evening. I'm Olivia Pisano, Grace Cornell's mother. She's expecting me.'

'Yes. I know.' Olivia was shown into the lift. 'I'll let her know you're here,' Joe said as he pressed the button. 'Second floor,' he added with a smile.

Olivia nodded. Not even on the day she had married Gerald had she felt this nervous. Her knees buckled as she stepped out of the lift and she steadied herself against the wall before walking the last few yards. Framed in the doorway was the daughter she had not seen for fourteen years. Her face crumpled despite her intention not to cry. Looking at Grace was like seeing a younger version of herself. She's beautiful, she thought, biting on her lower lip, transfixed, unable to believe it was happening at last. 'Hello, Grace.'

'Hello, Olivia.'

Neither woman moved. Olivia. Not Mum or Mother. It was like a slap in the face.

'Come in.'

Olivia stepped inside, close enough to Grace to smell her perfume and the shampoo she had used when showering after reaching home. No longer caring what Grace thought, she reached out and pulled her to her chest, breathing in the scent of her skin and feeling the wetness of her tears when Grace could no longer hold them back. Oh, God, help me. What do I say to her? How can I ever make up for the pain? But no one answered her silent prayers.

Grace pulled away and tried to smile. 'Come in here, I'll pour us a drink.'

'What a lovely room.' Instinctively Olivia walked towards the window and looked out over the city. How different from the view from her apartment windows. And Tony, she suddenly realised. She had not spoken to him since Sunday night.

'Grace, I had to be here for the trial, even if you'd refused to see me.' She spoke without turning around, terrified that anything she said might be misconstrued.

'I wasn't sure whether I wanted to. It's been a long time. What would you like to drink?'

Another small dart. But how would Grace know what she drank? She had been a child of fourteen when she left. 'Do you have any gin?'

Grace poured a large measure and added tonic, ice and lemon before pouring herself a glass of wine. The bottle was already open. She had needed that one glassful before she felt able to face Olivia. There was so much to say but where did they begin? She felt an overwhelming need to touch her mother, to pour out all her troubles, but she had kept her own counsel for so long she had no idea how to go about it.

'Grace, if this is all too much for you on top of the trial, just say the word and I'll leave.'

'No. Stay. There are so many things I want to know.'

'Like why I left?'

'Yes. Why you left us, Luke and me. That most of all.'

Olivia had been expecting this but was not ready to answer the question. To do so would have been disloyal to Grace's memories of her father.

'Please? I'll accept whatever you say as long as it's the truth.'

'All right.' Olivia took a long sip of gin then placed her glass beside her. 'You may not forgive me for what I'm about to say, Grace, but that's a chance I must take. Your father is dead, he cannot defend himself any longer. I will tell you the truth but I'm afraid of what it might do to you.'

'Might do to me?' Grace stood. Her eyes were alight with anger and her hands were clenched at her sides. Look what it's already done to all of us, she was thinking. 'I don't think there's anything that can hurt me now.'

Olivia held her breath. She is so beautiful, she thought, watching the light catch the glints in her daughter's hair and her

169

slender figure silhouetted on the far wall, the shadow thrown from the table lamps which lit the room. Olivia bowed her head. It had been a stupid, tactless thing to say. 'Forgive me. May I tell you?'

'Yes.' Grace sighed and sat down again.

'Your father was having an affair. I found out by chance and when I challenged him he didn't deny it. I had been suspicious but I just couldn't believe it of him. I always felt safe with him and that he loved me. But, you know, I started noticing those small tell-tale signs such as hanging up if he was on the phone when I came into the room, occasions when he said he had to go out. It was always on business, so he told me. Then, one day, I overheard more than I was intended to. I had been in the garden and I was coming into to the house from the back. Gerald was in the library with the french doors wide open. There's no need for me to repeat what I heard, but it made the situation irrefutably clear.

'We argued. Gerald apologised and begged for forgiveness, which, loving him as I did, I gave him. Three times this happened, Grace. He just could not give the woman up. And then, in the heat of yet another row, he admitted that he had been seeing her since before we were married and that he couldn't help himself.' She stopped to take another sip of her drink. How hard it was to say these things to a girl who had idolised her father. Olivia had no idea how Grace was taking the news because her face was set and expressionless.

'I had two choices, put up with it or leave.'

'Not three? Couldn't you have asked him to leave?'

'Initially I wanted to throw him out of the house bodily. But it was his house. I knew how the law worked, of course, but I just couldn't do it. It was his family home and had been for generations. I could not expect him to give it up, nor you and Luke to do so either. I needed time to think. It had to be me who left and I needed somewhere to take you both. But it all came to a head far more quickly than I had anticipated. After that last row he made no secret of it. It was almost as if he was flaunting this woman, not that I ever saw her. I never even found out who it was. He came and went as he pleased. I think he thought I'd decided to stay. Anyway, he came in late one night and, oh,

170

Grace, there was a smear of lipstick at the side of his mouth. He hadn't even bothered to shower before coming home.

'That was the end for me. I knew the one place where I'd be safe and treated with respect was with Tony. I can't expect you to believe me but there had been nothing whatsoever between us other than friendship. I guessed how Tony felt about me but not once did he abuse our hospitality. I told him what had happened and how I couldn't stand it any longer. You see, I still loved Gerald but I couldn't live with him knowing what he was doing, knowing that he'd never give her up and I'd always be second best.

'Grace, I took the coward's way out. Tony was about to go back to Italy. He offered to take me with him and you two children, of course. I had no idea how you'd take the news but I'd already decided that I had to be fair to Gerald because he loved you both as well. You'd spend the holidays with him whenever it was possible. Well, as you know, it didn't work out like that. I knew how much you both adored Gerald, but I didn't know how much you hated me for what I'd done.'

'What do you mean?' Grace spoke quietly, her face was white.

'I know moving to Italy would have been an upheaval, but Luke hadn't yet started at his new school and you were mature and sensible enough to treat it as a challenge. And, of course, there are English schools. I thought we'd cope. But when neither of you wanted to come . . . I just didn't know what to do.' Olivia was near to tears.

'We were never asked.'

'What?'

'There was never any mention of us going to live with you.'

'But my letters? I left you each a letter and I wrote afterwards. Neither of you replied. And Gerald knew. He had agreed to my terms. It was only when he wrote to say he was divorcing me that he said you and Luke had told him you never wanted to see me again.'

The room span and Grace thought she might faint. On top of the trial this was too much to deal with. 'We never received your letters.'

There was a long silence as the implications sank in. Gerald must have destroyed the letters she had left at Gorstone for her

171

children. But there had been others. 'I wrote to you both regularly. I cannot believe Gerald kept the letters from you.'

'I swear to you, I never received any letters. God, I see now why Dad changed his mind at the last minute about Luke's school. He didn't want you to know where he was. But how did he stop me receiving mine? Did you write to the school?'

'No, because I knew you were both at home at weekends.'

Grace felt sick. The man she had idolised had deceived her.

'The divorce went through very quickly. I didn't make a fuss. That he had instigated the proceedings spoke volumes. He had already written to express your feelings, to tell me I was no longer a feature in your lives. I wrote a few more times then, for both your sakes, I made no further attempt to contact you. But surely someone must have talked to you and Luke? I thought the child welfare people or someone would have wanted to know how you felt?'

'They did. I suppose they could see how comfortable we were at Gorstone, that we lacked for nothing, but you see, Dad told us you'd left because you didn't love any of us any more and that you didn't want to see us again. Luke told the woman who came that he hated you. He didn't, he was just hurt and angry. I don't remember what I said, not very much, I imagine, but she was obviously satisfied. And we hadn't heard a word from you, you must see how it looked to us.'

Olivia was speechless. All those years of believing her children hated her, all those years she could have had with them if she had not acted so hastily. If only she had remained in England none of this would have happened. But what other choice did she have at the time? Who would have taken her side against Gerald? Freddie, maybe, they had always got on well. He was the one person who was not completely bowled over by Gerald, who had never totally trusted him.

Olivia stood up and moved towards Grace, tentatively touching her shoulder. 'If only I'd known. If only I'd made more of a fuss. It was for you that I didn't. You could both have been with me all the time. And Gerald could still have had his share of you. Tony wanted you both, he'd have treated you well.

'One thing always puzzled me. I never could discover who the woman was. I don't imagine Gerald was crass enough to have picked on one of our circle of friends, but after what you've just

172

told me, nothing would surprise me now. Do you know who it was, Grace?'

'No.' She turned away, hating herself for having to lie.

Olivia cried in the taxi back to Monica's house and did not stop until the early hours of the morning. Adultery was one thing, but Gerald had robbed her of her children, and them of a mother. What he had done was unforgivable. Now she wished he was still alive because then she could have taken pleasure in killing him herself.

Only in the small hours of the morning did she realise that they had both forgotten that Grace had booked a table at a restaurant and therefore they had failed to cancel it, and neither of them had eaten.

Emotionally drained from the long day in court, Grace was barely able to assimilate the enormity of what Olivia had told her. The deep sleep which should have eased her mind was elusive, nightmares filled her dreams and she awoke exhausted. There were dark smudges beneath her eyes but they could be disguised with some green-tinted cream she had bought for just that purpose. By seven o'clock she was dressed and ready to face another day but it was too early to go to the courthouse. Almost a full pot of coffee had not helped. She was shaking from an excess of caffeine. A walk might rid her of some nervous energy.

There was an expression of surprise on Joe's face when she stepped out of the lift. 'You're up early, Dr Cornell. Couldn't sleep? No wonder. Not with what's going on.'

Joe had been following the news in the paper although nothing had yet been reported on the trial itself. One or two of the tabloids had tried to get in touch with Grace but so far she had managed to avoid reporters.

But only so far, she realised as she opened the plate glass door and saw the car. In it sat a man who might have been asleep. His arms were folded and he was slumped forward. But Grace wasn't fooled. 'Oh, shit!' she exclaimed in frustration. The man had seen her and was opening the driver's door.

'Dr Cornell?' he said with a small smile.

173

Joe, who had been watching from inside the building, came out and stared at her anxiously.

'It's the press.' Grace said, glad to have an ally.

'Do you want me to have a word?'

'I don't think it'll do much good, Joe, but thanks anyway.' I will not be beaten, she decided as she began to walk along the pavement and past the car.

'Dr Cornell? Could I have a word?'

Grace turned and smiled sweetly as he fumbled for something in his heavy overcoat pocket. 'You may have four. Go and fuck yourself.' The minute the words were out of her mouth she regretted them. I'll be quoted, she realised. Verbatim but with two stars inserted between the f and the k if he's from the tabloids, or I'll be accused of using an obscenity if he works for one of the better papers. And what will everyone make of that? Only that Dr Cornell is by no means the lady her friends are trying to portray her to be.

'Dr Cornell, please wait.'

He's not easily offended, I'll give him that, Grace admitted silently. 'Go away.'

'I don't want an interview.'

She waited, knowing that he wasn't going to get one, nor would she allow him to trick her into holding a conversation which could be edited and used as one.

'Look, this is going to sound unbelievable, but I think Lance Harrington may have known your father.'

'What?' Could this be possible, was there some evidence other than her own to put Harrington in a bad light? If what this man was saying was true, she might be rid of him for ever.

'Where's your identification?'

He dug into his pockets eagerly and produced it. His name was Dean O'Hearne and he was a freelance journalist. Instinct told Grace that he was all right. But she could not believe hearing herself ask if he wanted some coffee.

'I've got a flask.'

'Proper coffee. Come up to the flat.'

His mouth dropped open, then, like a puppy, he followed her into the building.

Grace liked the look of him, despite his roughly shaven chin. There was a boyish innocence which belied his way of earning

174

a living and his pale face topped by ginger hair was friendly and open. Be careful, she warned herself, those are the worst kind.

Joe let them in to save Grace fishing for her keys. He made no comment as they got into the lift together, there was no need, his expression was enough. Grace knew he thought her to be a fool.

'Hell, this is some flat,' Dean O'Hearne remarked when she let him in.

'Sit down. I won't be a minute.' Was it possible he had discovered something about Harrington that the police had missed or had he simply hit on a perfect excuse to speak to her? If Harrington had known her father . . . The thought trailed off. It was better than she had dared to hope for. She went back to the lounge and handed Dean a mug of coffee. She had made tea for herself. 'Tell me about yourself, Mr O'Hearne. What are you doing here and what do you know?'

'I was born here, in Exeter, though I haven't worked here for years. Naturally I heard about the awful things which happened to your family. I never expected to meet any of you, and I really didn't expect you to talk to me today.'

Get on with it, Grace thought, realising that time was passing.

'I worked on local papers until I felt ready to go it alone. But I want you to know that I'm not here on behalf of anyone but myself. I'm freelance now. Before I moved away I came across Harrington by chance. It was in a pub. One of those quiet nights when you think you might as well make conversation with the only other bloke standing at the bar. We introduced ourselves and I mentioned I was a reporter. Harrington said I must know all about the Cornell family in that case. I didn't. Only what I had read. I'm the same age as you, I was too young at the time your mother left to have taken it in but naturally I was fully aware of the strange circumstances surrounding your father's death because I was working on the paper by then. Our coverage mentioned your mother.'

Grace was surprised, she had assumed Dean was younger than her. 'I don't think anyone knows the full circumstances.'

'No. True. But this was just after it happened. Harrington said he knew you – that you were at Southampton together.'

Grace went cold with shock. Dean had met him here! How

could she have forgotten about that arranged night in Exeter, how had this vital memory escaped her until now? Dean meeting him like that placed Harrington in the area at around the time of her father's death. 'What did he say?'

'Well, that's the thing. He didn't actually admit he'd met Mr Cornell but he gave the impression he had. He'd had a few, quite a few, I'd say. He was rambling on about what an arrogant bastard he was, his words, I hasten to add. Dr Cornell, I know I said I didn't want an interview but can I ask you one question?'

'Go on.'

'Do you think he could've killed your father? Obviously the thought didn't cross my mind at the time, but now, after what he's done to you, I've been wondering if it was possible.'

'Yes,' Grace answered without hesitation. 'I really think he could have done.' Thank you, she thought, thank you, Dean O'Hearne. If he could somehow be persuaded to testify in court he might help clear her name by offering evidence against Harrington, incriminating him in the death of her father. 'So it's not me you're interested in, but my father.'

'Put like that it doesn't sound very flattering, but yes. I'm on leave at the moment, you see. The publications I work for will carry a report of the outcome of the trial, but little more than that. I'm not here on their behalf to dig up any dirt.'

'Then what are you here for? Look, I don't understand any of this. If you really did meet Harrington back then why didn't you go to the police?'

'Dr Cornell, I couldn't read into the future. He made a passing comment in a pub. Your family were well known. How many hundreds of people must have come into contact with them? I assumed it was a remark made out of jealousy or that he'd lost out to your father in business in some way. I also assumed that if Harrington was known to your father he would have been questioned at the time of his death.'

'And now? You knew what happened to me, why didn't you go to the police with this information before the trial started?'

'Until I returned, I didn't know it was the same man. I'd forgotten his name. I was in court yesterday and I recognised him. And, lastly, I'm a reporter.'

Grace understood. The police would believe he was trying to

elicit information by claiming prior knowledge of the defendant. A few words over a couple of drinks eight years ago was not exactly hard evidence.

'Before you continue, I am not prepared to discuss that night again now or ever. However, I have to ask you, would you be prepared to tell the police what Harrington said to you that night?'

Dean O'Hearne thought about it. 'I don't see why not.'

'Thank you.' Grace's mind was racing. If Dean O'Hearne was prepared to repeat this to Harry Jordan it would certainly add weight to the case against Harrington. But would it help her now? Probably not. If the information came out too soon the jury might think Harrington had been invited to her home, that she had known him far better than she had said. It was still one person's word against another's. 'Look, let's leave it until after the trial. Where can I get in touch with you? I have to go now.'

'Perhaps I could drive you to court? My time's my own for the next few days. I'm staying with my parents and they're both out at work.'

'Thank you. I think I'd like that.'

There was not much time to spare but at least there were fewer reporters waiting to delay them. Most of them would only be interested in the verdict. Grace felt buoyed up and optimistic but had to hide these feelings. It was hardly appropriate to arrive in court grinning.

Settled into a seat with Dean beside her, Grace's mood changed the moment that Harrington walked towards the witness box. With his hand on the Bible he was sworn in whilst he stared straight at her.

She listened in horror as he explained that he had met Grace when they were both students and that he had taken her out on more than one occasion.

'Was your relationship platonic?' Alan Lamberton inquired.

'No. It was sexual.'

'Miss Cornell says otherwise.'

'That may be. Why don't you ask her about the small birthmark on her left buttock?'

'Oh, God,' Grace whispered, her whole body stiff. Sensing what she was going through, Dean O'Hearne reached for her

177

hand and held it tightly. 'Do you want to leave?' he asked as quietly as he could.

'No. I can't. Not now.'

And for the next hour everything Harrington said only confirmed that he knew Grace well. Grace had helped him get a job at the hospital and Grace had invited him to the surgery that Saturday morning. 'I had absolutely no intention of abducting her,' he said in answer to Tanya Gregory's question.

'When did she ask you to go there?'

'The previous week, the day before Mr Roach told her to take some leave.'

Grace didn't faint but it was the nearest she had ever come to it. Someone in the courtroom was wearing Devon Violets perfume. All she could think of was that she did not realise it was still produced.

'For what purpose?'

'She told me she wanted to talk, that it was important. I never did find out what it was.'

It was over by lunchtime. All that was left now was for the jury to make up its mind. Dean O'Hearne grabbed Grace and rushed her out to where his car was parked. She caught a glimpse of Harry Jordan who stared at her without speaking. The sun had come out. It seemed an impossibility that it could shine on such a day. She made no comment but got into the car and fastened her seat-belt.

Dean pulled out into the traffic with a screech of tyres. When the car fish-tailed Grace had to steady herself with both hands against the dashboard. She started to laugh, almost hysterically, as alliterative headlines flashed through her mind: CORNELL KILLED IN CRASH! CURSE OF THE CORNELLS CONTINUES! 'I doubt very much we're being followed,' she said. 'Do you think you could slow down a bit?'

'Sorry, I didn't want to take the chance. I'd like to buy you lunch if I may.'

'And I'd like to live long enough to eat it. But why?'

He blushed. 'Because you were decent enough to speak to me. And I think we ought to talk about your father a little more.'

The pub he chose was not far from the city centre. It was called the Honiton Arms and was the cleanest pub Grace had ever been inside. The thick carpet was spotless, and all the surfaces and glasses gleamed. It resembled someone's living-room more than a bar, with pictures and ornaments and huge jugs of early daffodils. Grace ordered a large white wine. She was in need of it and she didn't have the car. Dean had a bitter shandy and asked her what she wanted to eat.

'I couldn't, my stomach's in knots.'

'In that case, you must. I insist.'

They sat down and waited until their baguettes arrived. Grace shook her head; she knew she would not be able to get through hers. 'What else did you want to talk about?'

'From what Harrington said this morning it seems he really did know your father.'

'How do you mean?'

'Well, you said you'd been out with him casually and that was that. How else did he get to know so much about you? I mean, I bet your father was proud of you, he probably talked about you all the time.'

'Yes,' Grace said, thinking just how useful Dean could be. 'Yes, he was proud.'

'It's an explanation anyway.' He bit into the overfilled bread and chewed. 'It might have helped if I'd thought of it sooner.'

Grace nodded, although Harrington would simply have denied having met Gerald Cornell.

Nothing seemed to impair Dean's appetite. Having finished his own food he stared at the half baguette Grace had left. 'May I?' he asked as he picked it up.

It was time to go back. The short interlude away from the court had given Grace time to come to terms with the fact that, apart from the verdict, it was now over.

She barely took in the judge's directions. She watched the jury being led out and realised there was nothing more to stay for. Dean glanced around and suggested they went somewhere else to wait.

They pushed through the small crowd in the foyer and there, waiting, was Olivia with Ruth and Harry Jordan. They're here for me, Grace thought. She was full of gratitude. Harry tactfully looked away as Olivia reached out to Grace and held her tightly. No one knew what to say. It was Ruth who was as practical as always. 'For heaven's sake, don't start snivelling. We're taking you for a drink. Oh, sorry, who's this?' She looked at Dean in surprise, not having realised he was with Grace.

'Dean O'Hearne.' He held out his hand and introduced himself to both women and then Harry.

'He's with the press,' Grace added, noticing the surprise on everyone's faces.

'And there's more of them outside,' Harry commented.

But between them they formed a sort of human shield around Grace's petite figure. Someone stepped on her foot in the process. Harry had foreseen this circus and a taxi was parked, its engine running and the driver ready to carry them off. It was only licensed to carry four passengers so Dean volunteered to drive himself. It seemed he had been accepted as one of the party because no one objected. 'The Papermakers. I don't imagine anyone'll think of looking for us there.'

The two cars stopped in the narrow street one behind the other. Harry paid the cab driver and told Dean where he could park legally. It was Olivia who went straight to the bar and ordered a bottle of rosé. 'No, make it two,' she added, starting to walk away.

They sat around a rectangular scrubbed wooden table and within minutes Dean joined them. A couple just finishing a meal soon got up to leave. The only other customers remained at the bar talking together.

'How long do you think they'll take?' Grace asked Harry.

'It's very hard to say. What were the judge's directions?'

'They didn't strike me as biased one way or the other,' Dean answered, aware that Grace had not taken them in.

'It might be some time then.'

Grace looked at Olivia sitting so calmly and looking so beautiful on the other side of the table. At least one thing had worked out and that made up for all the rest. Once Luke knew what their father had done he surely couldn't refuse to see her. Grace felt bad. She had not spoken to him yesterday. But Luke didn't ring me to ask about the trial, either, she admitted.

'And first they have to decide upon a foreman,' Olivia added.

'But how will we know? I have to be there. I shouldn't have come here.'

'Calm down, Grace,' Ruth said. 'What difference will it make?'

'I want to see his expression when they send him to prison.' The silence which followed this remark caused Grace to look into each of their faces. 'You don't think he'll go to prison, do you?'

No one replied. Dean watched them all while Grace wondered if he was mentally recording all that was happening for future reference or if he was simply stunned by being part of such a gathering. No other reporter had got near her.

'Yes, I think it'll be a while,' Harry said quietly 'and I wouldn't place any bets on the outcome. What it boils down to is the same as before, basically, your word against his. I warned you we were lucky that the case went to court at all.'

Grace knew this to be true. And how had the jury seen her? As a well-dressed, attractive professional woman with money. They'd know about that if they were local. Harrington would be contrasted as the low-paid courier who had provided a bit of fun for her before being cast aside without thought.

'I'll ring the court soon,' Harry said. 'I know most of the staff there. Someone should be able to give me an idea on time.'

'Please don't worry, darling,' Olivia interrupted before Grace could speak. 'And you've got us.'

Only then did Grace realise that Ruth must have introduced herself to her mother while they were waiting outside the court. She could not have failed to recognise her. And Ruth would then have introduced Harry. Grace had half expected Olivia to be there but not the other two. 'Shouldn't you be at work?' she asked Ruth.

'I took the afternoon off. And Harry's still on leave.'

She knew he must have planned it in advance, which said a lot about how he felt for her. That was not something to think about just yet, although she was grateful for his presence.

'You have lovely friends, Grace, and none of you know how wonderful it feels for me to finally meet you.' Olivia reached across the table and held Grace's hand but it was Harry she addressed next. 'What happens if he gets off? How will that affect my daughter?' She asked the question no one else had dared put into words. Her face was pale and her hand shook as she took a sip of wine.

'There's nothing we can do, not unless he makes a nuisance of himself.'

'Makes a nuisance of himself? Is that how you see what happened to me? He stalked me, for Christ's sake. He wrote those letters and he tried to abduct me.' Grace's face was whiter than her mother's. She was livid. She shook her head and took a deep breath. She had come close to hitting Harry. No other person had ever managed to make her feel so angry. She wondered why that might be.

Harry was startled but let it pass. 'He says he didn't. Look, if he bothers you in any way you can take out an injunction.'

'You see, you're talking as if he's going to walk free. And since when did a piece of paper stop anyone?'

'Sometimes it's enough.'

'A whole bloody court case isn't enough. Don't be so naive, Harry.' The wine was tasteless now that she knew Harry was preparing her for the chance of an acquittal.

'If it should turn out badly you must come and stay with me. Grace. Come anyway. Have a holiday, stay as long as you like. Tony would love to see you again. Whenever I mention your name he shakes his head and says, "Oh, that determined little chin!"'

Grace nodded and rejoiced in the fact that her mother had turned up the one time when she really needed her. Perhaps she should take her up on the invitation . . .

'Yes,' Harry said with a smile, hoping to lighten the mood. 'I know what you mean about that chin.'

'Too right,' Ruth chipped in. 'Stay clear when that juts out.'

Grace had to smile, even though they were humouring her. A week ago she could not have pictured her mother, Ruth and Harry Jordan discussing her as if she wasn't there.

Dean O'Hearne still hadn't said anything and was frowning in bewilderment. He was wondering if there would be any chance of having a quiet word with Mrs Pisano on her own. He was aware that she had been in Italy at the time of her husband's death and seemed to have no knowledge of Harrington, but it would be interesting to hear what she had to say about her family. And where was the brother? Had there been a falling out?

182

'It's a family thing, that chin, on the distaff side,' Olivia explained. 'Grace was a very determined little girl.'

Grace was aware they were trying to distract her but she panicked when Harry stood up and went outside to use his mobile phone. He returned to the table shaking his head. 'No news. They're still out.'

There was another silence as each of them attributed their own interpretation to this piece of information.

There was still no news when they repaired, at Grace's invitation, to her flat. From there Grace rang Luke and explained what was happening. 'Olivia's here,' she added, speaking from the privacy of the bedroom extension. 'Before you say anything, there's an awful lot we didn't know about. Please come, Luke. For my sake if not for hers.'

'All right,' he said after a long pause. 'I'll see you soon.'

She joined Ruth in the kitchen where she was putting together a makeshift buffet of cheese and biscuits and bread and salad. 'We need something to soak up the alcohol. I hope you don't mind.'

It had been four thirty when they left the Papermakers. Harry now informed them that the jury, still no nearer a decision, would have been sent home. He knew what having to wait through another night would mean to Grace but there was nothing he could do about it.

'Would you like me to stay?' Olivia asked when they brought in the food. 'Overnight, I mean.' She caught the relieved expression on Harry's face and realised how much he cared for her daughter.

'I'd love it.' Grace kissed Olivia's cheek.

'Then may I ring Monica and let her know?'

'Of course.'

Dean helped himself to bread and cheese and wondered what he was still doing there. He now had a strong whisky in his hand. Having driven back from the wine bar he saw that there were no parking restrictions on one side of the road outside Grace's building and had decided to leave the car there. It had been a strange day and he knew, if he stuck around, there would be lots to learn. For a start he was about to meet the brother.

It was half an hour before Luke arrived in a taxi. He had ordered it then fortified himself with several fingers of vodka, drunk neat. But he still trembled, unable to understand why he longed to see his mother when he hated her so much.

Olivia had been warned that he was on his way. Her face had paled but she said nothing, thinking that perhaps it was better that they met with others present. Don't let me cry again, she prayed, recalling the little boy of seven she had last seen.

When the buzzer sounded Grace pulled Olivia out of the room as she went to answer it. 'Not in there with the others.' She turned to the intercom. 'Come on up, Luke,' she said.

They waited in the hallway until he appeared at the door then Grace left them and rejoined her guests.

God, he's so like Gerald, Olivia thought. She pressed her lips together, but it was Luke who cried. He took one look at the mother whom he had been devoted to yet believed he had hated and tears ran down his face. Olivia held him tightly, her own tears ruining her make-up. There were still traces of the little boy she had last seen – but how very, very much like Gerald he was. She stroked his hair gently, aware that Grace had gone back into the lounge, closing the door to leave them alone. She could think of nothing at all to say and wondered if words were really necessary.

It was fifteen minutes before they joined the others, who were all too tactful to make any comment. Olivia had outlined everything to him and Luke was still in shock. But Grace was smiling, happy that they were finally together again.

'I must go,' Harry said, not wishing to outstay his welcome, especially now that Luke was there. The family needed some time alone together. He and Ruth would share a taxi.

Dean said he must also make a move. 'Will you ring me?' he asked Grace as he left.

'Yes. I've got your card.'

'Before I go back to London, I mean. I've already arranged to have a word with Harry about what we discussed earlier. I didn't let on what it was about, though.'

'Thank you. Of course I'll ring if you give me your parents' number.' He did so, scribbling it on the back of the card which Grace handed him.

'Take care of her,' were Harry's departing words to Olivia, which only confirmed what she had already guessed.

At last the three of them were left together. Olivia patted the cushion next to her on the settee, inviting Luke to sit down. 'I'll make us some proper supper,' Grace said, leaving Olivia to fill in the details for Luke.

Much later, when Luke had gone, Grace dragged herself to bed. Fatigue washed over her and she knew she would sleep. She could hear Olivia moving around in the next room. Feeling like a small child she hugged herself with happiness in the comfort of her mother's presence.

By the following lunchtime Grace was experiencing a strange sort of calmness, a lassitude that gave her limbs a peculiar fluidity. The limbo of waiting had taken on a sense of permanence. She and Olivia had realised it would be useless arriving at court too early because nothing would have happened during the first hour. They had not set off until ten thirty. At eleven fifteen Harry had joined them. 'Still nothing?' he asked.

Grace shook her head. 'Let's go home,' she said miserably to Olivia. 'I can't stand any more of this.'

It had started raining heavily. The pavements shone and tyres hissed as they made their way back to the flat in Grace's car. The sky was as dark as Grace's thoughts.

Neither woman felt like eating and there seemed little to talk about as they watched the minutes ticking slowly by. At four o'clock Harry telephoned.

'What's happening?' Grace asked, unable to keep the panic out of her voice.

'They've been given a further two hours. And no more.'

'At least we know it can't go on much longer,' she told Olivia who had taken away the tray which still contained uneaten sandwiches.

'I know, darling. We'll just have to be patient. Shall I make some tea or would you prefer a drink?'

'A drink. I don't care how early it is.' Several messages had been left on the answering machine during her absence that morning but she had ignored them. Later, when there was news, she would reply to the inquiries of Anton and Judith and Ruth. At the moment she would not be able to hold a rational conversation.

They sat on either side of the large window cradling their

drinks and gazing out at the darkening sky. Lights came on and a plane from the airport droned overhead. I wish I was on it, wherever it's going, Grace thought.

'Fly back with me at the weekend,' Olivia said, as if she had read her mind. 'We can easily arrange it.'

'I think I might like that. Thank you.'

Olivia nodded. It was unbearable seeing Grace so unhappy.

The phone rang again, startling them both. Grace bit her lip; her body felt like ice.

'Grace,' Harry said, 'the verdict. It's not one I foresaw. It's a hung jury.'

'What? What does that mean?'

'It means they were deadlocked, six for, six against. The Crown has the option to start a fresh trial with a new jury.'

'But they won't, will they?'

'No, it's highly unlikely. The case'll be discontinued.'

'Which means?'

'Which means Harrington will be acquitted.'

'I see. Thank you for letting me know.' Her knees buckled and she sank to the floor, still clutching the telephone receiver. Olivia was by her side at once and took the phone from her. 'Is that you, Harry?' She listened for several minutes. 'Yes. I see. Thank you for letting us know. Yes, she'll be fine. Hold on. Grace, Harry wants to know if he can come over. You speak to him.' Anything to distract her, Olivia thought.

'No! No, you can't come.'

'Grace, I –'

'No!' she shouted. 'Just leave me alone.' She replaced the receiver and stood motionless until she felt Olivia's hand on her shoulder.

'Oh, God, is there no end to this?' What would Harrington do to her daughter next?

Grace gripped the back of one of the settees until her strength returned. Dean O'Hearne was going to speak to Harry. If he could somehow convince him that Harrington was involved in her father's death, then he'd get an even longer sentence than he would have done if they'd found him guilty today. But she was clutching at straws.

Olivia was thoughtful. If only they still had Gorstone Manor. She could have taken Grace there and kept her protected.

186

Grace's flat was safe enough physically, but her daughter needed a change of scene, somewhere to spend some time rebuilding her life. If it hadn't been for the fact that the Cornells were known to be wealthy the whole thing would only have made a paragraph or two in the papers and Grace would have been able to forget it. Knowing the press, Olivia assumed they would now perform their own inquest on Grace's part in the affair. But there was also the worry that the man was mad, that he wouldn't stop now. Olivia knew she must persuade Grace to go back to Italy with her. She was sure Inspector Jordan would back her up on that. It was no use talking about a change of job and moving because Harrington, if he was determined enough, would find her. Better for Grace to remain where she was known and where people cared about her.

'A hotel. Why don't we go to a hotel? What do you think, Grace?'

'No. We'll go the farmhouse. I'll ring Judith to warn her.' And within days Judith would be gone, another chapter in Grace's life was to end.

'We? You want me to come with you?'

'Of course I do. Hey, you haven't rung Tony once that I know of. Won't he be worried?'

'No.' She smiled. 'He knows I'd have rung if anything was wrong. He'll have guessed I've got my little girl back. And Luke, too.' Luke had promised to ring that evening and had even mentioned taking his mother out for a meal. 'Look, I'll have to collect my things from Monica's. How about I do that while you get ready?'

Grace had nothing to pack, everything she required was already at the farmhouse, but an hour on her own would give her a chance to get her thoughts in order, to decide how to play her next move. And she could not go with Olivia. There was no way she could face Monica.

Ten minutes after Olivia had left in a taxi Harry arrived. Grace, too weak to argue, let him in.

'What do you want? I said not to come. It's all over, there's no need for you to be here. There's no need for you to see me any more.'

'I wanted to see for myself how you are. To make sure you're all right, which you obviously aren't.'

187

'I'm fine.' They were still standing in the hall. 'We're going to my place on the moors. Unless you're about to arrest me.'

'No, of course I'm not.'

He looks exhausted, Grace thought and for a second wished she could fall into his arms and they could both sleep for a week.

'When you've had some time to yourself may I see you again?'

'What for?'

'Because I'd like to.'

'I'll think about it. At the moment I've no idea what I want other than to get away.'

'You ought to take up your mother's offer. Go to Italy, have some fun.'

'I still have to come back.'

'Would you like me to drive you?'

'To Italy?'

'No, of course not. To Dartmoor. I can pick you up when you want to come back.'

She had no idea why he was being so attentive but it was a tempting offer. The thought of driving was not a pleasant one, although her mother would probably have offered. 'Thank you. It's very kind of you.' His expression was unreadable. 'You'd better come in and wait for Olivia. Do you want some coffee?'

'If you're having some. Why don't you allow me do it?'

Let him get on with it then, she thought. They were drinking it when she planted the first seeds. 'Harry, did you check Harrington's fingerprints against the ones found in my father's car?'

'No.' He was puzzled. 'Why on earth do you ask that?'

'Well, you know Dean O'Hearne wants to speak to you – he thinks – well, he has some information which might be relevant to my father's death.' She paused. Was it too soon to voice Dean's suspicions? 'He says Harrington was in Exeter at the time.'

'What?'

'Well, think about it. Harrington already knew me then and he seems to know everything about me now. Dean claims Harrington knew my father and that he spoke disparagingly about him. Anyway, you can ask him about that yourself.'

Harry swallowed some coffee. It had not occurred to him, or anyone else for that matter, that there could be any connection between the two cases as far as Harrington was concerned. Not once had it been suggested that he knew any of the Cornells other than Grace through university.

Olivia's arrival put an end to his immediate thoughts. Grace told her that Harry had offered them a lift. She looked from one to the other, gave a small nod of approval and went to fetch Grace's coat. 'Come on, then. Let's get going.'

Harry knew the route out of Exeter and Grace had made the farmhouse sound easy to find, but once they were on the winding narrow roads he lost his way several times. When he craned his neck in order to reverse a second time he swore in exasperation. He could even see the house, or at least the chimney, there was no other dwelling for miles, but there seemed no way of reaching it. Once Grace had given her instructions the journey had been conducted in silence because she had closed her eyes and he and Olivia hoped she was sleeping.

'Turn right and take the first track to the left,' Grace said, woken by his swearing. 'You seem to be lost.'

Eventually Harry pulled up on the soggy grass outside the farmhouse. Even the sheltered parts of the moors were clear of snow now and a lush green was beginning to appear beneath last year's dead growth. He heard an underground stream, still running fast with its added burden of melted snow.

He approached the front door hoping that Grace had remembered to bring the key with her, although he recalled there was a local girl who came in who must be in possession of a spare one. In the event he need not have worried. The door was flung open before he reached it.

'Is she all right?' Judith came out to the car where Olivia was helping Grace out. She flung her arms around her employer and squeezed her. 'I had to be sure you was all right,' she said. 'Now why don't you all sits down and I'll make some tea.'

Grace was used to Judith's Devon way of muddling verb endings. Usually they made her smile. 'No thanks, Judith. We're awash with liquid. Unless Harry wants some.'

He didn't and said he would start making his way back.

Olivia realised how loyal Grace's friends were and how much they had replaced the family she should have had. Only in retrospect had she seen how little real caring there had been on Gerald's side. Oh, there had been laughter and fun and sex and she had loved him with every part of her and without question, but there had always been too many people around for them to interact in such a personal, caring manner as Grace and the people she knew did. Perhaps it hadn't all been honey, after all, she decided as Harry said his goodbyes. 'I'll let you know how it goes with O'Hearne. Can I ring you?'

No one apart from Luke and Matthew had had the farmhouse telephone number but she had given it to Harry during the week before the trial hoping that she would not regret her decision.

'There's a letter for you, Grace.' Judith handed her a thin envelope which she took from the pocket of her duffle coat. 'It was on the mat when I came in.'

Grace took it. A half smile formed on her lips. It was from Harvey in America. She did not open it but placed it carefully in her own pocket, smoothing it as she did so, surprised that he had written again so soon.

'Grace? Are you sure you'll be all right?' Harry was still on the doorstep.

Judith studied the group. Of the three, she only knew Grace. But the elegant woman in the tan leather trenchcoat could only be her mother.

'Grace, did you hear me?'

'For heaven's sake, Harry, of course I'm all right.' She had been thinking that as well as a trip to Italy, she might follow it up with one to America . . .

'I'm off too,' Judith said, wrapping a scarf around her head against the rain.

'Do you need a lift?'

She stared at the tall, gangling man with the broken nose. He was nice even if he wasn't much to look at. 'No thanks. I walked today. It's the first time I've been able to cut across the field for months. It's not far.'

'Please don't rush off,' Olivia urged.

'I must. I've got to see to my daughter and I've still got some packing to do. My husband can't wait for me to join him. Grace, I'm really sorry about what happened. At least that man doesn't know about this place. Anyway, Mrs Tucker's daughter'll come and do for you if you want her. I already asked.'

'Oh, Judith, you don't know how much I'll miss you and Zoe.'

'Me too.' Judith turned away. The last thing Grace needed was to see her in tears. 'I'll write. And mind you do too.'

'Thanks for everything.'

Harry and Olivia were watching Grace's face, each of them wondering how much more she could take.

'Does she need a doctor?' Olivia whispered.

'She is a doctor,' Harry commented drily, 'but no, I don't think so. Rest is what she needs.'

'I wish you two would stop talking about me as if I wasn't here.'

'I'm sorry. Well, I'll leave you to it. Are you sure about that lift, Judith? It's no trouble.'

The rain was now lashing against the windows. Judith looked at it and changed her mind. 'Go on, then. Thanks.'

'And thank you,' Olivia said to Harry as she showed them out. Did Grace know how the man felt about her? Olivia did not think so. Nor would she ever tell her, it was up to her to discover it for herself. If she wanted to.

'Grace, I think you ought to go straight to bed.'

'I'm not tired.'

'You're right, you're not tired, you're exhausted. Harry was right, you need rest, lots of it. There's to be no more discussion about this today.' Quite firmly she took Grace's arm and led her from the room. 'Come on, show me where the bathroom is. I'll run you a bath and then it's bed. No arguments.'

Grace smiled wanly, feeling like a child again. Somehow she would survive, but she was, as everyone had pointed out, on the verge of collapse. What luxury it was having Olivia take charge.

Olivia, not certain of her daughter's mental state, did not close the bathroom door fully. In what was obviously Grace's bedroom she found a nightdress. What a lovely room, she thought. The window was in the eaves and looked out over miles of unbroken countryside. In daylight the view must be spectacular. No wonder she had chosen such a place to get away from it all. Many people would have picked Laura Ashley designs and over-prettified the place but Grace's tastes were nearer to what the original owner would have been able to afford. The bed was ancient and must have been constructed *in situ* because there wasn't a door or window large enough to have allowed it entry, and the bend in the stairs would have prohibited it anyway. There was no duvet here. Spread over the sheets and blankets was a handmade patchwork quilt. Olivia wondered if it was Judith's handiwork. Instead of a wardrobe there was a small walk-in cupboard and an oak pedestal desk served as a dressing-table.

The second bedroom was smaller and contained a single bed which was almost all there was room for. Then there was the bathroom. Once the whole of the first floor had been a storage area. Over the years conversions and adaptations had taken place, the addition of the bathroom being the main one because of the work involved in piping the water from the nearest mains.

Olivia switched on the electric blanket, pleased to note that some modern inventions were deemed important. They had not eaten all day but sleep must come first for Grace. She heard the water running down the drainpipe and allowed enough time for Grace to have wrapped herself in a towel before knocking and handing her the nightdress she had found in a drawer. 'Everything okay?'

'Yes.' Grace followed her mother to her bedroom and waited while the sheets were pulled down. She got into bed and pulled the bedclothes up around her neck.

Olivia bent and kissed her gently on the cheek. 'Sleep well, my darling.'

Downstairs she took stock of the rest of the place, allowing her mind to dwell only upon trivial matters: the contents of the fridge and the freezer, where the tea and coffee were kept and where the light switches were. Practical things were all she could help Grace with at the moment but tomorrow she would decide if other help was needed.

Half an hour later, exhausted herself, she crept upstairs as quietly as she could to check on Grace. Very gently, hoping it wouldn't creak, she pushed open the bedroom door. Grace was sound asleep. Her eyelids fluttered slightly but her breathing was regular. Sighing with relief Olivia closed the door and went back down, closing the sitting-room door behind her. She reached for the telephone and rang Tony in Milan. She gave him only the barest of details and said not to ring back in case the phone woke Grace. He offered to fly over immediately, a suggestion to which Olivia agreed readily, surprising herself by realising just how much she needed his support and constancy at that moment. Then Olivia went to bed herself.

The following morning, before Grace was awake, she made another call, this time to Anton at the surgery. His voice, even after many years, was so familar she was shaken. How quickly the time had rolled by since she had last seen him. But the slightly pompous manner was still in evidence. Olivia recalled how often he was mistaken for being rude because of the abrupt pattern of his speech. As she had been put through to him immediately, Olivia guessed that Anton was more than curious as to why she was ringing.

'Good God, woman, where did you spring from?' were his opening words.

'Didn't Grace tell you?'

'Grace? That you were back? No.'

So she wasn't sure if she wanted to see me, Olivia realised. 'You're in the middle of surgery, I take it?'

'I am, but carry on. Mr Halford won't mind waiting a minute, I'm sure.'

Olivia could picture the sweet smile Anton would turn on for his patient's benefit thus allowing him no chance to complain. 'I won't keep you then. I thought you ought to know the verdict. A hung jury, It's very unlikely there'll be a retrial so it looks as though Harrington will be aquitted. I didn't think it would have made last night's paper.'

'I know. We heard it on the local news. We can't believe it either.'

'Grace is worried about her job, Anton. She's got this crazy idea that if Harrington's innocent, then she's guilty.'

'What rot. I thought Grace knew us better than to believe we'd ask her to leave. We've coped without her before and we're doing so now. Tell her to take a couple more days off.'

'Thank you, Anton. Actually, I was going to ask you a favour. I'd like her to come back to Italy with me for a while. Can you spare her for as long as a week?'

Anton sighed deeply. 'I suppose so. But this whole thing bothers me. If Harrington is acquitted he'll keep his job. I don't know what that'll do to Grace. I suppose we could find a way around it. Leave it to me. Look, I must go, Olivia. It was good to hear from you.' There was only the slightest hesitation before he added, 'If you've time, come and have a drink with us.'

'I don't have time, Anton. We're at the farmhouse and I hope to persuade Grace to fly back with us tomorrow or the next day. Thank you anyway.' Olivia replaced the receiver. One obstacle was out of the way, now all she had to do was to convince Grace. Thank goodness Tony was on his way. He would be in Exeter by that evening and with them in the morning. I should have found him somewhere to stay, she thought belatedly. It was doubtful Grace would welcome him into her home. Still, Tony was a seasoned traveller, he'd find his way around. Apart from which he knew Devon well from their early days.

At ten she made a breakfast of fresh orange juice, boiled eggs and toast. Knocking on the bedroom door she nudged it open with her knee. Grace was still asleep, her hair spread over the pillow and half concealing her face. Olivia bent to kiss her and Grace opened her eyes and smiled. The smile faded as the memory of the verdict resurfaced. There was still a long way to go. It was far from over yet.

HARRY

Although he had tried to prepare Grace for the possibility of an acquittal it was a shock when it came in the form of a hung jury. It was such an unsatisfactory end to a trial. Bad enough in any case but worse for Grace because she might never be free of the man. She hadn't been far wrong in her estimate of what people would believe. If the jury couldn't decide whether or not Harrington had lied, the reverse was also true; they did not know if Grace had lied. He tried not to worry about her as he joined the A30 and headed back towards Exeter.

Coming off at the roundabout at Alphington Spur and merging with the traffic flowing into the city, he wondered if he would ever see Grace again.

At least she and her brother had been reunited with Olivia. And how alike she and Grace were. If the old adage about looking at the mother to see the daughter was true then Grace would retain her beauty. But how would Luke come out of it all? He seemed to have no direction in life and no trace of ambition. Harry was aware that he had lower expectations of the human race than most people. This was due to the job, to witnessing so much of the shitty side of life and rarely the decent. The worst aspects of man's character no longer surprised him.

Where to now? he thought. What is there left for me? He could take the car home, find a pub and drink to forget, except he was wise enough to know that that was only a temporary solution. He could go home. And do what? Watch television? Read the paper? Or he could go into the station. But now this case was over he didn't want to be there either.

'I can't go on like this,' he said aloud in desperation. If his mind wasn't occupied he would start replaying the trial. But there was the possibility that Harrington had a part in Gerald's death. It was yet another problem. He acknowledged wryly that anything to do with Grace was his problem because he had made it so. 'Jesus.' He slammed the palm of his hand against the steering wheel. He couldn't be in love with her. There was no future in that idea. Even now, with all that had happened, Grace appeared not to need anyone. Glad of her mother's support she might be, but she certainly had no need of Harry Jordan. It was a long time since he had seen his own mother. It was the perfect remedy. A good deed done in the form of a dutiful visit and a dose of his father's vitriol would set him straight. As soon as he was able he turned the car around and headed back in the opposite direction. With gritted teeth he prepared himself for what lay ahead.

He no longer kept a key to the house and had to knock. As his mother let him in he recoiled at the familiar smell of the place: his father's socks and his mother's flowery perfume. Mrs Jordan managed a quick smile and said she would make tea. Harry opened the living-room door, where, predictably, his father sat reading a paper whilst the television talked to itself in the corner. In deference to the weather he wore a sleeveless knitted jumper over his grubby shirt and trousers.

'The prodigal son,' he sneered without looking up. 'I suppose you've come to brag. We saw you quoted in the paper the other day. Win the case single-handed, did you?'

'No. It was a hung jury.'

'Lost the case? Wonder boy fails, eh?' The thought seemed to delight him. 'So you've come home to grovel to your mother instead.'

'I don't grovel to anyone. Unlike you.'

'What the hell do you mean by that?' Frank Jordan was on his feet.

'You and your bosses.'

'I've never grovelled in my life, son, not like you with those snot-nosed teachers at school. And I bet you're half-way up the arse of the man above you now. How else could you have become an inspector?'

'It doesn't work like that, and you know it. You just resent the fact that I've used my brains, passed exams and worked bloody hard to get where I am.'

'You make me sick. You think you're better than me, that I haven't worked hard, too. You're a snob, that's what you are, ashamed of me because I work with my hands. And think about it, you must've got your so-called brains from somewhere.'

'Yes. From my mother, the woman who's always been superior

to you in every way. Your wife, you bastard, who you treat so very badly.'

Frank took a step forward, his face red, his fist raised.

'No!' Celia Jordan stood in the doorway with two mugs of tea in her hand. Her eyes widened when she saw her son's fist draw back ready to retaliate. Her husband was in a half crouch, elbows raised, both fists ready now.

'Shut up. Leave this to me. It's your fault, you spoiled him.'

Before his father could move, Harry struck him. The blow sent him reeling back into the settee, overturning an ashtray on his way. 'I've wanted to do that for years, you snivelling coward. And I should've done for the way you've treated my mother alone.'

Frank Jordan was wiping blood from his lip. 'She's a woman, they need handling. That was your trouble, son, you'd have kept Gill if you knew how to handle her.'

'Gill found someone else. She's the guilty party, not me. I'm sick of you and your bloody self-righteousness. For someone who's so completely self-absorbed you have no self-awareness whatsoever. Forget the tea, Mum, I'm off. If you want to see me, you know where I am. But him,' he pointed a finger at his father, 'he'll never be welcome.'

'You won't set foot in my house again either, I can tell you that much,' his father shouted at his back as Harry thrust his way to the door.

He stopped, looked hard at his father and said, 'Do you know, that's the best news I've heard in years.' He slammed the door behind him, no longer bitter, but cleansed, although sad that his mother was in tears and would probably have to pay the price of his outburst. It was useless agonising. His mother could have left at any time. She had sisters to whom she could turn and even alone she could hardly be any worse off.

It wasn't his father who had angered him so much as the verdict. Deep down he had suspected how the visit might end but he had not planned it that way. He had, he realised, used his father quite literally as a punch-bag.

He didn't want Grace to go to Italy, he didn't want her out of his sight. That was impossible, of course, and there was no way in which anyone could keep a constant watch over her, not that she would have allowed it. The irony of the situation struck him.

If Grace went back to the surgery, what would happen about Harrington? He was not employed by the practice – would they have any say in who came to collect the samples or would Grace have to face him every day? Harry guessed that the trial would not deter the man. He had no ties, perhaps he would cut his losses and leave. But what if it was Grace who left? What about the gaping hole she would leave in his life? The old routine of work and drinking no longer seemed so appealing. He would not allow himself to sink that low again.

His house was as unwelcoming as ever. He poured a beer and sat by the phone in the kitchen willing himself not to ring the farmhouse to inquire after Grace.

He was tired himself, tired to the point where his nerves jangled when his own telephone rang. It was a colleague from work asking if he fancied an evening out. Harry told him he didn't.

After a makeshift meal there seemed nothing to do other than to go to bed and hope that he could finally shake off his cold and that his dreams did not centre around Grace.

GRACE

She had no idea how long she had been asleep except that light now showed through the curtains and it had been early evening when they had arrived at the farmhouse. Grace sat up and brushed her hair out of her eyes. 'It's quarter past ten,' she said with surprise when she looked at the bedside clock.

'I know, but you needed the rest and you look a lot better today,' Olivia said, placing the tray on the bed. 'I thought a boiled egg was light enough on an empty stomach. We can eat properly later.'

'Thank you.' Grace reached for the orange juice. 'I could stay here for ever and forget the rest of the world exists.'

'That's impossible, my darling. You'll have to make some sort of plans. I hope you don't think it presumptuous, but I've spoken to Anton. He said to take a week off. He also said he was going to think what he could do about that man.' Like Grace, Olivia hated speaking his name.

They ate in silence and Olivia took away the tray. Grace got out of bed slowly. She felt as if she was convalescent after a long illness; stronger, but not yet ready for the real world. She showered and dressed and went downstairs, only noticing in full daylight how tired Olivia looked.

'Come and sit down. Can I get you something? More coffee?'

Grace smiled. It was lovely to feel so spoiled. 'No, I'm fine, thanks.'

'I didn't know whether to light the fire. I'm warm enough, but I wasn't sure if you would be.'

'No. Don't bother.' Grace walked to the window unaware of Olivia's narrowed eyes on her bony hips. She's too thin, her mother was thinking.

Outside the sun shone over the moors where the hills cast their large purple shadows. The sheep were clearly visible against the brownness of dead bracken beneath which early new growth sprouted green. Grace turned to her mother. 'Do you think I'm mad?' She asked quietly.

'Good heavens, no. Of course you're not.'

Olivia's eyes were as large and dark as Grace's. They softened as she smiled. How beautiful she is, Grace thought, taking in the narrow-legged checked trousers, the silk shirt and matching jacket. Her ear-rings were gold shells with a pearl in the centre and a gold clasp held back her hair.

'Surely you've talked to Ruth? She'll have confirmed there's nothing whatsoever wrong with your mind.'

'I'm not sure she believes that. She told me we can do all sorts of things then block them out if they make us ashamed or frightened.'

'But you haven't done anything, darling. Grace, you mustn't torture yourself. Why don't you ring her? I'm sure you'll feel better.'

'No. She'll be seeing clients.' Grace turned back to study the view.

'Is there anything you'd like to do today? A walk, maybe? Or would you rather rest?'

'I think a long walk would do me good.' She paused. 'Would you mind if I went alone?'

'Not in the least. I've been outside, the wind's cold, but you'll soon warm up. I'd forgotten how quickly the weather changes here. You'd never imagine it was pouring down yesterday.'

Grace went to get her coat. 'I'll be about an hour, maybe longer.'

'Well, while you're out I'd like you to decide about Italy. I spoke to Tony and he's flying over. He should arrive sometime later today. We'd both like you to come back to Milan with us tomorrow. Tony will hire a car and collect us or we can get a taxi if you don't want him here. Please, think about it, Grace?'

'I will.' She leant forward and kissed the top of her mother's head.

Olivia grabbed her hand and swallowed back tears. 'I still can't believe this. I still can't believe we're together again.' But neither of them mentioned the fact that it was Gerald, adored husband, worshipped father, who had turned out to be a liar and a cheat and had kept them apart.

'What about flight seats? No, don't tell me.' Oliva's embarrassed smile answered for her. They were already booked. To someone in Tony's secure financial position the cancellation fee would not have mattered. 'See you soon.'

Grateful for the coldness of the wind in her face, Grace strode out over the moors. In places the ground was boggy beneath her feet but her stout boots, into which she had tucked her jeans, kept her dry. At one point, when she could no longer see the farmhouse, she stopped to look around. The road was hidden in a hollow and she might have been alone in the world. I have enough money, she thought, I could come and live here and have no need to work. Then what would all my training have been for? And how long before I missed my job and my colleagues? First things first. Milan. Yes, she decided, because at least for a week she could forget everything. Feeling more settled she returned to the farmhouse.

'Was that in the freezer?' Grace asked, open-mouthed, when she saw the chocolate confection on the kitchen table.

'No. I made it. You used to love them.'

'But you don't eat sweet things.'

'It's for you.'

Grace always remembered what a bad cook Olivia had been and how glad she was to leave things to Mrs Collins. But baking cakes was a different matter. And the mincemeat, Grace recalled. How could she have forgotten all the good things? 'Can I have a piece?'

She ate two slices, which pleased Olivia. 'I shall put on the weight I've lost in no time. It's delicious.' Have we regressed? Grace asked herself. Are we trying to relive the years we did have together? She smiled. 'I have thought about it and, yes, I would like to come to Milan.'

'Oh, that's wonderful.' Olivia, leaning against the sink as she watched Grace eating, came across and hugged her. 'What about clothes? Will you need to go back to Exeter?'

'Yes. I dress like a farm worker out here. I'd better let Ruth know or she'll be calling the police again.'

It was not much of an attempt at humour, but it was a start, Olivia thought as Grace went to the telephone.

'Where's Tony staying?'

'I've no idea. He'll find somewhere.'

'Why didn't you invite him here?'

'I wasn't sure he'd be welcome. And, besides, I didn't want to share you until I had to.'

For the rest of the day they talked. Grace explained all that had gone wrong with Matthew and the misunderstanding about the letters. It was almost perfect, except for the things which Grace knew and Olivia didn't, things which could never be said.

They ate steaks and salad and opened a bottle of wine as the wind grew stronger and rattled the back door. Grace made coffee and they took it through to the lounge and drank it with brandy. 'What's Angelina like?'

'Fearsome. She's one of those women whose bum seems to stem from their ankles and she wears a permanent scowl. She has a wonderful mole on her chin complete with sprouting hair, just like her armpits, a sight to which we are treated in the summer. However, on the minus side . . .' They both laughed. Grace was shocked at the sound of her own voice. How long is it since I last laughed? she thought.

'What should I do about Luke?' Olivia asked. 'Do you think there's any chance of him coming too?'

Grace doubted it. 'Ring him anyway. He's finding it very hard to forgive you even now he knows the truth. He doesn't want to be hurt again.'

'I won't hurt him, Grace.'

'I know that, but he doesn't yet. Go on, use the phone.' Grace left the room and when Olivia came to find her she was smiling.

'He prevaricated but he more or less promised he'd come out in the spring. I think it'll be better that way, he won't be over-awed by you. He always has been, you know. Now, what's happened to Tony? I thought he'd have rung by now.'

Ten minutes later he did so and the arrangements for the trip were concluded, but the moment Grace had been dreading arrived. Olivia wanted to know about the night Gerald died.

Calmly and quietly, Grace told her, but there were things she left out, had to leave out . . .

OLIVIA

She isn't going to tell me, Olivia thought, her eyes fixed on her daughter's face. I had so hoped she would, there are so many things I would like to know. But Grace surprised her by beginning to speak.

'He received a telephone call and told me he had to go out but that he wouldn't be long. By then I'd realised that he was seeing someone, a woman, that is. Like you, I'd read the signs, he didn't actually say so, but there was no other explanation for the way he was behaving. I wanted to know who she was, why she never came to Gorstone. I'm ashamed to admit, I often thought of following him but I couldn't bring myself to do it. Anyway, I assumed he was meeting this person that night.'

Olivia sighed. 'I wish you'd found out who it was, Grace. I've always wanted to know the name of the woman who held such power over Gerald – well, over all of us really.'

'I know, but we'll never know now. Perhaps it's best that way.'

Why won't she look at me? Olivia wondered. Is she protecting me? Does she know but thinks I couldn't bear to hear the truth? I can, because it doesn't matter now, not now I know what Gerald was and what he did to all of us. 'Go on,' she prompted as Grace stared at the window, not seeing anything.

'He left and I carried on studying. Luke was with Maggie, in the flat. Dad rang me on his mobile. He said he had some trouble with the car and could I go and collect him because on such a night and out on the moors it would be hours before the AA reached him. He'd decided to go back for it in the morning.

'I saw the car and pulled in behind it. I wasn't sure he'd be alone, I thought he might have already picked up whoever he was meeting. Oh, God. He looked so smug, sitting there, knowing I would do his bidding. I was angry, angrier than I'd ever been before. I challenged him, don't ask me why I chose that moment but it just felt right, the two of us on neutral ground and him at a disadvantage.' Grace inhaled deeply and shook her head in disbelief. 'We had a row, a terrible one. I accused him of all sorts. He said I was hysterical. Maybe I was. I couldn't stop. It all poured out. He hit me, not very hard but enough to shock me out of it. He was angry now and I was frightened. He kept walking towards me saying his life was his own. I started running. He came after me. I was crying, the tears stung my face because it was so cold. I just kept running. He called my name several times. He was running too. I was gasping for breath, I had to stop. I looked back but I couldn't see him. The next thing I recall is being in someone's car and then being in hospital.'

'So what do you think happened to him? Grace?' Olivia lifted Grace's chin with her finger. 'You can tell me, none of it matters now.'

'I think he slipped. I think he fell and hit his head. It's the only explanation. I left him there, you see. I didn't go back. I didn't go back because I didn't want to. I wanted to punish him but I honestly didn't imagine he'd die. When he started shouting I should've just got back in my car and driven off and made him wait for the rescue services. By the time I realised that it was too late.'

Olivia closed her eyes. She could picture the scene clearly, the deserted moors, covered in snow, no sane person out on such a night, Gerald getting out of the car to welcome his daughter. And Grace? Grace finding him, full of hate, already having guessed a little of the harm he had done.

'I had to tell you. I had to tell someone the truth.'

'He must've slipped into a ditch and hit his head. You know how the place is littered with boulders, darling. You mustn't blame yourself, not if you were scared.' Olivia felt sick. Grace must have been living in hell since that night. She got up and went to her and held her tightly. Never had she seen such anguish in anyone's face. 'It's all right, really it is. You think I'll hate you now, but I don't. How could I now that I know how he kept us apart?'

'I lied to the police. How could I explain what I had done? They would never have believed me. I just wanted to know who he was going to meet and that was what caused the row. Everything else I told them was the truth.'

'The post-mortem showed he died of hypothermia. I never did understand why the police made such a thing of it.'

'I was there. I'd seen him. Both our cars were there. I'm found in a state on the main road. It's easy to see why they were suspicious. You can't imagine how I felt afterwards. I was training to become a doctor and I left my own father to die.'

'Harry Jordan told me you could have died too. When that couple found you wandering around on the main road you were close to hypothermia yourself.'

'I think at the time I was crazy. My phone battery was dead. I know that was careless. He insisted we had them if we were out at night but I doubt if I'd have thought of using it anyway.

'It was such a bad time, but not as bad as when you left, when he told us that you didn't love us.'

Olivia bit her lip. She must not cry now. 'What would you have done if he hadn't died? What would you have done afterwards? Would you have challenged him another time?'

'That's something I'll never know.'

How odd that I can understand her, Olivia thought, that I feel neither shock nor disgust. My daughter has just admitted she was partly responsible for Gerald's death yet I don't love her any the less for it. She's been carrying this around with her for eight years and then all this Harrington business. She's paid the price, that's for certain. 'I expect you wondered why I didn't come over for the funeral. It wasn't that I couldn't face it, or any criticism that would be thrown my way. I simply felt that you and Luke would not want me there intruding on your grief. Maybe if I had done . . .' But it was too late now for regrets. The future was more important than the past. 'The main thing is the police believed you and, don't forget, if he hadn't frightened you he might still be alive.'

Her guilt was so ingrained the idea had never occurred to Grace. But was what she had done worse than her father's actions, were her own justified? Her mother believed that they were.

Olivia could now guess what it was that Grace would never tell her. The woman Gerald had been seeing throughout their marriage and afterwards was someone she knew. 'You've been through enough, Grace. Let's go to bed now. No one else will ever know what you've told me, you have my word on that.'

Olivia lay awake for a long time. How sordid life was. What

an absolute fool she had been not to have seen what Grace had worked out. Gerald had been playing close to home. The woman involved was possibly one of her old friends. She thought of them each in turn but could not recall one suspicious incident or a conversation ending abruptly when she entered a room. But for Luke's sake, she, like Grace, would not bring it out into the open.

GRACE

The following morning Tony arrived in a large comfortable-looking car. Grace opened the door to him, feeling a little nervous of the man she had maligned silently for so many years.

'Grace, you've grown as beautiful as your mother.' He grinned, then, as he held her lightly by the shoulders, he dropped a kiss on her head and it all felt so natural.

Grace smiled back. She had forgotten how much she had liked the man, how much a part of the family he had once been. Although only fourteen when she had last seen him she would have recognised him instantly. His faced was more lined, the short cropped hair more grizzled, and he had gained about a stone in weight but it was the same Tony who had always reminded her of his namesake, Tony Bennett.

'Unquestionably your mother's daughter and, oh dear, that same stubborn chin.'

'Oh, Tony, come on in,' Grace said, taking him by the arm. He was so easy to be with, unlike Gerald who had made life exciting but never comfortable. Once it would have been anathema to have compared her father unfavourably to another man. She watched the interaction between Olivia and Tony. Tony walked towards her, holding out both his hands. I understand what the expression feasting your eyes on someone means, Grace thought, because there was no other way in which to describe how he was looking at her mother. Olivia smiled and kissed him as she took his hands in hers. With a deep sadness, Grace turned away. She had never felt that way about anybody, not even Matt, and even if Olivia didn't recognise the fact, she loved Tony.

Throughout the drive, by way of many small gestures, Tony demonstrated how much he thought of his wife. Was my father as caring? she tried to recall. No. He made her laugh a lot, but that's different. There was one occasion when Olivia had had an urgent letter to send. Their postman, who was happy to carry away the odd bit of mail for them, had already been and gone. Gerald was going into Exeter and Olivia had asked him to post it for her. 'I'm a bit pushed for time, my darling, and you know what I'm like, I'll probably forget to do it.' Olivia had had to get out her own car and drive to the village. Tony, she thought, would have gone out of his way to make sure it was mailed.

'I had forgotten how wonderful the scenery is,' Tony commented over his shoulder. 'Especially on a day like this.' The sky was a deep blue arc framing the dramatic countryside.

'I never forget,' Olivia said with a smile.

They were not stopping in Exeter after all. Tony had suggested she went on a shopping spree in Milan – he and her mother would foot the bill. 'To make up for all the lost birthdays and Christmases,' he insisted. He knew that Olivia's gifts to her children had always been returned unopened until she finally stopped sending them, but he had not realised that Grace and Luke did not know any had ever been sent.

Grace was not ready to accept such a generous offer but the idea appealed. She would use her own money. Fortunately her passport had been at the farmhouse to which she had returned from her last foreign trip.

The drive up the motorway was monotonous and little conversation took place. The hum of the tyres and the soft purr of the engine were hypnotic and Grace dozed on the back seat. They reached Heathrow with plenty of time to spare. Tony handed over the keys at the desk of the car rental firm and they checked in without a hitch. They had a drink in the bar before they went through to the departure lounge where Olivia said she'd like another. Tony smiled. 'She still hates flying. Shall we all have another?'

Arriving in Milan Grace barely had time to take stock of her surroundings before being whisked to the apartment where a delicious meal was waiting. Olivia had telephoned to warn Angelina they were having company. When they had eaten, Grace sank into one of the comfortable sofas and began to relax as she listened to her mother and Tony catch up on each other's news. For a few hours she was truly happy.

The next three days passed in a blur of shops and restaurants and noise and traffic. But she was enjoying herself. Both past and future were temporarily on hold as she was introduced to their friends and acquaintances, all of whom commented upon Grace's likeness to her mother.

They went to museums and galleries, and friends invited them for drinks. Grace realised just how popular the couple were and felt proud to be in their company. Tony had taken some time off but conducted a few bits of business over the telephone, insisting that he chaperone them everywhere, apart from a couple of occasions when Olivia insisted she wanted to be alone with Grace. There were no more confessions, no reliving the past, everything that had needed saying had been said. They simply enjoyed one another's company, drawing closer to each other all the time.

On the last evening Olivia excused herself from the table in the restaurant in which they were dining because she had seen a friend across the room and had a message to relay to her.

'Grace, have you forgiven your mother?' Tony asked quietly. It was the first time they had been alone, the first opportunity he had had to speak to her on a more personal level.

'Yes. I think, deep down, I forgave her a long time ago. It was just that I believed she didn't want anything more to do with us.'

Tony nodded. 'She told me. I've never been so angry in my life. You'll never know how hard she tried to contact you. Gerald kept writing to say you both hated her. She was so very hurt, Grace.'

'Did you know who the woman was? The one responsible for the break-up of my parents' marriage?'

'No. I always thought I should have been able to guess. I knew you all so well, your family and your friends. To give Gerald his due, he was extremely discreet. He didn't boast about it or make any reference whatsoever to the fact he was seeing someone else. In fact, until your mother explained the situation I had no idea. Do you know who it was? Your mother has always been curious. He never moved anyone in with him, did he?'

'I . . .' Olivia was returning to the table. Grace swallowed, grateful that she had not had a chance to continue. She had been dangerously close to confiding in Tony.

'I know you haven't got much time left,' Olivia said, as if their previous conversation had not been interrupted, 'but Tony and I have been discussing the future. We're in total agreement that if you're worried about Harrington, or even if you aren't, we'd like you to come and live with us. We have masses of room, we wouldn't be in each other's way. I'm not sure how you'd go about working here, though.'

Grace had enough Italian to scrape by with on holiday but not enough to be able to practise as a doctor. But it was another demonstration of Tony's love for her mother that he was prepared to have her daughter under his own roof. There was also Harvey's suggestion to consider. If she was to change direction in her career, now would be the time to do it. 'I love working with Anton but until I know what'll happen with Harrington I'm not making any decisions. If he stays in the area then I'll certainly have to leave it. I promise I'll give it some thought.' It was a tempting idea but one which Grace knew would never work. She was too used to her independence for it to be possible. But she would spend her leave in Italy, probably every moment of it.

The following afternoon Grace packed her bags. A second had been purchased to contain her beautiful new Italian clothes. It was a cold, wet day and the weather reflected her mood, but there would be other visits, lots of them. Life would be almost perfect if it wasn't for the fear which she couldn't shake off.

The week had gone so quickly that Grace could hardly believe they were already back at the airport. They had coffee and rolls which were eaten almost in silence because the parting would be painful. The last call for Grace's flight was announced over the tannoy. There were tearful embraces then Grace, with one last look over her shoulder, made her way to the departure lounge where she had to board immediately.

There was a lot to consider during the flight home: not least, the question of how she was going to deal with Lance Harrington. It had become clear to her that she would have to meet him, that somehow or other she must put things right herself.

MONICA

The blackbird tilted its head, left then right, to ensure it was alone before stamping on the wet grass to bring the worms to the surface. Its one visible eye was bright with expectancy as its beak sank into the soil. Monica leaned her forehead against the cool window pane and watched it, guessing that the bird was as pleased as herself that the lawn was visible once more. No matter what the weather, tomorrow she would play a round of golf and thereby get herself out of the house. Luke had told her that Grace was in Italy. All she could think of were the conversations which might be taking place.

Olivia had spent only the one night under her roof but there had been nothing strained in the way in which she had explained she wanted to stay with Grace. On the other hand she had not been in touch again before her departure.

Monica decided to invite Luke for dinner. Although she saw him infrequently the tell-tale signs of too much drink had not gone unobserved. She would insist that he stayed the night. There was so much unsaid and a lot which must remain that way within the Cornell family, but Monica needed Luke as an intermediary between herself and Grace. It was the quickest way in which to learn if the whole truth had come out. Of course, if Luke refused the invitation she would know at once.

The robin had not put in an appearance. 'Fickle friend,' Monica muttered, realising that now the thaw was complete the bird would be able to seek its own food more easily and no longer needed her daily ministrations.

'Did I get you up?' Monica asked when Luke finally answered the phone. It was after ten.

'Sort of. But I was about to surface.'

'Would you like to come over for dinner tonight? It would give me pleasure to see you again.' It was emotional blackmail but it worked. Monica had done much for Luke during his schooldays, she had tried to take the place of his mother and he

211

had seemed to appreciate it. A little something in return was deserved. To put it crudely, she thought, you owe me.

'Of course I'll come. I didn't have anything planned anyway.'

Does he know he's so thoughtless? she asked herself as she went to the kitchen to study recipe books. She shrugged. Perhaps he's just more honest than most, she conceded.

The menu planned, she put on her coat and picked up the car keys. It would be exciting to shop for someone other than herself. Her dietary preferences were plain but tonight there would be a sauce with the meat and she would buy some handmade chocolates to go with the coffee. And a good strong Cheddar and some squidgy Brie. That boy always did love cheese, she reminded herself.

Having made her purchases she returned to prepare the meal, laying the table well in advance. She was pleased with the effect. Her bone china crockery was white, edged with a thin silver band, and the glasses were crystal. The linen was spotless and the only splash of colour came from the fruit bowl which she placed in the centre. Flowers, she thought, just get in the way. After a bath she dressed in a softly flowing suit with a matching silk vest and dabbed her wrists with a small amount of the perfume she had used since she was in her twenties. Entertaining a man, even though he was her nephew, and dressing for dinner made her feel younger and more feminine. She poured a gin and tonic knowing that Luke would have had a head start.

He arrived on time, having, she noticed with pleasure, made an effort with his own appearance. He had bought wine and flowers and he was completely sober, for which she thanked him silently. As she stood on her toes to receive his kiss she smelled only toothpaste and aftershave. 'It's good to see you again, Luke. I've missed you.' She squeezed his hand. It was true and she felt ashamed that she planned to use him. He had been as close to a son as was possible for a childless woman to have, but she needed to know what Grace might have told Olivia.

'I'm glad someone has.'

'Drink?'

'Please.'

'Beer, or would you prefer one of my specials?'

212

'The latter. Definitely.'

So that's the lie of the land, Monica thought, assuming he was making reference to his mother. He's suffering from a bout of self-pity.

'Ah, a woman after my own heart.'

'What?' She stared at the tall glass of Bloody Mary in her hand.

'You're doing it properly, with a dash of dry sherry.'

'I'm a great believer in doing things properly.' She added tabasco and a celery stick and handed him the glass.

'Do I detect a touch of auntly criticism?'

Monica smiled and swept her pale hair behind her ears, impatient to introduce Olivia into the conversation. 'Just a soupçon. Seriously, though, Luke, I did want to talk to you. You've seen your mother now. Can't you forgive her?'

'I'm not certain I can, it's been such a long time. But I'd like to get to know her again. She doesn't seem to have changed much.' He sat down and crossed his legs, one foot swinging. He had always been restless, unable to sit without fidgeting.

'Why not? Why can't you let go of the past?' Monica took the armchair on the opposite side of the grate. 'People make mistakes, people have their own lives to lead and they do things which might seem cruel but which are, in fact, the very opposite.'

'My mother was being kind in leaving us?'

'I didn't mean it literally. But you have to understand she had her reasons. Very good reasons.'

'I see. So why has no one, especially her, until recently, that is, ever bothered to enlighten me?'

'Because, Luke, hard as it may seem, they are none of your damn business.' Monica bit her lip. 'Forgive me, I could have phrased that better.'

Luke grinned. 'Nothing like a bit of straight talking. I think there hasn't been enough of it over the years. Do you know, I often wish we could have been a normal family.'

'You've been watching too many documentaries. Don't classify us as a dysfunctional family. You look closely enough at any family and you'll find they're all the same underneath no matter what sort of front they put on for the outside world.' Not strictly true, she amended silently, at least, not in my case.

'Do you believe that?'

'Most sincerely.'

'So, Aunt Monica, what's my problem?'

'You want the truth?' She studied his face, unsure if this insecure nephew could face it.

'Try me.'

'Well, you're lazy. I know you've got money but you need a purpose in life, something to get up for each day.'

'What do you get up for?'

'Point taken, Luke, but we're not talking about me. Unfortunately my mother brought me up to believe that marriage was the only career for a woman. Even in her time she was extremely old-fashioned in that respect. I was unprepared for anything. However, she taught me organisational skills and many ways in which I could pass the time which equipped me well as an army wife, and I'm never bored. I have plenty of hobbies. I think you're bored, Luke. Am I right?'

'Yes. But what do I do about it? If you ask me, I should say I'm unemployable.'

Monica hid a smile as she got up to pour more drinks. 'At least you don't deceive yourself. We'll eat as soon as we've had these. I've got some rather good wine to go with the meal. Now, I can't see you working for anyone else. You're of age, the money's yours to do with as you like. Why don't you set yourself up in business?'

'Doing what?'

'I don't know. I can't work out your life for you. It was just an idea.'

'What if I fail? I'll be worse off than I am now and I'd have to get a job.'

'That's another of your faults. You're scared. You were scared to make real friends as a child, you're scared to commit yourself to a girlfriend now and scared of failure in almost every respect of your life. No doubt you blame all this on your mother and maybe you're partially right but not completely. Some people become stronger in the same situation.' She paused, about to cite Grace as an example, but saw that this would have been a terrible mistake. Luke idolised his sister but he was also in awe of her and, in a way, he was jealous of her strengths. 'You see, you've allowed the situation to control the rest of your life.

214

I should've said all this to you years ago but you were such a sad little boy at times. I suppose Olivia coming back has brought this on. Stop me if I'm preaching.'

'No, there's nothing I like more than hearing someone talking about me.' It was said with wry humour.

'Well, there're choices you can make. You can carry on as you are but I think you'll end up very unhappy, or you can simply try to forget the past. Wipe it out of your mind, pretend it happened to someone else.' She sighed. 'None of it was really Olivia's fault, you see. She was driven to it in the end.'

'Do you know why, Monica? I've grown up with the feeling that everyone in the family has secrets they won't share with me.'

Monica swallowed. Did he mean Grace? If so, that really was something to worry about. 'No, what happened belongs in the past, my past, not yours. It is something I prefer not to think about. Now, you sit there and consider my lecture about your future and I'll see to the food.'

She hoped she hadn't gone too far. It was a long time since she had seen Luke and she did not want to antagonise him. She also hoped he hadn't noticed that when she blew her nose it was to disguise the tears which had threatened. As he shifted position and lifted his head it might have been Gerald who sat there, who had sat in that same chair on so many occasions when it had been beside the large fireplace in the lodge.

'I hope you're hungry,' Monica said, returning to the lounge with a puzzled frown. She had not realised just how much food she had cooked. 'Shall we start? You can do the honours with the wine.' Luke followed her to the dining-room.

The evening was a success after all and Luke slept in one of the spare bedrooms. After he had gone up, Monica loaded the dishwasher and went up, too, suddenly feeling rather old and tired. She had been close to telling him – not the whole truth, that was impossible, but as near to it as she could get. For so many years she had wanted to get it off her chest, but it was, as she had said, her past and none of his business, and she would have lost him for ever by doing so. But did Grace really know? Had she already told Olivia? If so, then all was lost anyway.

As she undressed she thought again of the row between Gerald and Freddie. Mostly she assumed it was about the

215

amount of time she spent at Gorstone, but now with Olivia's return she began to wonder if Freddie, who had always taken Olivia's side, had tried to persuade Gerald to allow his wife to have access to her children. One thing was certain, it was not over the thing which haunted her and yet which had given her so much happiness. Even Freddie would not have stood for that.

HARRY

It was Ruth who telephoned Harry to let him know that Grace had gone to Italy with Olivia. He wondered why Grace had not rung him herself but hoped it was simply because she had left in a hurry.

By the time he knew he had already spoken to Dean O'Hearne who told him he had met Harrington, by chance, in a pub, around the night of Gerald Cornell's death. Harry was now going to speak to Harrington, to discover just what he had been doing in the area at that particular time. He hoped he would be able to control his temper. The man had been acquitted but he had almost ruined Grace. No one was aware of Harry's feelings for her; had they been, he would not have been the one sent to speak to Harrington. But he would not go without the company of another officer.

Harrington was alone. He looked haggard when he opened the door and sighed when he saw who his visitors were. 'I thought I'd heard the end of it,' he said. 'You'd better both come in.'

Inspector Jordan and a young detective constable stepped into the shabby house. There was evidence of female occupancy: a hairbrush on the settee, a blouse over the back of a chair.

Lance noticed the direction of Harry's glance. 'She's left me. Anna, that is. I'll never understand women. She stood by me throughout the trial then buggered off once I was acquitted. Still,' he shrugged, 'I can't really blame her, mud sticks, doesn't it? Do you want to sit down? Is this going to be a long visit?'

Still so calm and rational, Harry was thinking, as if he's done nothing wrong.

'Some tea? I believe that's the usual form.'

'No, we're fine, thanks. There's something we want to clear up, something unconnected with the recent trial.'

'Fire away.' Lance sat on the hard-backed chair draped with the blouse. He had given up his courier's job and had not been expecting anyone, but even so his clothes were clean and smart and he had shaved that morning.

'Did you ever meet Dr Cornell's father?'

'I thought you said this was nothing to do with her.'

'With the trial, I said. Did you?'

'No. I knew of him, of course. I'd heard he was charismatic and very rich and that no one could understand why his wife had run off.'

'You never visited the house?'

'No. I was never invited to.'

Harry felt no need to control his temper; he wasn't angry. He did not know exactly what he felt. He would analyse it later. 'So what were you doing in and around Exeter at the time Gerald Cornell died?'

'I was supposed to be meeting Grace. It was during the Christmas vacation and I'd got a room in a small hotel. She had arranged to meet me there. She never showed up. I was furious. She was always doing things like that. I went to the pub instead and got quietly pissed.'

'Can you recall the name of the hotel?'

Lance could. 'I hung around a bit the next morning in case she rang again, then I went back to Southampton. It wasn't long after that that I dropped out of university.'

'Did you meet anyone that night?'

Lance frowned and rubbed his forehead. 'Yes. There was someone. Can't remember his name now. We were in this pub and it was really quiet. The weather, I suppose. I don't know what we talked about, nothing much. He had ginger hair, that's as much as I can recall.'

'Might you have said that you hated Gerald Cornell?'

Lance smiled. 'It's very likely. I'd been looking forward to spending the night with Grace. I thought it might have been his fault she hadn't turned up.'

'After you left Southampton, how did you come to be working at the same hospital as Dr Cornell?'

'Come off it, we've been through all this at the trial. We kept in touch. When she fancied it we met. It was an extremely one-sided relationship. But you've seen her, I couldn't resist when she rang up. She told me there was a job going there, the path lab were looking for an assistant technician. A grand but meaningless title considering the work I was allowed to be involved with. Like she said, we hardly set eyes on each other at work. She felt sorry for me, I suppose, she said it was such a waste and that I reminded her of her brother. And before you ask, I never met him either.'

All Harrington said had the ring of truth. Both he and Grace had confirmed that his collecting from the surgery was pure coincidence, that Harrington had not known where Grace was working when he applied for the job as courier. 'I didn't make it as a doctor,' he had said at the trial, 'but I still wanted to work in or around medicine.'

'But why Exeter?' he had been asked.

'I like the area and I was born in Devon.'

'What did you think when Grace didn't turn up and then you learned her father had died?' Harry felt sick with dread at what might follow.

'I didn't know what to think. She often mentions that night, she can't shake off the guilt, you see. She feels she could have saved him somehow.'

'Could she have done?'

Lance got up and walked to the window, his hands in his pockets. There was nothing to see but a row of parked cars and a patchy blue sky overhead. 'I've no idea. She's a bit of a drama queen, our Grace. Look, she wanted some attention, I gave it to her. I've no idea why you want to hear all this again, but I'll answer your questions once more then I shall ask you to leave. If I ever see or hear of you again after today I shall file a complaint of harassment. I arranged the hotel booking. At the time she seemed very keen on me but there were occasions when she stood me up or got in touch at the last minute to say she couldn't make it. That night was one of them. To this day I've no idea why she didn't show up.

'Anyway, she arrived back at Southampton after everyone else but we'd all heard about her father. She didn't show it, not outwardly, but she needed a shoulder to cry on – figuratively, that is, she never shed a tear. I believed the relationship was on again, which just shows how naive I was. She dumped me again. As I said, soon after that I left. My decision was nothing to do with Grace.'

Oh, God, Harry thought, swallowing down bile. I believe him.

I'm glad he was acquitted. Grace is either paranoid or playing some horrible game with him.

'And if you want to know why she did it, why she wanted me to stand trial, then I've no idea. I've never knowingly done anything to harm that woman. She was too good for me, I knew that, but when she called, I went running. Not any more though, you can take that for definite.

'And those letters, they were meant to incriminate me in some way. Why, Inspector? Why would a woman go to those lengths? All she had to do was not contact me or tell me she didn't want to see me any more. I wouldn't have made a fuss, I never imagined it would last so long anyway.

'I'd like you to go now, please. I've got to pick up the pieces of my life again. I can't stay here, not now. No matter what the verdict was the fact that I stood trial for such a crime makes me guilty in many people's eyes.'

'Thank you for your time, Mr Harrington. You won't be hearing from us again.'

Lance nodded and watched as they walked to the door. Anna was coming back for the rest of her things in two days' time. He had paid the rent until three weeks after that date and then he would move. He didn't know where just yet, but it did not matter, as long as he could put as much distance as possible between himself and Grace Cornell.

Back at the station Harry sat at his desk with such a grim expression on his face no one made any attempt to speak to him.

Why? he kept asking himself. Face to face with Harrington, on his own ground rather than in a court of law, Harry had recognised the truth. But what had Grace possibly to gain from it? Had she planned it all in order to draw attention to Harrington, to incriminate him in her father's death via another crime? How much easier to have simply said at the time that the man was in the area. No, there was something missing, there was some reason she wanted him locked up and considered to be unstable. Which meant he was some sort of danger to her. Maybe she thought he knew more than he did, maybe she wanted revenge for some unintended slight. He had seen Gill in action and knew how vindictive women could be, what lengths they would go to for the sake of revenge.

The best thing I can do is to put Grace Cornell out of my mind, he decided as he picked up the phone. They would check Harrington's account of what had happened. It was possible he was lying, it was even possible he had been in the car with Grace that fatal night. Now, almost anything seemed possible.

Later that afternoon he wondered why the Cornells all acted as if they had something to hide and why there was such a deep rift between Grace and Monica. Both women had once been unusually close to Gerald, there might be some relevance. He picked up the phone and dialled Monica's number, unsure what to say because the questions he wanted to ask were not official and might cause offence.

'Inspector Jordan, how nice to speak to you again,' she said unexpectedly. 'I hope nothing's wrong.'

'No. Just a couple of points I wanted to clear up.'

'Well, if it's convenient why don't you come now? We can have some tea.'

It was only the second time he had called on Monica but he was made to feel welcome. In a casual two-piece over a Viyella shirt she was very much the lady of the house as she let him in. She smiled as she opened the door and said how pleased she was to see him again as he followed her into the lounge.

'Tea first, handcuffs later?' she asked with an amused smile.

'Thank you. I'd love some.'

'I've laid a tray, I won't be a minute.'

When she left the room Harry looked around, taking in the few but expensive ornaments and the photographs of Grace and Luke which stood in frames above the fireplace. Grace was about eighteen when the most recent one had been taken. Her hair was loose and she was smiling but even in the photograph he saw the wariness in her eyes as if she had never really been carefree. He picked it up and studied it.

'It's rather a good one, isn't it?' Monica said, pushing the door closed with her elbow as she carried in the tray.

Harry hastily replaced the frame but Monica appeared unconcerned that he was handling her things.

The ritual of pouring the tea over with, they both sat down. 'Have you heard from Grace?' Harry asked.

'No, but there's no reason why I should have done so. She's only away for a week. Is something the matter?' Monica placed

221

her cup and saucer on the tray. Her hand shook a little. Harry Jordan obviously had no idea that she and Grace had had no contact for some time.

'No. I just wondered how she was.'

'Ah, so this isn't a professional visit.'

'I'm not on duty, if that's what you mean. Mrs Andrews, this Harrington character, did Grace ever mention him to you?'

'No. And I'm sure I would have remembered had she done so.' Monica sat back and leant her head against the sofa cushion, her eyes half closed. 'The past. It always comes back to haunt us, doesn't it?' There was silence for several minutes as she studied her guest. By no means a handsome man, she thought, and rather ungainly. He was well spoken and intelligent and, she guessed, dogged. He would not rest until he knew their family business, until he had dug up all the dirt and displayed it before the world. Could she, could any of them survive another onslaught from the press? And what would it do to the tenuous relationship re-established between Olivia and her daughter?

And yet this man loves Grace, she thought. Monica blinked, unsure how, after only two meetings, she could be so certain of this. 'Do you have skeletons in your family cupboard, Inspector?'

When Harry grinned the contours of his quirky face softened. 'More than most, I suspect.'

'Really? Would you care to tell me about them?' The grin faded as she had known it would. 'Just testing. You see, we Cornells have had a basinful of it over the years. Our old bones are dragged out with monotonous regularity and subjected to scrutiny. It is not a pleasant experience. It's all down to Gerald's death, of course. Inexplicable as it was I really don't think there was that much of a mystery surrounding it. He went out to meet someone; knowing Gerald, probably a woman. He should never have left Gorstone on a night like that and Grace should've had the sense not to follow but to call out the emergency services. However, she idolised her father. The roads out there weren't gritted and the temperature that night was well below freezing; all too easy to slip over in those conditions. You see, Inspector, it's like reading a thriller, people aren't happy unless there's a resolution, no one wants to finish a book and find there are loose ends. But that's the way life is.

'I know what's concerning you. You believe that Lance Harrington knows something about that night. There are probably thousands of others out there who think they can work out what happened if they took the numerous press suggestions seriously. He got his information from the newspapers, it's as simple as that. The man's an obsessive, he's already proved that by his recent behaviour. He just can't let go of his connection with the family, however minor it is.'

Harry did not explain that Lance Harrington was not making any claims about that period of Grace's life, other than that he had been seeing her at university.

'May I ask you something? Why this interest in us, as a family? I hope I cause no offence when I say I suspect it's because you have unresolved problems yourself, that it's your way of avoiding them.'

'Mrs Andrews, my private life is not up for discussion.'

'No? I can't see why not. Mine seems to be. You've admitted you're not on duty, you're here as my guest. You see, Inspector, money and unwarranted notoriety have deprived us of any sort of private life. There is nothing to discover, you're wasting your time if you think otherwise. Now, court my niece by all means, but please leave history alone.'

Harry's deep laughter took her by surprise. 'Mrs Andrews, I can see where Grace gets it from. She doesn't beat about the bush either. I think I'd better go now. Thank you for the tea.' He stood up, towering over Monica who remained seated until she remembered her manners as a hostess and went to show him out.

At the door she hesitated before speaking her mind again. 'Matthew wasn't right for Grace. I never met him but I gather from Luke that although he was a good man and he loved her, he was weak. He'd have hurt her at some point, did hurt her, in fact. I'd hate that to happen to her again.'

'Point taken, Mrs Andrews, but I don't play games.'

She nodded and closed the door on a chilly but sunny afternoon. 'No,' she said as she went to fetch the tea tray, 'I don't imagine you do play games but I wonder if you have any fun at all?'

Washing the delicate china in the sink she found it odd to

realise that she did care if Grace got hurt. Perhaps it was because Grace was Gerald's daughter as much as Luke was his son.

Harry got into his car and swung it around in the wide driveway of the house. Was he, as Mrs Andrews had suggested, clinging on to this case because his own life was such a mess? Or was it merely an excuse for keeping in touch with Grace? The old emptiness had returned but it was not Gill he missed now. Yes, he thought, I probably do love Grace. But something either in himself or within Grace prevented him from following it up. Instinct told him that she would only ever be one step ahead of trouble and he had had enough of that. It was best to forget her.

There was a message on his answering machine. It was the news he had been waiting for. The small hotel where Harrington claimed he had stayed had dug out the old registration forms and the handwritten invoices they had used before becoming computerised. A double room had been booked in his name and he had paid in advance in cash. The place was run by a family, a man and his wife and their married daughter who came in to help in the kitchen on a daily basis. They had been there for thirteen years. Harry thanked whatever gods there might be for people like the Blakes who kept records long after they might legally have been destroyed. It now looked as if Harrington was telling the truth.

GRACE

Two days after her arrival home, Grace returned to work. Through the slatted oatmeal blinds of the surgery window she saw the spikes of daffodil buds and the tiny shoots on the forsythia hedge which would flower before the leaves unfurled. The bitter winter was at an end but she shivered. Anton had told her that Lance Harrington had left his job of his own accord. She frowned and reached for her coffee cup. He might be leaving the area, might have done so already. How foolish she was to have waited. She ought to have telephoned him immediately upon her return.

Anton Roach had taken her into his room before morning surgery. He needed to convince himself that she was one hundred per cent fit before she resumed her responsibilities. 'I can't risk you collapsing within a week, Grace, you do understand that, don't you?'

'Anton, you've been marvellous throughout all this. I promise you I won't let you down again.'

'Good. Then go to it, woman.'

Grace did, more glad than she would have thought possible to be back at work. Being reunited with her mother filled her with joy but it had left her drained emotionally. Knowing she could not contact Lance from the surgery she got through the day by paying extra attention to what her patients were saying. At last she was free to go home.

The flowers in the corridor at the flats now consisted of narcissi and hyacinths and filled the air with a sickly, funereal scent. It was overpowering. Grace let herself in, took off her shoes and picked up the phone.

Half an hour later, satisfied with the way the conversation had gone, she was gratefully sipping a glass of wine when the telephone rang. It was Harry Jordan.

'May I come over?'

'I'm exhausted, Harry, I'd rather –'

'It's important.'

'All right, if you must.' Good news or bad, Grace no longer cared. She was sure nothing could surprise her now.

Harry arrived empty-handed. No wine, no nothing. He did not intend to outstay his welcome. 'Grace, Lance Harrington had nothing whatsoever to do with your father's death. Why are you trying to persecute him?'

'What?' She was laughing.

'I think you know what I mean, Grace.'

She sank into her chair and gestured for Harry to sit too. A chill wave of panic ran down her spine. Had Harry spoken to Lance ahead of her? 'He's the one who was persecuting me.'

'The jury didn't think so.' She was so beautiful he wished he could forget all he knew and start afresh.

'Yes, but as you pointed out, the law isn't about justice.'

'Grace, what is it that drives you? What is this all about?'

'My God! How much more do you need from me? Isn't it enough that he got away with it?'

'Or you did.'

Please, God, no more, she thought as she got to her feet. But her legs wouldn't hold her. She swayed and clutched at the side of the armchair.

Harry jumped up and grabbed her arm. 'Are you ill?' She shook her head. 'Have you got any brandy?'

'I think so.'

'Where is it? You're white as a sheet.'

She told him and waited until the glass was in her hand before speaking again. 'I don't know why you're here, Harry. You've done your bit, the case is closed. I think it would be best if you left now.'

He nodded. How odd that she had almost echoed Harrington's words. Harry Jordan was being dismissed. He walked slowly to the door and let himself out. Grace did not move from her chair, nor did she look at him. He wasn't worth a backward glance.

The lock of the door clicked automatically behind him and Grace reached for the brandy bottle. Once, it had all seemed so simple but now there were no longer any certainties. There had to be a way out of this. But she wasn't going to run, not any longer. She had to face Lance and put things straight. Only then would she be able to face the future.

226

MONICA

She had always enjoyed the company of those younger than herself but company of any description had been rare for several years. Now that Luke was more of a regular visitor Monica realised how close to cutting herself off from human contact she had been. She felt happier and there was the added bonus that Luke was trying to sort out his life. Although his petulance still surfaced occasionally he had started to talk about his future. When he telephoned to say that Grace was home and looking much better, she invited him over for dinner later in the week.

Luke still enjoyed a drink, more than was good for him if she was honest, Monica admitted, but if he did, as he had mentioned he might, go and see Olivia at Easter, he might find a little peace. It seemed, as nothing had been said, that she had been wrong about how much Grace had known.

On the morning of the Thursday that Luke was coming she started to write some personal letters but soon abandoned the task as her mind kept reverting to the time of Gerald's death. All those years ago she had half believed that Grace had had something to do with it. It had even crossed her mind that Freddie might have been involved. He had not been at home that evening, although that was not unusual. Especially if they knew, she thought.

The pen to her lips, Monica stood framed by the open doors leading to the garden, which was flooded with sunlight. For the first week in February it was unbelievably mild. Dew still sparkled on the grass but it was early in the day yet. It wouldn't be long before the man who came in once a week to do any heavy work would get the mower out and give the lawn its initial spring trim: 'Just the top off it the first time, I'll lower the blades next mowing,' he would explain year after year. There was nothing more evocative than the smell of freshly cut grass. It made her nostalgic, although for what she did not know.

She had made a list of jobs to occupy her. There was too much

227

to do to stand around daydreaming. Upstairs she pulled down the ladder leading to the loft. Here was stored the usual accumulation of old furniture, clothes, books and papers which Monica imagined everyone kept. Learning of Luke's possible interest in the restaurant business she had decided to clear out the attic and see if there were any papers of Freddie's which might be of any use to him. The past was finally that. Any reminders of it could go, she thought as she carefully ascended the wooden steps, the hem of her skirt in her hand. I might even sell this place and buy somewhere smaller. I might even become the woman everyone thinks I am.

In one corner was the box containing Freddie's paperwork. There were paying-in books, old cheque stubs and invoices. Below them were sets of the restaurants' accounts and a record of staff wages, all of which she had cleared from the room he used as his office a month or so after the funeral. The room had been redecorated and turned into a small sitting-room but Monica rarely used it. Freddie had been a meticulous man and had encouraged Monica to keep written records. She carried the box downstairs and began sorting the contents into piles to check them thoroughly. If she overlooked anything of importance it would be too late once she had lit the bonfire.

She was surprised to find a copy of Freddie's will amongst his things because she could not recall seeing it in his desk. It had not been required after his death because the original was with their solicitors who were also his executors and he had never altered it since the day it was drawn up soon after their marriage. Everything went to Monica, regardless of whether or not they had children. It must have been slipped between the old invoices at some point. Out of curiosity she decided to read it. She had forgotten the exact wording. Monica withdrew the folded sheet of paper from its buff A4 envelope, puzzled when a second, smaller envelope fell to the floor. The writing caused a peculiar sensation in her stomach. It was Freddie's and the letter was addressed to her. Putting the will to one side she slit open the envelope with her nail and pulled out three pages covered in his bold hand. As always he had written with a fountain pen.

'My dearest Monica,' it began.

228

I will no longer be around by the time you read this but I want you to know that I have never loved any woman apart from you. You have made me happier than I can express in mere words despite what I have always suspected and now know for certain. You, I can forgive because I always knew that you loved me in your own way, but not Gerald.

Monica put down the letter. One hand was at her throat, clutching her blouse as if it was a lifeline. Freddie knew? It was incomprehensible. Why had he never said anything? She was shaking, afraid to read on, but did so when she had regained her composure. There was more about his feelings for her which made her wish she had been a better wife. No, she thought, I was a good wife, I was the perfect army wife, at least for a while until I got too homesick, and I always ensured his comfort came before mine. Meals were well cooked and served on time and there were always clean clothes. The house and garden had been kept immaculate over the years, admittedly with outside help, and she had never denied him sex. She had loved him but not in the way in which he deserved. Only in one respect had she failed him but she had always believed that he would never find out. How long had he known? How many years had he suffered? Frustratingly, there was no date on the letter.

And then the final paragraph. It filled her with horror and revulsion until she realised that to a man like Freddie it was the only course of action. He had been to see Gerald and had it out with him.

So that was what the row was about. At least I know, she thought, but what on earth do I do about it? But something wasn't quite right. If Freddie had known how could he have kept it to himself, how could he possibly have lived under the same roof as her? Impossible to think straight until she had digested what she had read. Whatever happened she must not let Luke see that anything was the matter. Oh, poor, dear Freddie, she thought. I never meant you to suffer, I never meant to hurt you.

Monica put the letter in her handbag and snapped it shut, then she turned her attention to the papers on the dining-room table, her hands trembling only a little as she continued sorting them into heaps.

By the time Luke arrived for dinner there was only a small pile of documents for him to read. Everything else except for Freddie's letter had been burned and she had showered away the bonfire smuts. With a glass of sherry inside her she was ready to face her nephew.

I was meant to read it as soon as he died, she realised later. Freddie would have assumed I'd check the copy of the will immediately. But there had been no reason to do so. She had already known what was in it.

'How do you feel about it, Luke?' Monica asked as soon as she had handed him a drink. 'Do you think you could make a go of it? It would be nice to think of someone following in Freddie's footsteps. You were almost like a son to him anyway. And, selfish as it sounds, it would please me to see you involved in such a venture.'

Luke shrugged and brushed back his hair in the way which was so familiar to Monica. She held her breath. 'I think, with your help, it's not beyond the bounds of possibility that I could become a restaurateur.' He grinned and Monica hugged him. 'I'd like you to come with me to look at properties, and I'll need help in choosing staff. Would you mind?'

'I'd love to.' Mind? she thought. Little does he know it'll give me something to do. Perhaps I should simply have taken over from Freddie. It was the least he deserved.

'Luke, have you given any more thought to the matter of visiting your mother?' It would be another step in the right direction towards making a man of her nephew.

'Let's put it like this. I've booked a flight and we'll take it from there.'

'Tony's a good, decent man. Don't allow your feelings for your father to influence what you feel for him.'

Luke's hair flopped forwards as he sat, hands between his knees. 'My feelings for my father are no longer what they were. I had no idea what he'd done to us, and to Olivia. I just wish I'd known sooner her reasons for leaving.'

'You know?' Monica trembled.

'Yes. Grace told me. Another woman. One he'd been seeing for years and refused to give up. But he must've been an evil man to stop us from seeing our mother, to tell us she didn't love us any more. He was your brother, Monica, did you think he was evil?'

'Totally selfish rather than evil.'

'I'm sorry. Let's forget it. You were right, the past no longer matters. And something smells good.'

'Let's hope it tastes as good.'

But she hardly tasted the food. Freddie's letter was still much on her mind.

Over dinner they discussed Luke's future. She gave herself credit for his growing enthusiasm when he said he would make an appointment with one of the advisers at his bank to discuss how to set up a business.

In the privacy of her bedroom she reread the letter for the third time. It explained the severing of the relationship between Freddie and Gerald to which no one had ever referred and which marked the beginning of the end for them all in a way.

'Oh, my God.' Monica laughed aloud, then put her hands up to her mouth in case Luke heard her and thought her mad. She had misread the letter. Freddie didn't know, he only thought he did. 'You, I can forgive, because I always knew that you loved me in your own way, but not Gerald for his part in it,' he had written. His part in it. He had absolved her of her infidelity but he could not forgive Gerald for 'allowing you to meet him at the manor'. Freddie had thought Gerald had permitted Monica to bring her lover to Gorstone where they conducted their affair.

Now both men were dead and she, like the rest of the family, must try and put the past behind her. She would not have been able to do so had she believed that Freddie knew the whole truth.

LANCE

Lance was waiting at the end of the towpath of the River Exe. Head Weir was to his right, St David's Station to his left but out of sight beyond the trees. It was Sunday morning and Grace was late. He wondered if she would come. Despite the biting wind children poked sticks in the water and walkers were out with their dogs.

'Yes. But this is the very last time, Grace. No matter what you do or say from now on I never want to see you again,' Lance had told her when she telephoned.

Lance had received a response to an application form he had posted off. Next week he was to be interviewed for a job as laboratory assistant in a hospital in Plymouth. Yes, he was going to remain in Devon, not because of Grace but because it was where he wanted to be and he would not, as he had initially imagined, allow her to drive him away. He had had no idea she would get in touch again but sensed that she wanted to offer an explanation for her behaviour. And I'm too curious to have said no, he realised.

He turned and saw her in the distance, hands in her deep pockets, head down against the wind, her lovely hair flying about her face. He felt only a small surge of regret that he would never set eyes on her again. She had, after all, attempted to get him sent to prison.

'You're late.'

'I'm sorry.' She stood beside him as they both stared at the fast-flowing water. It raced over the weir, rainbows of colour catching in the foamy spray.

'What do you want, Grace? Have you thought up some new way to torment me?'

She did not raise her head. 'What'll you do, Lance, now that you've left your job?'

'I have another one.' Not quite true, at least not yet, but he would find something if this one fell through. 'I'm leaving Exeter soon.'

'Why did you blackmail me over all those years?'

'What? My God, Grace, I'm not joining in another of your

stupid and dangerous little games. Have I ever asked you for a penny?'

'I don't mean financially.'

'Then how?' Already he wished he had refused to see her.

'You know perfectly well how. But you don't know what a misery it's made of my life.'

'You're fucking crazy, you do know that, don't you?'

Grace turned to face him. She was white, her own face pinched. In his she saw the truth, that he had no idea what she was talking about. He was right, she was insane. But she had to continue, she had to make sure. 'But you knew about the night that my father died. I told you.' She had been drunk, very drunk, her only reaction to his death after she returned to university. Already she had decided against seeing Lance again, which was why she did not turn up at the hotel. But that night she had been desperate and when he had walked into the students' union she had already had too much to drink. Back in his room she had admitted that she killed her own father.

'Not that old chestnut. Can't you forget it?'

'No, I can't. How would you feel in my position?'

'I'll tell you how I'd feel, I'd feel sorry my father was dead, sorry he'd had an accident of his own making, but I'd also feel at least I'd gone when he telephoned for help. What happened afterwards was not your fault. There was nothing you could've done, Grace, and you nearly got yourself killed for it. Oh, I know, you and your guilt trip. I think you wanted to believe you were responsible, it would be a bit of excitement in your rather dull life. Yes, Grace, despite your glamorous lifestyle you were rather dull, you know. Nothing but work where you were concerned. Okay, it got you where you are today but you're still dull, do you know that? Well, you must do, to have fucked me around the way you have. Enjoy it, did you? Your fifteen minutes of fame in court? What if they'd convicted me? What then? Something else for you to feel guilty about, I suppose. And you've got the nerve to say I was blackmailing you.

'That time you came back, after the funeral, and I took you out, that was the only time I ever saw you out of control. You had too much to drink but I took you back to my room and there you were, the drama queen, sobbing into my pillow and saying you'd killed him. You were far too together, far too interested in

233

making a career for yourself to have done it. Were you trying to impress me or something?'

She did not answer because she couldn't. She had made that confession just as he'd said and for eight years she had thought he believed her. 'But you said . . .'

'I know what I said, that it was our secret, that I'd never tell a soul as long as you kept on seeing me.'

'I have done so. I kept my part of the bargain.'

'Grace, you're sick, it was hardly more than a joke, the sort of thing people say when they're young. I imagined myself in love with you back then. It was lust, it's always been lust. You've used me, but I always knew you were doing so and I can't deny I enjoyed screwing you now and again over the years.'

'But you've never been far away, I thought . . .'

'You thought I was obsessed with you. It was the other way around. Did you really imagine you were the only one over the years, that I lived only for the odd occasion when I could see you? Grow up, Grace. Don't forget, it was you who helped me get a job in the lab of the hospital where you worked. Was that to keep an eye on me or did you just like having me around? Or maybe it just made you feel superior. Come on, tell me, why did you do it, why did you go to the police with that ridiculous story?'

'I don't know.' She was rigid, unable to believe what she was hearing. 'Why did you say those other things? Those jokes about patricide? And that time you called me your little murderess?' She had believed them to be reminders of his power over her.

'I thought you enjoyed it. You certainly seemed to. I was humouring you, okay? You can't blame me for taking you up on your offers. Girlfriends or not, there's nothing like a bit of illicit sex with a good-looking woman.

'Look, Grace, there's no point in going on with this conversation. You find someone else to lay your guilt trip on. If you want to carry on believing you're some sort of notorious femme fatale, then go ahead. I'm sick to death of you to be honest so, if you'll excuse me, I'm off.

'You,' he added, looking back over his shoulder, 'don't have it in you to murder anyone. It's people's feelings you kill.' As he strode along the side of the water he wondered why she looked so ill. But he was free of her. It was time to move on.

GRACE

Grace couldn't move. Mesmerised by the weir she wondered whether to throw herself into it and be done with everything. *All those years I thought he believed me. I was drunk, I didn't know how much I'd told him. And I was young, too,* she admitted. *Young enough to believe I was the only person who mattered to Lance, that he really meant it about keeping the secret as long as I still saw him. I've been safe all the time. I need not have done any of it.*

But she had known she had to act, to get the world on her side by making Lance appear dangerous. On one occasion he had spoken of that night again, had made some crack about turning her in and asking for a reward. 'Shall I call the police?' he had asked. 'Maybe you'd enjoy being handcuffed.' She had laughed, but she had thought he meant it. She had not seen that he was doing what he thought she expected of him. She really believed the past had caught up with her. Guilt and fear had been her companions for so long they had made her irrational. Paranoid, she admitted. If Lance had really been blackmailing her he would have insisted they lived together, or even married. And she, Dr Grace Cornell, had been driven to imagine that Carl Roberts, an innocent blind man, had been Lance in diguise when all they had in common was their build.

So she had asked him to call at the surgery at a time when she knew no one would be there. She had planned the scene knowing that Ruth would contact Harry when she didn't show up, she had antagonised Lance beyond endurance, taunting him about the past and his failure as a medical student until he had lunged at her and she had tripped and fallen. It had been an accident although she still wasn't sure if he really would have hurt her. But if the police were convinced that he had stalked her then tried to abduct her, no one would take him seriously if he turned around and said she'd told him she'd killed her father. But the guilt was there because, in a way, by not going back, she had. And then Dean O'Hearne had come along and placed

235

Harrington in the area at the relevant time. For a while Grace had hoped that Harrington *was* responsible for Gerald's death because then she would be free of him and her own guilt might evaporate.

Ironical that she had made her decision never to see him again just at that time. Grace had not been totally sure of her feelings. She had liked him a lot, enough to sleep with him, and he had made her laugh, but it wasn't quite enough. There had always been something missing. Now she realised it had been missing on his side, too.

She sat on the grass, uncaring that it was slightly damp. There was so much to think about, not least of which was the way she had behaved towards Lance and the events which had culminated in her father's death.

By that time Monica and Freddie had moved to Exeter. Grace had inadvertently picked up one of the extensions at the same time as her father. There had been no mistaking the voice on the other end. About to hang up she had heard Gerald say, 'Ah, my darling, I was hoping you'd ring. Is Freddie out?'

'Yes. Shall we meet?'

'Of course. The usual place. I've missed you.'

'Me, too. See you soon.'

Grace had never discovered where they did meet. Obviously not at the lodge when she and Freddie lived there and not at the Exeter house. And it certainly wasn't at Gorstone. But her father was rich, rich enough to have bought some hideaway. She had felt sick with disgust. She recalled the time she had walked into a room and Gerald and Monica had pulled apart quickly. Only then did she realise why no woman ever slept in her father's bed. Monica was his lover. Monica, his own sister. That was when she had begun to hate Olivia more than ever, for leaving them in the care of such a man. But Olivia had never found out who it was and Gerald had prevented her from seeing her own children; had cheated them all of happiness, except for himself and Monica. Olivia used to say how unusually close they had been as children, thrown together because their parents travelled a lot. When did it start? Grace wondered, unable to understand. How old would they have been the first time? Teenagers? Or did they climb into each other's beds as small children and it developed from there? She found it impossible to visualise the two of them together in that way but she knew it had happened. A shudder ran through her as she wondered how they could have done such a thing. Comparing her own situation she felt only revulsion at the idea of having a sexual relationship with Luke.

The wind tugged at her hair. She tucked it into the collar of her coat and tried to smile at two small boys who ran past her. So where had Monica been that night? Had she gone to their meeting place, waited, then realised something had cropped up and gone home again? She had not rung Gorstone that night, not according to Maggie Collins who told the police that the telephone hadn't rung again after Grace had answered it. Why didn't I tell Maggie I was going out? she wondered. Did I have some sort of premonition about what would happen? She could no longer remember. Perhaps she simply hadn't wanted to disturb them.

There were things Grace would never know but it no longer mattered. She was free. Her own guilt at leaving her father had made her see danger where there was none, she had lived with what she had done hanging over her like a black shadow, afraid that at any minute the police would come back to her and charge her with murder. She could have lived a normal life, married Matt, maybe. No. If not Veronica there would have been someone else. She could think of Matt with fondness now, but nothing deeper.

Yes, she thought, I set Lance up. I knew that no one could prove I wrote those letters. But without them how could she have sown the seeds of doubt, had reason to be so afraid?

But now I have my mother, she thought, and that was all I ever wanted from the day she left.

And Harry? I mustn't think of him. I mustn't. I know what we could have had had things been different. He believes Lance, he'll never be able to trust me. He's a good, honest man and I don't deserve him.

Grace walked slowly back along the towpath, deep in thought. I didn't kill him, but I left him to die. Mum's right. If I hadn't gone to help him he might still be alive but then we would not have been reunited. That does not lessen my sin. I ought to have gone back to see what was wrong. But was my neglect any worse than what he did? Grace did not know. He had been conducting an incestuous affair since before his marriage, he had withheld his children's mail, he had let their mother believe they hated her and his children that she hated them. Harry Jordan had a lot to say about the difference between law and justice. Grace could not help thinking that justice had been done where her father was concerned.

She thought of Monica who must have suffered too, who had lived a lie all her life and who had watched when her friend left her family. And Monica had been Olivia's friend, as hard as it was to accept, because Monica loved anyone who was part of Gerald's world. Had she tried to stop Olivia leaving? Had she ever tried to persuade Gerald he was wrong in keeping his children from their mother?

There were secrets Grace still had to keep and a deeper sense of guilt to live with for what she had almost done to Lance. I shall go and see Harvey, she told herself, and there will be trips to Italy and my mother will come to the farmhouse. Forgive me, Lance, she thought as she hurried home on foot.

Luke turned up that night. He carried a folder of documents and laid them out in front of her. Grace watched him closely as he spoke of his plans, his enthusiasm obvious. How like his father he is, she thought. No wonder Monica adores him. 'Luke,' she said sharply, 'has Monica ever . . .?' She stopped. The question could never be asked.

'Ever what?' he frowned.

'Nothing. Go on, it sounds fascinating.' This, Grace saw, was Monica's way of making amends. She would see to it that Luke pulled himself out of the gutter. In that she would succeed where Grace had failed. It would not make up for the past, nothing could do that, but maybe Luke would have a chance in life.

'Why don't you two speak any more?'

'Oh, it's a long forgotten argument. We both prefer it the way it is.' Grace knew he would repeat what she had said, that Monica would know that Grace knew. But there was no reason for them ever to meet. It was best left like that.

'If this goes through will I qualify for free meals?' Grace asked later over a supper of cheese on toast.

'Not until I'm making a profit.' He winked, but Grace knew that for once in his life he was taking himself seriously.

'Good boy,' she said.

'You haven't said that for years, sis.'

Grace grinned. 'No. But things are different lately.'

'Ah, yes. And I believe a certain Inspector Jordan might be responsible for that.'

'In a way, yes.' She looked away, wondering if she would ever hear from him again. If she did, would she accept any invitation he offered? Yes, almost certainly. The ambivalence of her feelings for him confused her. She missed him when he wasn't around; she felt safer when he was, although he often managed to infuriate her. Deep down she recognised that they had a lot in common: if they gave each other a chance, a satisfying relationship was possible. But Harry might have other thoughts. If he knew the whole truth, about the night her father died and about those letters of which she was now so ashamed, he would think even less of her than he seemed to do now. But she would not compromise him. Any advances had to come from Harry. She tried to put him out of her mind and entertain her brother.

Grace continued to put him out of her mind as she went through the daily rituals of getting up, getting ready for work and arriving at the surgery. Once there her patients and her partners filled her mind. She spent time with Ruth and Luke and other friends in the evenings and wrote long letters to Olivia and Tony and Fay who always mentioned Harry in her replies. At the weekends, if she wasn't on call, she went to the farmhouse. Enjoying the solitude and the beauty of her surroundings did not make her feel the loss of Judith and her daughter any less. But Judith was happy, she said so in her letters, and she sent photographs which Grace kept in an album. 'We'll be back in August for a fortnight,' she had recently written. 'I can't wait to see everybody again, especially you.'

And then, out of the blue, Harry telephoned. She was in the bath, up to her neck in vanilla-scented foam, when she heard the telephone ring. The answering machine was on but when she heard his voice she was out of the water in seconds and running, naked and dripping, to grab the receiver before he finished leaving his message.

'Oh,' he said, surprised when her voice interrupted him. 'How are you, Grace?'

'I'm fine. I really am. And you?'

'Too much work and not enough relaxation.'

239

There was an awkward silence. 'I was in the bath,' she said. 'I'm going to America in a couple of days. I'm going to see Harvey. It's only for a week, though. I want to spend the rest of my holidays in Italy.' I'm babbling, she thought, I'm babbling to keep him on the line.

'Well, I hope you have a wonderful time.'

'Thank you.' She paused. 'Was there any particular reason you called?'

'Yes, to make sure you're all right. And from what you've told me it seems that you are. Grace, can I buy you a drink before you go?'

She had not realised just how much she had been hoping to hear those words. Her reaction surprised her. Her hand shook and she felt her face redden. 'I'd like that very much.'

'Can you manage tomorrow?'

'Yes.'

'I'll pick you up at eight.'

'All right. I'll see you tomorrow.'

Grace hung up. What did his invitation mean? Why had he rung if he wasn't interested? She shook her head. She could only wait and hope, and time would tell. Whichever way it went there would always be Gerald's death and those letters between them but she felt sure that if Harry did suspect anything he intended to keep it to himself. He had had plenty of opportunities to expose her. She had lived with her guilt for so long that it had become second nature and if it meant a chance for her with the man she had come to respect and admire then she could live with it for the rest of her life.